ALSO BY JAMES D. HOUSTON

FICTION

Between Battles (1968)

Gig (1969)

A Native Son of the Golden West (1971)

The Adventures of Charlie Bates (1973)

Continental Drift (1978)

Gasoline (1980)

NON-FICTION

Farewell to Manzanar,
with Jeanne Wakatsuki Houston (1973)

Open Field, with John R. Brodie (1974)

Three Songs for My Father (1974)

Californians: Searching for
the Golden State (1982)

One Can Think About Life After the
Fish Is in the Canoe (1985)

Love Life

Love Life

A NOVEL BY

James D. Houston

McGRAW-HILL BOOK COMPANY

New York St. Louis San Francisco Auckland
Bogotá Hamburg Johannesburg London Madrid
Mexico Milan Montreal New Delhi Panama Paris
São Paulo Singapore Sydney Tokyo Toronto

Reprinted by arrangement with Alfred A. Knopf, Inc.

First McGraw-Hill Paperback edition, 1987

1 2 3 4 5 6 7 8 9 A R G A R G 8 7

ISBN 0-07-030487-4

LIBRARY OF CONGRESS CATALOGING-IN-PUBLICATION DATA

Houston, James D.
    Love life.
    I. Title.
PS3558.O87L6 1987   813'.54   86-27824
ISBN 0-07-030487-4 (pbk.)

Love Life

The scene is an American household. Mom. Dad. Two kids. Dogs and cats. It was late in the day for the nuclear family, but this one was still intact. The wife, the keeper of the nest, that was me, Holly Andersen Doyle, and this is her story. My story. Which means it is also the story of the husband, the father, the roamer and the gatherer, since their lives, our lives, could not be disentangled. She happened to be that kind of woman, what they used to call the marrying kind. These two had been together ten years. The story begins on the day she found out he was cheating on her, knew for sure, after all the months of not-wanting-to-know, knew for sure it was serious cheating. That is to say, he was not just playing around. He was giving great chunks of himself to another woman. He was losing his judgment. The blind-eyed, deluded fool was losing his grip. . . .

P A R T I

I'm drinkin' muddy water,
Sleepin' in a hollow log,
Because you treat me, baby,
Like a lowdown dirty dog.
    —Old blues

1

Balls of Fire

I rose early that day, half an hour before the alarm went off. It was my birthday. I wanted to make time to think about that. I didn't want a party or a lot of people calling in. I wanted some time to savor it, maybe brood awhile. I deserved a little time off for brooding. I saw my life at some kind of crossroads. I wasn't sure what I meant by this. It needed thinking through. I knew I couldn't give myself to it properly until Grover and the kids were out of the house. I woke with a sense of premonition, a foreboding that was tied—or so it seemed at the moment of rising—to the fact that I was now thirty-two. One of my grandmothers had died at the age of thirty-two, in a freak September blizzard in Alberta, Canada. The other grandmother had met her second husband at that age.

An orange light had set our bedroom curtains smoldering. The curtains were orange. When it wasn't raining they smoldered most of the time, which is what I had hoped for when I bought them at Macy's. But this light passing through the window seemed about to burst them into flame. I drew them back and saw the sun filling a low notch in the eastern hills, the sun's most southerly point, only rising through that notch for a couple of weeks before starting north again. If I had been asleep for twenty years and had awakened that morning I would have known the season in an instant, the month, perhaps the week, by the sun's angle and the winter clarity of its flame, igniting curtains, backlighting the camelia bushes and the spindly saplings I had planted on the slope behind the house, backlighting the creek whose waters then were high enough and full enough to make a glossy surface under the trees, and backlighting the light itself, so that all the air around the house and above the creek and all the air between the window and the farthest ridge seemed polished by this ball of new fire.

For two days rain and overcast had obscured the light. Now the sky was rinsed and the returning sun should have been a sign of renewal and rebirth. I always look for signs. This one had a double edge. With the nonweight of its early glow coating me, I felt protected, and yet I felt exposed. It was odd. It was like being naked in a warm room you suspect is walled with one-way mirrors. This light was full of memory. Birthday light. The bright slanting light of early winter that in childhood was the day I could do no wrong. Out of nowhere I felt a sob rising. I quelled it and turned toward the bed where Grover still lay sleeping.

I wanted a hug from him then, a good long hug with no questions asked. There had not been many of those lately. A lot less touching in recent months. I took that too as a sign. And yet I didn't. I preferred not to. I preferred to look for other explanations. There were plenty around. We had reached what I look upon as the Unidentified Flying Object stage, when obstacles seemed to appear from every direction at any moment of the day or night to land between us, each one a little meteorite thrown into our midst from somewhere in outer space—the kids, the phone calls, the visitors, people staying overnight, part-time jobs, and sick animals, and the gang of musicians Grover practiced with. Standing there by our bed and looking down at him sleeping in his early-morning sprawl, on his side, with one leg drawn up and one arm out, it occurred to me that maybe a little shock therapy was what we needed. Before the household came to life. A shock to stir the still waters.

I called out, "Grover!"

His eyes sprang open in wide alarm.

I took a quick step toward him, like an Olympic diver stepping to spring, and dove into him shouting, "Aaaaaaarrgghh!"

Underneath the mattress something cracked. The bed sagged in the center. He said, "Oh shit, Holly, you just broke one of the slats."

I said, "You want to play *County Fair?*"

"I am going to have to take the whole bed apart just to patch that slat."

"It's a new game. I just heard about it. Only two can play."

He groaned and closed his eyes. Early morning is not his playful time.

"The way it works," I said, "is I sit on your face and you try to guess my weight."

He couldn't help laughing. He fell back onto the sagging mattress giggling and looking at me with a sly glance that said he was considering it. "Where the hell did you hear that?"

"At the health club," I said. "I should sneak you into the women's locker room sometime. You wouldn't believe some of the stuff they talk about."

"What do I get if I guess your weight?"

"You get a free pass."

It might have worked, my shock therapy, if the door had not squeaked open just then. I have often wondered what difference it would have made in the way things turned out. Buddy was standing there, our eight-year-old, in his *Star Trek* pajamas.

For just a moment he seemed strange to me, a stranger in the doorway, someone I was seeing for the first time, both familiar and unknown, saw his young face in sharp detail, the red hair like his father's, the wedged chin like his father's, the same jutting insistence in his whole boyish body. I felt pinned between them, the man I had a sunrise hunger for, and this little stranger, the mirror-son. I didn't like the feeling. I tried to smile it away with a welcoming, motherly smile.

"What happened?" Buddy asked. "Who yelled?"

I said, "Mommy was trying to get Daddy's attention."

"Why were you talking about the county fair?"

"That was a joke," I said, wondering what else he had heard.

"You're still gonna take me to the game, aren't you, Dad?"

"I wouldn't miss it, tiger."

"You didn't get hurt?" Buddy asked him.

"That was the bed that cracked," I said, "not your dad. Come over here. I want to tell you something."

When he was within arm's length I ran a hand through the hair behind his head and pulled him close. He was a great kid, especially first thing in the morning, before the dance started, the long boy-dance of all-day bursting energy that would give to the world by the end of any Saturday a torn pair of pants, one or two broken toys, a fluid spilled, a cat tormented, a mother unhinged.

"You going to win the game today?" I asked.

"I think so. We beat them once already."

"Your daddy going to get you a pizza if you win?"

He had a grin like Grover's, full of charm. A few more years and it would be a devastating, lady-killer's grin. "Either way," he said. "We always get a pizza."

Grover was out of bed by that time, stepping into his jeans. He picked up Buddy and swung him around like a sack of wheat, then they both started down the hall toward Buddy's room, where there was a soccer shoe to be repaired, Grover talking all the way.

"Okay, kid, we need the glue, we need the scissors, we might need a dab of touch-up paint. I mean, we don't want these little nicks to show if we can help it. We want you out there on the field with good-looking *shoes*, don't we now? So you run out to my workbench and get that little can of tire blacking. It's right there where I keep the paint thinner and the brushes. . . ."

The voice and the footsteps faded, and I found myself alone in the bed feeling vaguely betrayed by the speed of this maneuver. Was it the eagerness of the father to be with the son? Or the eagerness of a husband to avoid his wife? Or both? Or neither? Was Grover glad for the distraction? And did I, Holly, really want to know? Or was I glad, too, for the next distraction, which came thirty seconds later, and allowed me not to think it through?

It was Karen, our three-year-old, wailing from the bathroom that she had locked herself inside.

It took Grover twenty minutes to bring his stepladder around to the back of the house, and shove Buddy up through the bathroom window to liberate Karen, and put the ladder away, and give her a little refresher course in how the knobs and latches work, and get back to Buddy's shoe. By that time I had breakfast on the table, the eggs, the whole-wheat toast, the marmalade, the orange juice, the out-of-season cantaloupe trucked up from Mexico. Then Grover and Buddy were into the pickup with a thermos of Gatorade, and that was how it went on Saturdays.

He has been a good athlete all his life. Not a performer. Not a star. But a swimmer and a hiker and a reliable team man whenever a team forms up for softball or basketball, whatever comes along. From the day Buddy was born, Grover wanted his son to be like him, had the kid swimming laps by the time he was four, playing soccer in the county league at six.

This was Buddy's third season on the six-to-eight team. Grover would taxi him to the Wednesday practice. When there was a weekend match I stayed home till noon or so to keep an eye on Karen. It was classic. Father and son go off and do sports. Mother and daughter stay home and be domestic. I was not pleased by this arrangement, and I had told him so a number of times, in those very words. "It is fucking classic, Grover, if you want my opinion!" And yet I put up with it because, well . . . what was the alternative? Should the mother take the son to the soccer game, while father stays home to watch Karen destroy the yard? In the end, the answer was no. Father and son did not do that many things together, and it is hard enough these days for a kid to find the role model and grow up feeling good about his own masculinity, et cetera, et cetera. Should the whole family then go to the game together, so that mother and daughter don't have to sit it out at home? No. That was no solution either. Why? Soccer was "Buddy's activity," and the sibling rivalry could disrupt his concentration. We tried it once, the four of us. Karen repeatedly broke loose to scamper out onto the field every time a ball came rolling toward the sideline. Maybe when she was a year or two older we would try it again. But positioned as we were, in the midst of the UFO stage of family life, the easiest pattern was the classic pattern. And that day had all the signs of being another soccer-season Saturday, with Holly stoically enduring her fate, until I found something, quite by accident, that I would later tell Maureen and Leona and a few other friends I wished I had never found, although that wasn't true at all.

It was on the floor beneath the desk where he did his paperwork, an old rolltop desk he'd inherited from his grandfather and namesake, the original Grover Doyle, a scoundrel from Tennessee who, it is said, won this desk in a poker game. It had drawers wide and narrow, dozens of pigeonholes, and a few secret compartments where I never looked. I had my own desk, you see, next to my piano, and a filing cabinet stuffed with sheet music and all the letters of my life. We were both keepers. We kept all sorts of things. I figured everyone had the right to a few secrets. It just added to the shock and distress of the way things unfolded when I thought back on how easy it would have been for him to conceal anything he truly wanted to conceal, in a desk like his, where a snoop could spend hours just going through all the scraps and loose ends and marked pages and old leaflets crammed into the compartments you could see.

Karen was out in the play yard at last, the gate to the creek trail was barred and locked. I was making a quick pass through the house to pick up the loosest pieces of trash and clutter, "clearing a path," as I might have joked to one of my colleagues in the child-care co-op, when I came upon a printed flyer. It announced a conference going on that weekend at the local community college, called "Mothers of Us All."

Violet in color, it lay half folded on the hardwood floor beside his chair and seemed to vibrate and still vibrates for me now as I recall the way its edges were heightened by the floor's dark polish, so that I grasped it gingerly, by the corner, as if it were alive. A shiver of unaccountable dread ran through me as I began to read.

It was not like Grover to have such a flyer among his papers. He kept his distance from seminars, self-improvement gatherings, weekends or workshops of any kind, unless they connected to his own line of work and/or one of his personal obsessions, which boiled down to three or four subjects he was passionate about: installing solar panels, worldwide applications of solar energy, authentic bluegrass music, and authentic western swing, particularly the music of Bob Wills and his Texas Playboys. What's more, Grover had never mentioned this seminar to me, and that made it stranger. The morning's agenda read like this:

8 - 9 A.M.	Coffee and registration
9:15	A New View of Archaeology
10:45	The Reemerging Goddess
11:45	The Power Within: A Ritual Gathering
12:15	Lunch

Next to the schedule of events, a little note had been penciled into the margin and partially erased. It said, *Parking lot. 9:15. S.*

This could have meant any number of things. And I could have let it go. On another day I might have let it go. Later I often wondered, to myself and out loud to others, what turns my life might have taken if I *had* let this go. But I had been letting too many things go. I was still rankled by his sudden exit from the sheets and blankets, when in times past he would have ushered

Buddy down the hall and plugged him into the Saturday cartoons and locked the door and climbed back into bed. Rankled about that, and feeling stuck out there on our country road, and wanting an excuse to drop Karen somewhere so I could be out and about, I picked up the phone and called Eleanor, that month's co-op coordinator. She would take Karen without complaint, whether or not it was an emergency. She herself was the mother of three. Even if they were all driven indoors by another squall, one more youngster would usually get lost in the crowd.

2

Speaking in Tongues

When Grover and I met, ten years before this happened, I was driving a 1949 Packard sedan. I drove it for five more years and finally sold it to a collector, only because parts were so hard to find. I loved that car. It was baby-blue and had plenty of legroom. You have to keep in mind that I am tall and high-waisted, and legroom matters more to me than mileage or maintenance costs or insurance rates or any of the rest of it.

Just before Karen came along we bought a 1960 Chevrolet station wagon, one of those single-owner dream cars with less than a hundred thousand miles on the meter, a car that had spent most of the sixties and seventies inside a dry garage waiting for its elderly owners to make the weekly run to the shopping mall or a moviehouse. It had legroom to give away, and plenty of space for hauling two kids. The upholstery smelled musty from the years of garage dust settling on the pool-green Naugahyde, a smell both musty and new. The body was forest-green and white, with broad bands of chrome gleaming across the front and along the sides. Driving that car made me feel powerful. I still have it, by the way. It has reached the vintage stage. People often turn to watch me pass. They will smile or wave or make some hand signal that means, "Good going!" Every month or so someone asks if the wagon is for sale and how much will I take. It makes me feel significant. It makes me feel unique.

After I dropped off Karen and swung around, heading back along the creek bed, through the corridor of alders and sycamores that connects our place to Eleanor's, a mist began to drizzle down from a high translucent fog and make the road slick and gather on my hood in tiny globules that gleamed in the midday light. The first owner used to wax that car once or twice a month. I myself will run through a car wash whenever it occurs to me, and throw in an extra dollar for the coat of sealer wax. That's why I have never minded driving in a light rain. It lifts my spirits to see those droplets dance across the glossy and original paint job. Behind the wheel I began to feel a little rush of liberation. Though I would have to pay back Eleanor sooner or later, and fill my own house with another layer of anarchy, I had bought myself a slice of unexpected time. I thought, Maybe this is what my expedition is all about, looking for some space and time, and making Grover the excuse. I wanted this to be true.

I wanted to trust him, after all. I wanted trust to count for something in the world. That in itself had more than once warded off my housewife's paranoia. Can I follow him all over town? I would ask myself. Every time I get a little sniff of something funny going on? Whatever happened to trust? I would ask myself. It is trust that is getting kicked to pieces these days, when everybody is on the make, and the very clothes you get to wear must keep every male in a state of high agitation and put him to the test. Grover had said as much to me, said he wished he'd been born in 1850 instead of 1950. "It would have been a whole hell of a lot easier to keep your mind on your work" is what he said to me. He was only half-joking. He is a Puritan at heart, always was, always will be. Just like his father. Nobody falls harder than a Puritan when he falls. I didn't know that at the time, of course. It is only later that you piece these things together.

At the first bridge I had to stop. It was a one-way wooden

bridge with raggedy asphalt paving. While two cars eased toward me from the far side, I looked down at the water, trying to remember where the level had been the last time I stopped and looked. Not this high, it seemed. When the cars passed, I switched off my engine, to hear the rush, and that too lifted my spirits, the restless tumble of dark water pouring past the bridge. I like shows of natural power. Not the big and devastating ones. But the moderate shows. The high wind on a mountain top, but not the tornado. The thundering shorebreak that can tear loose beach sand and move it miles along a coastline, but not the tidal wave.

Soothed by the gush of this rain-swollen creek, I gazed for a long time and almost turned around and went back home, thinking that this, and not another drive into town, was what I really needed.

Someone came up behind me just then, someone in a GMC van, who honked once. Glancing in my rearview, I saw a man I did not recognize. He seemed to be in a patient sort of hurry. To back up and turn around I would have had to ask him to back up. I started my engine and crossed the bridge. With him riding my tail, itching for some wide space to pass, I kept going, across the second bridge, winding along until the creek road joined the two-lane state highway that follows the long river valley the rest of the way in.

By the time I reached the campus the drizzle had disappeared. The sun was shining. I was having second thoughts, or third thoughts. By the number of cars spilling out of the parking lot I could tell this was going to be a mob scene. I don't like mob scenes. By the panorama of bumper stickers I could tell it was going to be a very specialized kind of mob scene. They said:

GIVE A SISTER A RIDE
A WOMAN'S PLACE IS ON TOP
TRUST IN GOD: SHE'LL PROVIDE

Dozens of these slogans in one parking lot filled me with apprehension. I can take just about anybody on any subject, one at a time. But give me even two or three people gathered together on some kind of crusade, it makes my jaws hurt. What's more, it now occurred to me that I was going to have to pay money to get inside, something like fifteen dollars for the morning session. It was fifteen I didn't happen to have, unless I wrote a check. That would get me through the door, but there was an outside chance it would overdraw the account, unless I got to the bank early Monday morning to transfer some cash from the business account, which would mean explaining it to Grover, plus an extra trip on a day I had hoped to put in an hour or two at the piano, which in turn could mean loading Karen and the carseat into the car, since Grover would be gone by that time and Buddy would be in school, and so on and so forth—my life a jungle/network of these niggling details.

Thinking such thoughts as I crept along the crowded rows, I had almost forgotten what brought me there, when I came upon the vehicle I was looking for, and the last one I wanted to see. My foot slipped off the gas pedal, and my engine stuttered dead. It was Grover's Dodge pickup, which could be distinguished from several similar pickups in this assemblage by two bumper stickers pasted to the tailgate:

I'D RATHER BE A ROPER THAN A DOPER
and
EXPECT A MIRACLE

I slumped back against the seat, as if someone had hit me in the chest with a two-by-four. I sat there shaking my head and thinking, That sonofabitch, that dirty dirty bastard.

In the lobby, at the registration table, between the sets of closed double doors that led into the auditorium, two women were counting money and shuffling sign-up sheets. I recognized one of them, from a local ballot proposition we had worked on together a couple of years earlier. We were about the same age. I remembered not liking her much because she was a chronic "inside dopester," a person who had to appear to be right at the cutting edge of whatever was said to be going on.

We smiled at each other and I said, "Can I just stick my head in the door for a few minutes?"

With a glance at her companion she said, "I guess that's okay, since you'll have to stand up anyway. We already have a hundred more people than we expected."

"If I decide to stay, I'll sign up at the break or something."

"Hey. You'll decide to stay. There's some powerful people in there."

The way she said this, the look on her face, made me shrink inside. I could not help feeling she knew something, or had seen something. It was a look of the conspirator and seemed to say, "You and I both know why you're here."

I opened one of the doors and stepped into the hall. Wide semicircles of padded seats tiered down toward the stage, where a woman wearing knee boots and tight jeans stood at the podium talking into a bank of microphones. One mike fed into the sound system. The others snaked down to tape recorders scattered around the podium. They seemed to be floating in a pool of bright light. At first that was all I could see, the circle of light and the woman. In a clipped voice she was talking about the Virgin Mary.

"Female deities were prominent in all the so-called pagan cultures. The Goddess was visible everywhere. In the eyes of Judeo-Christian culture, of course, those pagan beliefs were looked down upon as inferior and therefore expendable. And what was the effect of this attitude? You reduce the significance of the pagan culture, and by definition you reduce the significance of the female deity. At least that is what they *tried* to do. But you cannot suppress the Goddess. . . ."

My eyes were slowly adjusting to the light. I had begun to scan the rows when, as this last line was uttered, a chorus of bedouin trills swelled from somewhere down near the front. Two rows of women were lifting their heads and trilling approval. I could not see their faces, but I could see their backs, the shawls and scarves on some, combat fatigue jackets on others. I knew who they were, a coalition of witches and moon-cycle activists and dyke/astrologers. Probably trying to take over the conference. The speaker waited until they were finished, while I studied the rows one by one. I saw some girls who looked like college students, in their jeans and T-shirts. I saw some middle-aged women who looked like club women, wearing polyester pantsuits and carrying matching umbrellas. I saw heavy women and slender women, grandmothers and lonely teenagers looking for something to join. I saw very few men. Maybe ten, in this crowd of three hundred or so. I did not see Grover anywhere.

"In the very stronghold of the Judeo-Christian patriarchal tradition," the woman at the podium continued, "she began to emerge in a new form. As early as 374 the worship of Mary was being listed as a heresy by a bishop of the Catholic Church. And where had she come from? Well, there is nothing in the New Testament to justify the elevation of Mary to sainthood. She is only mentioned once or twice in all the Gospels. And it was not the church fathers who let her out of the closet. They were very content with the Father, the Son, and the Holy Ghost. And it was not the church mothers who elevated Mary, because in those days there weren't any church mothers. What we are looking at is the original grass-roots movement, a new emergence of the goddess who has never gone away. Mary is one name for her. Ishtar is another. Isis is another. Hera too. And Demeter. Kuan Yin. Diana. Kali. Parashakti. Astarte . . ."

With each name in this litany the speaker's voice rose. Now the trilling women were on their feet, filling the space in front of the stage with their gypsy skirts and wild, comb-filled hair and baggy Marine Corps fatigues decorated with camouflage. There were tambourines among them. Their arms were darting toward the microphones with fingers outstretched, as if they were throwing handfuls of rice. I knew this gesture. Handfuls of approval were being thrown toward the stage, a dark blessing from these women making ancient tribal sounds that prickled my skin. All those shrill tongues fluttering—I didn't like it. And yet they called out to me. They cut through the heavy words, and I have always listened to anything that cuts through words. I have never been entirely content with words as a means of expression. I felt my own tongue against my palate, ready to begin trilling with them. This surprised me. My tongue itself seemed to understand that here was another kind of speech. I looked around to see how others in the crowd were taking the demonstration. That's when I saw Grover.

He was sitting on the far side of the hall, in the topmost row, between two women, one of whom had just stood up in obvious disapproval of what was going on, a very heavy woman in lemon pantsuit and something around her neck, a layered pendant or several necklaces that caught the light and thus caught my eye. When her seat was vacant, when she had made her indignant exit, a sightline was cleared. I saw him sitting straight-backed as he always does, paying close attention, bent slightly forward, and so absorbed in the scene below he might have been alone. In that first moment I wanted him to be alone, even though it was totally out of character for him to be here, and though it meant he had abandoned Buddy on their one morning together, which was worse than out of character.

I could have lived with all that, and wanted to. But the woman at his right chose this moment to turn and whisper in his ear. I saw long black hair fall across his sleeve. From the way he responded, leaned toward her, or rather, leaned *into* her as she spoke, and from the way her hand grazed his chin to tip the head an inch closer, I knew that whoever she was—and I could not yet see her clearly, though a name was right between my tongue and my teeth, the first letter hissing S. S. S. S. S. S., while the coven trilled below me—I knew those two were more than random conference companions.

I knew him too well, you see, knew all his body language, knew the parts of himself he saved and the parts he might offer casually, to anyone. They say your veins run cold at such moments. I know it's true. Mine turned to ice. I couldn't move. But something in me caused him to move, perhaps some current as strong, or stronger, than the handfuls of energy being hurled toward the stage. He turned and saw me staring at him across the auditorium. I saw his triangle face, his cap of reddish hair, his eyes catching a hint of light from the bright pool off the stage, and the side-lit neck tendons, corded and stretched by the turn, looking chiseled. There was no expression on his face, nothing I could see from that distance. He is capable of registering nothing. He was a piece of sculpture, a freeze-frame, until I found my will and took a step, heading toward them, along the wall's back curve.

Seeing this, he turned to whisper something, then rose quickly, striding up the aisle to intercept me. I watched the black hair. It did not move. I reached the second set of double doors and changed my course, pushed them open, rushing into the empty lobby.

3

The Song with No Words

I had crossed the broad veranda in front of the hall when I heard him calling, "Holly! Holly, wait!"

I kept walking, almost running down the concrete steps. At the edge of the parking lot he caught up with me and grabbed my arm.

"Holly, wait a minute!"

"Get the hell away from me!"

"It's not what you think it is."

I looked hard at him and almost laughed. "How do you know what I think it is?"

"She's just a good friend."

"It's no time for bullshit, Grover."

"I swear to you."

When I finally stopped walking, we had reached the far end of the lot. I looked at him again, searching his eyes. "Then why didn't you say anything about coming over here?"

"It was just a last-minute thing."

"Don't lie to me, Grover, whatever else you do, please don't lie to me."

I reached into my shoulder bag and pulled out the flyer and told him where I had found it, then stood there watching his mind begin to work overtime.

"I guess I didn't mention it," he said, "because I knew you'd probably react just like you are reacting, and if there was any way to avoid that, well, I'd rather try and avoid it."

"How am I sup*posed* to react? Where the hell is Buddy? If she is just your good friend, why isn't Buddy with you?"

"He's playing soccer like he always does. I dropped him off. I'll pick him up. Is that a crime?"

"Do you know how that looks? Don't you realize what that says to me?"

"Hey. How many soccer games are you supposed to watch in one lifetime?"

I was still studying his eyes for some sign of what could be trusted. When he glanced away, unable to meet my gaze, when I saw the guilt he could not conceal, I felt sick, nauseous. I said, "When is the game supposed to be over?"

"I dunno. Ten-thirty, eleven. Someplace in there. It varies, depending on when the first game ends and when the referees show up."

"Do you know what time it is now?"

He did not wear a watch in those days. He carried an old-time pocket watch with a second hand, on a thin hammered silver chain hooked to his belt loop. Carefully he pulled it out. I knew he was stalling, buying whatever shred of time he could. When he looked at the watch I saw his face fill with fear. I waited for him to speak, but he didn't.

I said, "The game was over an hour ago, wasn't it."

"It's no big deal, Holly. They pile into the cars, and they all go to the Pizza Hut. He knows I'll meet him there."

"How old is she, Grover?"

"Jesus, don't get so upset."

"How old is she?"

"She's twenty."

"That's perfect."

"What does that mean? That I've been running around behind your back just to get something going with another woman?"

"Did I say that?"

"She's not a kid. And she's not a band follower, if that's what you're thinking."

"Stop telling me what I'm thinking! If you had any idea what I'm thinking you wouldn't be sitting in there playing lickyface with a girl that age. Do you have any idea how that looks? You think people can't see you? You think you are some kind of invisible man you can just run around the county and have the world believe you are soul mates?"

"I go a lot of places, Holly. I do a lot of things with a lot of different people. If I have to put an age limit on who I can spend time with . . ."

"But you don't go sneaking around like this, on a Saturday morning, without telling anybody . . ."

"I am not sneaking around! All we're doing is sitting in an auditorium, for Christ's sake!"

"Then why did you dump Buddy?"

"I didn't *dump* him. He's on his own for a couple of hours."

"He is barely eight years old."

"He can take care of himself. We baby him too much anyway."

I almost reacted to that, but held it. I did not want to debate the way we were raising the kids. Not that day. I waited, trying to calm myself, find my center, then I said, in what I thought was a controlled and reasonable voice, "Do you think she's still inside?"

"Why?"

"I like to meet your friends, Grover. Maybe this would be a good time to meet her."

I could see him weighing what was clearly a no-win situation. At last he said, "I think you've already met her. Maybe not. You remember that big party last summer at Earl Mason's? The Fourth of July?"

As he said this, the picture appeared in vivid detail. I saw the two of them dancing, and I remembered that it had gone on much too long, and I remembered the name—Sarah—because we had argued drunkenly about her and the dancing on the interminable drive home. There had been margaritas followed by Humboldt sinsemilla. The dancing had been wild, with dozens of bodies shining in the summer light. Grover had been splendid. Too wild. Too splendid. This little girl had chosen him then, small, dark-haired, big-breasted, predatory. I knew it was happening, and that is why the picture stayed. She had painted her eyes for the party, the top lids silver, the dark corners lifted for the feline and pouncing look.

That drive home was not the first time we had argued about women. Grover had his flirtations. I had mine. We all do. You learn to put up with a great deal of that as the years go by. I would not say he is a philanderer. But he likes to be around women and to perform for them. Nor is he what I would call handsome. There are flaws in his appearance. His tooth, for instance, a molar on the upper left, broken off in a diving accident when he was a kid and never replaced. Now he refuses to replace it, says it is part of his "effect," this black hole at the edge of his smile. Not handsome, then, but vigorous. His vigor is like honey, so that women seek him out. And you learn to allow certain things. Certain intimacies become allowable if the two of you plan to go on living among other creatures made of flesh and blood. But there has to be a line, there has to be a limit. Maybe the arguing is one way to keep that line alive and visible, so you both know more or less where it is. As we stood in the parking lot I was hearing echoes of a dozen loud conversations. Yet I knew as I watched him squirm that he had gone too far. He was in too deep. Much later I understood why: At the moment I was ready to murder him.

He was saying, "She does graphics down in town. She has designed a couple of things for us. Announcements. She is a very talented woman. Very intuitive. You would actually probably like to see some of the things she has done."

I said, "Is she a good lay?"

"Is she what?"

"You're sleeping with her, aren't you?"

"Jesus, Holly, why do you make things sound so cheap?"

"Did I mention cheap? Since when is sleeping with somebody cheap?"

He took a deep breath, and waited a beat, gazing into the sky, as if for guidance. I had run out of patience with his charade, and I will say this much for Grover—so had he. He looked directly at me and said, "I don't like to play games any more than you do, Holl. I don't want to double-time or sneak around or any of the rest of it. So I am going to tell you straight out what is going on. For weeks I have been trying to figure a way to put this together. I really have. I don't like how things have been going. It is dishonest. It raises barriers between us. You and I have always been honest and out-front with each other. I want to keep it that way. Maybe this is the best thing that could have happened, you coming out here today. I mean, it forces the situation, doesn't it."

He said all this with such sincerity it defused the rage that had begun to well inside me. It made my head swim. The noon sun off the parking-lot gravel seemed to grow brighter. I had to squint. My voice got husky.

I said, "Put what together? What does that mean?"

"Don't you think it's possible to care about more than one person at a time? Where is the law that says it is something that goes on between two people? Why can't it be three, or four, or five?"

"Oh shit, Grover! You know that doesn't work."

"I'm serious. Think about this. The more people you love, the greater your capacity for loving. If you want to know the truth, I believe I care more for you now than I ever have before."

I saw something come into his eyes then, a brimming fullness. It was a look I might have trusted twenty-four hours earlier, but I couldn't trust it then. It was too close to weeping. He was close to caving in.

"And this is something you have discovered because of . . ."

"Sarah. Yes. She has helped me discover some things about myself."

"Discover what?"

"My ability to express myself. The deeper parts of myself have been dammed up."

"My God! You say that like it's a new idea! Haven't we talked about that, you and me, I mean for—Christ!—years on end?"

"Sometimes you really have to . . . reach out in new directions. In order to unlock it. Take new risks. You have said that yourself. That is what I want you to try and understand. I want the three of us to talk it through."

"How long has this been going on, Grover?"

"Not long. A while."

"When you called last month from Lake Tahoe, after that weekend gig at the ski lodge, and said your transmission went out and you were stuck for four days, was she with you?"

He didn't say anything.

"And the two-fifty that supposedly went into the transmission. Did she help you spend the money?"

Still nothing. He gazed past me toward a stand of scrub oak, as if trying to remember the episode.

"You know we went into the hole last month," I said. "We ate chicken wings for a couple of weeks, when we could afford them. Is that your idea of caring deeply?"

"I know that in your present frame of mind it seems hard to believe, but love is . . . my idea of love has changed a lot, Holly. It has opened up."

I closed my fists then and drove them into his chest with such unexpected force it threw him off balance. I had never hit him, nor had he hit me, though we had both come close to hitting. Now I wanted to go for his face. He knew it. He grabbed my wrists and held me at bay, his own arms stiff as logs. We are exactly the same height. We stood glaring eye to eye until I began to shake, then to shout.

"It is too much, Grover! It is too much to take! You think I have been busting my ass to keep the house together and work part-time and all the rest of it, the shitwork of life, keeping books for your goddam company, so you can spend weekends up at Tahoe with some little hooker and spend money we don't have . . ."

He started shouting back and squeezing my wrists so hard they ached. "Don't get self-righteous with me!"

"Let me go!"

"You think you are the only one busting ass around here?"

"Yes, I do!"

"Well, you're wrong!"

"Let me go, Grover! You're breaking my arm!"

"Everybody is busting ass!"

"You're breaking my arm!"

He released me suddenly, with a push, and stood looking down at his hands.

"Don't call her a hooker. She's a beautiful person. She has helped me see a lot of things. She has helped me see that I love you and the kids more than ever." When he looked up, his eyes were brimming again, coated with a shine of moisture. He was ready to weep. "That hasn't changed."

"What did you say?"

"I said I love you and the kids more than ever. You have to understand that, Holly."

"I hope you're serious."

Something about the way I said this confused him. "What is that supposed to mean?"

"I don't know yet."

Again I saw fear widen his eyes. I regretted putting it there. Fear in his eyes made me feel fear. This time I was the one who looked away. I looked back toward the broad veranda in front of the auditorium. A crowd of women had gathered there. I thought I saw Sarah watching us from the railing. Through a wide break in the cloud cover, the sun was shaping everything with bold brights and dark patches, and I could not be sure of what I was seeing, or who. At that point I really didn't give a damn. They were all too far away. Women were filing through the double doors, standing, as if waiting for something to begin.

I said, "I can't handle this, Grover. It is . . . just too much. It is too far over the line."

"We need to talk. We need to start right at the beginning."

"I don't think I feel like talking." I should have added, We have been talking for ten years and what has it accomplished? But I didn't.

He said, "We have to," and from the way he said it, I could tell he thought he had hit upon some kind of solution. Grover feels best when he has perceived a specific move he can make in order to deal with the problem at hand. It gives him a sense of purpose and direction. Having thought of something to do next, he seemed lighter, as if relieved of a terrible burden.

"We need to go where we can talk," he said. "Maybe we should both drive back to the house. I have to pick up Buddy anyhow, and . . . I know this sounds like a strange thing to say right now, but . . . I just want you to know I didn't forget your birthday. I have been talking to the kids about it. I actually have a present right there in the pickup."

"Did Sarah help you pick out the present?"

There was a long pause while he looked past me at the scrub oak beyond the lot. His brow furrowed as if he were gradually recalling something that had escaped him. He looked like a man surrendering to police.

I felt sick again. Emptied. I did not know what to do, what to say, where to go, who to turn to, whether to follow him home or get into my car and just start driving. Underneath my grief I had the sense of having played a scene, and now it was ended—not only the scene, but the pattern and flow of my life up to that moment. There I stood, Holly Belle Andersen Doyle, eight and a half years married, B.A. Berkeley, mother of two, seven hours into my thirty-third year, unhinged and unraveled and disrupted and suspended, and days seemed to pass before the sound of a single voice cut the air, singing a single note, in the middle register, a strong, clear alto, soon joined by others, some in unison, some above the first voice, some below it, a dozen voices, then ten dozen, then two hundred or more, singing a long chord of a choral note that sounded first like the echo of a Gregorian chant and became, as it swelled, a much earlier sound, a siren rising from that ring of women under the sun at high noon, taking resonance from the poured concrete walls and pillars that framed the veranda, filling the air above the cars and above the oaks beyond the lot and the redwood grove behind the meeting hall. They held it for many minutes, some stopping to fill their lungs, while others sustained the old, old note, older than anything visible there, older than cities. Older than speech. It rang in my throat and touched me and held me. Among the cars I stood as if alone, listening, I don't know how long, until the note subsided.

4

Sisters

Grover was leading. I was about twenty yards behind in the station wagon thinking, Why am I doing this? He treats me like shit and now I am following him home.

It was classic.

The back of his head framed in the pickup rear window made me think of a target. I remembered a book that had been advertised a year or two earlier. *Mom Kills Kids and Self.* It had struck me as a tasteless title, which is why I never bought the book, even after the paperback came out. Thinking of it again, I felt I understood the impulse. That was just how I was feeling, although I would have rewritten it to read *Mom Kills Kids, Dad, Dog, Cat, Self, Others.* The urges rising in my blood, the scenes of mayhem filling my mind, scared and alarmed me. I saw myself ramming his pickup's tailgate. It would be easy to do. I could force him off the road. I saw myself destroying both these vehicles in a rage of ramming and bucking. Sarah was part of this vision, mangled in the wreckage. Unrestrained tears were plopping down my cheeks and into my lap. I was glad we weren't at home where the knives and tools were located. A rush of hot fear poured through me as I realized that's where we were heading. I didn't want to go home. I didn't want to be with Grover. I did not want to be near him.

We were half-a-mile from the campus, approaching an on-ramp that curved upward onto the cross-county freeway. This was the shortest route to the Pizza Hut, where Buddy awaited his father's return. Once Grover was out on the freeway, I knew he would not be able to get off for at least two miles. I slowed, dropped back, let a couple of cars move between us. When he had taken the rise, I gunned through an amber light, across an intersection, under the freeway, out onto a boulevard that led in the opposite direction, away from the mountains.

I didn't know what I wanted to do or where I was going. At that moment my only goal was to put space between us. I don't know how fast I was driving. I almost rammed a city bus that pulled out right in front of me. The wall of yellow metal appeared like a nightmare tidal wave, and so suddenly the shock made me nauseous again. I thought I might have to throw up. A Texaco station appeared, one of the older ones, from the Sixties, surrounded with paving. I pulled in next to the restrooms and switched off the engine and sat staring at the sign on the door to the women's room:

CUSTOMERS ONLY

ASK ATTENDANT FOR KEY

When your will is at a low ebb, something like that can bring you to an absolute standstill. I could see the attendant, a black-haired kid wearing greasy white pants and a foul-weather jacket, out there at the full-service pump leering at two high school girls filling up a Mustang on somebody's credit card. He was the kind of guy who would gaze inside your blouse if you were sitting behind the wheel, look you up and down if you asked him for the key to the women's room. It was too much to deal with. I sat very still for quite some time.

When my nausea subsided, I backed over to the telephone

booth, intending to call Eleanor, to instruct her to wait until Grover called or, if he didn't, to call him in an hour or so. But I knew Eleanor would ask too many questions. Anything I told her or even hinted at would spread, by instant chain reaction, throughout the co-op. That would mean days of consoling house-wives coming around to gobble up the clinical details. I had done that myself a few times. It wasn't healthy. I didn't need it. I wanted to talk. But not to Grover. Not yet. And not to Eleanor.

By the time my dime rattled to a stop I was calling my pal Maureen, who knew some of the men in my life but almost none of the women. She and I, we traveled in two circles that just barely touched. Maureen had been married, now she was single again, working days part-time at the health spa and nights tending bar in one of the clubs where Grover's band occasionally picked up a gig. It was a country-and-western band, so the bars he played in were all of a type. This one was called The Last Roundup.

Maureen was home and told me to come on over for a bowl of soup or a sandwich, since it was close to lunchtime, then said the soup might have to wait until after some errand she had just re-membered, saying it was eerie I had called her when I did, and she would explain the rest when I got there.

She lived in a new apartment complex called Sunburst, a sin-gles ghetto at the edge of town, with a lot of sports cars around and a turquoise pool inside the compound. Two years earlier it had all been croplands. Now the whole district had been trans-formed into condos and subdivisions. When I reached the front entrance she was standing at the curb with an urgent face. She was wearing a red-and-white ski sweater and jeans. She signaled me to pull up next to her, then opened the door quickly and scooted in, talking.

The thing I liked about Maureen, she was not afraid to talk about anything, and yet neither was she the kind to betray your trust through free-form babbling. It was quite a balance, consider-ing how much she talked. It contributed to the strong sisterly feel-ing between us. Maureen was thirty-four. Sometimes I actually believed she was the older sister I should have had, the one who died at birth, born prematurely, right after World War Two. It was intriguing to think of the difference between Maureen and Eleanor, who was older than either of us. Eleanor seemed like a daughter to me. In her house full of kids she was another child. She sought my approval in a daughter's way. Perhaps that made it easier to leave Karen with her a while longer that Saturday afternoon.

"I have to go to Long's to get this prescription filled," Maureen said. "Do you mind if we drive down there? We can talk on the way. My car is in the shop. As usual. I'm supposed to pick it up today, *if* it's ready. You never know what they're going to do to you. It was supposed to be ready yesterday. Meanwhile there is this mini-emergency, so it was amazing that you called, but what's going on, Holly? You look terrible."

I glanced in my rearview, at the puffy eyes, the haggard brow, and began to tell her the story. Maureen knew us well enough to have an opinion. She knew what our relationship had been like. In her mind there was no doubt what my course of action should be.

"Kick him out," she said. "Right now."

"Don't think I haven't thought about it."

"Then do it. Don't wait another second. Call him from Long's. Tell him you don't want to see him there when you get home."

"It's not that easy, Maureen."

"Of course it isn't easy. I know. I've been through it."

"But you didn't have kids. If I kick him out of the house, it just gives him more time to do whatever he is doing. Meanwhile, who do you think takes care of the kids?"

She thought about this. I had just parked outside the store. We watched a huge woman push a cart through the automatic doors. It was filled with cartons of cigarettes, half-gallons of cheap sherry. Two fat youngsters followed her, stuffing sticks of gum into their mouths, five or six each, from a twelve-pack of Wrigley's on top of the load.

Maureen said, "Suppose you let Grover take care of the kids."

"What do you mean?"

"Kick yourself out of the house."

"He couldn't handle it. He'd never put up with it."

"How do you know? Give the guy a chance."

As we single-filed across the rubber pad that triggers the automatic door marked IN, I did not think I was ready for such advice. I attributed this to my concern for Buddy and Karen. I could not yet voice the deeper doubt, my own fear of some nameless power that girl might have over him, which was tied to the deeper fear birthdays always draw toward the surface, the age-old fear of aging, of losing your hold. I could not yet mention any of that to Maureen, nor could I think about it, and so found myself relieved to be entering Long's Drugs. It was, I saw later, exactly the right setting for my mood.

Long's will disorient me every time. The store is vast and full of very bright artificial light and artificial music. The light seems to spread down from invisible ceilings. The music is the endless tape loop of forgotten American standards, designed to lull and sedate you, while the display racks are so high, so crammed with small bits and pieces of merchandise, my memory goes blank. Inevitably I forget what brings me to such a place. It is so easy to surrender there. On that particular day, though I could not forget those past few hours, the surreal interior offered me a short season of detachment. I became the Zen wanderer of Long's Drugs. And something similar evidently happened to Maureen, because she did not move directly toward the prescription counter on the far side of the store, where tall panes of plate glass screened off the high-security shelves of tubes and tiny vials. Together we began to wander the aisles, touching things, letting our fingers graze plastic dishes, hairbrushes, gallons of latex paint, light-bulb cartons, garden tools.

I told her what Grover had said about love. "He says to me, why can't you care about three or four or five people at the same time."

She snuffed a mocking laugh. "Holly, this is what I am trying to tell you. They always want it both ways. If you're not careful, the next thing you know he will be trying to get the two of you into the sack at the same time. I have seen it happen."

As she said this, a young woman stopped and looked at us. We were standing by the refrigerator where the beer and cold drinks are displayed. Maureen took my arm and guided me past the fishing tackle and the baseball mitts to a corner where no one was standing.

She moved in close, with a lowered voice, and went on. "Listen, just before Charlie and I broke up, he said to me, 'I love you so much I really don't know which way to turn.' He was so agitated he actually had me feeling sorry for him. So one thing led to another, and one night we all got into bed together, me and Charlie and this woman Roberta he thought he could not live without."

"You must have been on something."

"We were on everything. This was at the end of a long night that began with Heineken's dark and ended with Quaaludes Roberta had brought along. And what happened was, she and I got turned on to each other. Charlie was so loaded he didn't notice. After he passed out, she and I just . . . continued."

Maureen had not mentioned this before. I thought she might be making it up. She likes to startle people. With a little edge to my voice I said, "I didn't know you'd done anything like that."

"What I found out was, the whole thing had been her idea. She talked him into it. Told him it would be the solution to his sense of being pulled in two directions. She was probably the most amoral and promiscuous person I have ever known. She totally destroyed Charlie. The poor bastard still hasn't recovered."

"Are you still . . . I mean, do you . . . ?"

"Make it with other women? Not in a long time. I still prefer men. But don't ask me why. I am just about out of patience with the whole tribe. They are all the same."

"C'mon, Maureen. You keep saying that. But you don't really think it's true."

"Of course it's not true. But it *is* true. Look at what I've got myself into. This morning I am awakened from a sound sleep by this guy I have been seeing for a month or so. Nice guy, as they say. Real considerate. Which is why he calls. We have made it a couple of times, and now he has picked up crab lice somewhere. He isn't sure where, and he isn't sure when, and he is trying, in his very polite way, to find out if I might be the carrier. And then, if not, to warn me there is an outside chance I could have picked up crabs from him, implying—again, in a very polite way—that there are so many women in his abundant life he cannot quite keep track of who has what or in what order. But if I want to be double-safe and go pick up a tube of this stuff you use, he will be happy to pay for it. A real gentleman, you see. And yet, ungrateful me, I am thinking, My God, not only am I but one more link in this gent's chain of fools, I am stuck with something as old-fashioned and out of date as *crab lice!* It isn't even V.D. It's just a disgusting pestilence!"

As she told this story, which ordinarily would have made me laugh, I was still thinking about Roberta and the three of them in bed, and the two of them in bed. It changed the way I looked at her, and the way she looked at me, or the way I thought she looked at me, as if there had always been in her eyes a gauging and a testing I had not recognized until now. It called to mind those trilling tongues, made me uneasy in that same way. And yet, like the long note that floated out across the courtyard from the mouths of all those women, it drew me toward her. I wanted to describe that one-note song, but didn't, did not know how to talk about it.

On our way past the liquor rack she picked up a fifth of Wild Turkey and carried this with her to the prescription counter, so that when the lotion finally arrived from the pharmacist's window she paid for the two together. I watched the cashier's face for any sign of surprise or amusement. But the clerks at Long's are trained not to react to any combination of merchandise at the checkout stand, no matter how bizarre. I have seen, in one purchase, gopher poison, Hershey bars with almonds, *Easy Rider* (the motorcycle magazine), and Preparation H. In such a world, perhaps it is nothing at all to ring up a bottle of Quell and a fifth of Wild Turkey.

Maureen would not let me help with the whiskey. Her little contribution, she said.

We drove back to her place and found some glasses and sat down in the front room, which was really the only room. At Sunburst they called it a studio—tiny kitchen, bathroom with tub and extra closet, and this one long room carpeted wall to wall. There was a sofa covered with something like terry cloth, two easy chairs that matched the sofa, and a double bed off in an alcove. She said it was all she needed, since she wasn't there that much, working two jobs. It looked that way, not a place where anyone *lived*. Sparse, and temporary, and lonesome. It made me sad to think of Maureen coming back to such a place every night. She had not done much to it. A couple of posters on the wall, one about whales, and one big blow-up of Patsy Cline, the country singer who was killed in an airplane crash back in 1963 at the height of her career. Maureen's favorite record was Patsy Cline singing "Crazy." It was already on the turntable. As the music started, she was pouring out two glasses of Wild Turkey over some ice cubes.

"I've been working in that club for three years now," she said. "I still haven't figured out whether it's the country music makes me feel like drinking whiskey, or if drinking whiskey makes me feel like listening to country music. But they go together, don't you think?"

We had talked about this before. We both liked Patsy Cline. For a long time I had tried to sing like her, when I was doing a lot of singing. Then for a long time I worked not-to-sing like Patsy Cline. That day, her rich lament, her voice on the ragged edge of breaking, affected me another way. I was standing at Maureen's window, looking down at the pool, when anxiety gripped me. I was ready to jump. I said, "What am I doing here, Maureen?"

She said, "Relax. You're right where you ought to be."

I found myself shouting at her. "He is somewhere with that bitch right now! I should have gone after her when I had the chance! She's only twenty years old, for Christ's sake!"

"If I know Grover, he has the kids, and right about now he is starting to worry about what to fix for dinner. That is the last thing this young lady wants to get involved with. Two hungry kids and a stove. She has already told him to call in the morning."

"If I know Grover," I said, "they are on their way to McDonald's for a sack full of Big Macs and fries and milkshakes. The four of them. They are having a party, and I am up here getting drunk."

"You want to call home?"

I turned and glared at her, ready to shout another reply, and realized I did not know what I wanted. I wanted everything. I wanted to be driving to McDonald's to get a Big Mac. I wanted things to be like they had seemed to be at ten a.m. I wanted that moment back. I wanted to pick up the flyer for "Mothers of Us All" and drop it into the trash. I wanted to be in San Miguel de Allende the year before Karen was born, when we left Buddy with Grover's folks and we had one whole month. . . . A month. You get to the point where one month in the clear is your idea of paradise on earth.

I sat down on the sofa, took another sip of the Wild Turkey, and looked at the glass. Maureen chose that moment to tell me Grover had come into the club one night a few weeks back with a dark-haired young woman she now figures must have been Sarah. I'd had the feeling she knew something she was holding back. I think she deliberately waited until the first glass had worked on me. But still, the news cut like a sword.

I said, "Was that the only time? Has he come in there with other women?"

"Not that I know of. But it struck me as a pretty cavalier and foolhardy thing to do. I figured he just forgot I tended bar, which was not likely, or just didn't give a damn how it looked. Some band was playing. He took her to a table on the far side of the bandstand and stayed quite a while. Now, Grover will usually come to the bar and pay his respects, tell me a new joke or something. That night he didn't even say hello."

"Jesus, Maureen! Why didn't you tell me about this?"

"It's always hard to know what to do, Holl. Hard to know how much you knew, or didn't know. Sometimes a wife knows everything that is going on and puts up with it anyway. Sometimes she doesn't know anything. Then you do not want to be the one nosing in. I have done that more than once. I mean, tending bar I see just about everything sooner or later. I have learned that more often than not people will despise you for being the one who tells them what they don't want to hear. They will figure a way to turn it against you. People are always looking for somebody else to be responsible for what they have done."

My mind was running wild again. What more had she seen? What had others seen? Or heard? Or talked about? They say Wild Turkey can make you paranoid. I sat there consumed with self-pity and with hate for Grover and with a vision of a worldwide network of grubby secrets shared by everyone but me.

5

The Last Roundup

We drank until almost seven, when Maureen had to report to work. During that time she had twice called the shop and been told her car still wasn't ready. I offered to drop her at the club. That was my intention, just to drop her off. By the time we got there I saw that I was not ready to go home, nor was I ready to be alone. I parked and walked in with her. I was taking one thing at a time.

The band started at eight on Saturday nights. They were already setting up. I knew a couple of the musicians, the drummer, and the pedal-steel player, Eddie McQuaid. I was glad to see Eddie. It meant the music would be good. He and Grover had worked a few jobs together over the years. He was known to play the sweetest pedal steel in the county.

When the mike levels were adjusted and all the instruments plugged in, he came back to the bar. He was wearing faded jeans and a custom-made white satin rodeo shirt with mother-of-pearl snap buttons. From a distance he had a lean and rugged look. Up close you could see how delicate his fingers were, how delicate his mouth behind the close-trimmed beard. I hadn't seen him in months. I stood up and gave him a big hug, let my hands linger on the white satin, the way it stretched across his back. This probably conveyed more than I meant it to convey. He sat down and asked me what I was drinking.

"Firewater," I said.

He signaled to Maureen. "We'll have two more of whatever Holly's drinking. I like what it's doing to her."

"Is this a new group, Eddie? Some of these guys I haven't seen before."

"We've been working out together for a couple of months."

"You feel good about the music?"

"Tonight'll be the test. I'm glad you're here. You can tell us how it sounds."

"You know I love to listen."

"Too bad Grover's not around. He might like to sit in later on. Where the hell is he, anyway? He meeting you here?"

"Nope. Grover is . . . occupied. It's ladies' night out."

I could see his mind working as I said this. I guess I wanted him to read it the way I knew he would. How can I describe the relationship I had with Eddie? A precarious friendship? For years we had flirted back and forth, before and after gigs, with innuendoes and glancing body contact, dancing up close to the brink of seduction, backing off. Somehow we had always agreed that was the way it had to be. Sometimes I told myself we were afraid to risk damaging the mutual pleasures that came with the music itself.

The drinks appeared, Wild Turkey over ice. When we had toasted our little reunion, Eddie held the glass to his nose and inhaled a snootful, for the aroma. With a fake Irish accent he said, as if this might be a gag line, "There's a sadness in you, Holl."

I tried to match it. "And what might you mean by that, Mr. McQuaid?"

"Is it because this Grover fella lets a handsome colleen like yerself run about loose on a Saturday night?"

"This Grover fella you mention is the one who seems to be doin' most of the runnin' about," I said and instantly regretted saying too much.

Eddie waited a few moments. He dropped the accent. "You want to talk about it?"

"Well . . . I do, and I don't."

"None of my business one way or the other."

His tone was brotherly and his eyes were sincere and my tongue was loose and my heart was full. "I've just found out he has something going with another woman. Basic stuff. It's a little hard to take, that's all."

"I'm sorry to hear that, Holly, I really am."

"Not as sorry as I am."

"You aren't splitting up, are you? I mean, it hasn't gone that far."

"I don't know how far it's gone, Eddie."

Onstage the rhythm guitar player was chunking chords into the mike. Eddie stood up.

"I hope you're not going anywhere between now and the time we finish the first set."

"I told you I love to listen to your music."

"Maybe you'll come up and sing one for us. You in the mood?"

"I could be, Eddie. I could be talked into it, depending on how good you guys are."

I watched him walk back to the bandstand and slide behind his three-tiered bank of metal strings and carefully slide the picks onto his slender fingers. I liked Eddie. I liked looking at him. I had known him for years, and he was still exotic to me. I think it was because he worked at night. Night people run on a different frequency from day people. With a row of buttons next to his right foot he could control the stage lights. They were white when he sat down. Now they went blue. The thick blue light flooding the band made me think of those deepwater fish they say have special radar for navigating through sunless waters.

The lights became bordello-red, and the band started the first tune, without any introduction, just to warm up the room. It was an old Jimmie Rodgers number called "No Hard Times Blues." As soon as I heard the first chorus I knew I could sing with this band. By the end of the second tune I was aching to sing with them, aching for Eddie to call me up there. I looked at my clothes. I had not thought of my clothes since I'd left the house. I was wearing the jeans that fit me best and a high-waisted buckskin jacket and underneath that a long-sleeve shirt with a collar. They would do. Maybe, for effect, I could take off the jacket as I started to sing. I had seen Emmylou Harris do it once at the start of a concert. In my unvoiced fantasy she was the singer I most hoped to resemble—long-legged and long-haired and sexy and earthy and elegant. If I ever got all the parts of my life and body in perfect running order, that is how I would look when I took the stage to sing a song.

I had already picked out the tune, running the words through my mind to make sure I could keep the verses straight. It was one of my own, called "Love Life." Thinking the words took me back to the last time I had sung it, at a country-music jamboree and benefit for all the Democratic candidates in the county. Eddie was playing that day too. A wave of remorse went cascading through me as I realized an entire year had passed. Where had it gone? I used to do this all the time. On and off through college I had sung with pickup bands, at parties, and with the various groups Grover had put together or played with in the years since then. It was not my profession, but it was part of my life, the part I often told myself would have the chance to blossom and bloom once the kids were older and the UFO stage had passed. I had not given it up. I had my piano. I was still writing songs, at least writing down lines when they came to me. But how had a year slipped past? I fell into a reverie of befuddled nostalgia, which was interrupted some time later by the sound of my name.

Eddie was leaning toward the mike above his steel. "I know you'll recognize the voice as soon as you hear it. She used to sing with the Bear Flag Republic band and after that with the Land and Title Company. She happens to be passing through the club tonight. We asked her to come up and help us with our debut. Holly—you ready to do it?"

There was a sprinkling of applause as I moved toward the stage. I stopped to confer with Eddie about the key, then stepped up to stand between the rhythm guitar and the fiddler.

It was a big room, about half full. The white lights were on, between numbers. As I gazed into the crowd, as I took my jacket off, I relived all the performances of my life. In the next instant I was reliving all the things I did not do, moves I had not made. Like this year that had just slipped through my fingers, they were the lost opportunities, the times I could have gone to bed with Eddie, and didn't, the time I almost took off with another man, and didn't, choosing Grover once again, the time I could have taken a full-time singing job with a traveling band, and didn't, because we both agreed, Grover and I (always Grover), that, as Willie Nelson says, "the night life ain't no good life"—better, we agreed, to maintain the amateur status and spend your days and years on something wiser, more substantial, less precarious. Did I let him talk me into that? Could I now be standing where Emmylou Harris stands, instead of here, a walk-on, in this half-filled saloon on a rainy Saturday night?

These memories came tumbling in the seconds before Eddie kicked the floor button, drenching the stage in red. He had worked out an intro that could make your eyes water and your nose run, it was so poignant and heart-wrenching. The sound of it pushed me right over the edge. All the rage and hurt and jealousy building these past ten hours or so were channeled into the song. I could not see the crowd, but I knew I had them, the moment I opened my mouth.

It is a song about a woman who has given all her love to one man and she has just found out he has betrayed her. She is sitting in a bar, which is where you have to be sitting in a country-and-western song when it is time to think about your love life. She is listening to other lonesome songs on the subject coming from the jukebox, and she is bitter because she has loved so many other men along the way, or could have. She is feeling the loss of all the love that could have been expressed and wasn't, when into this same bar comes the guy himself. Before you know it, he is begging for forgiveness. By the end of the song you know that underneath the hate and the bitterness she still loves him and that she will be able to forgive him because there is something that runs deeper than the misfortunes of her love life, and that is her love of life itself.

I am not going to write out the lyrics, even though of all the songs I have composed, it is still my favorite. Country-and-western lyrics hardly ever stand up by themselves. You have to feel the tempo, fast or slow, and the mood, whether raucous or mournful. And you have to hear the instrumentation at every crucial moment in the story, what the strings are doing to underscore the feeling. I wish you could have heard what Eddie did that night when he took the middle chorus. Something happened between him and the fiddler. It was angelic. It was as good as a Mozart violin sonata with harpsichord, but with the added flavor of a roadside saloon and a brokenhearted woman. Later, when I finally stepped off the stand, Eddie told me it was the best this band had sounded and that it was due to something in my voice, the power of my voice. I told him it was because I was so pissed off at Grover, and he said, "Well, purely in the interests of country music I would encourage you to keep that battle alive."

The crowd got so much more than they had expected they went wild when "Love Life" was over. They were banging on the tables and calling out for more. I confess it did me some good. At that point I needed any encouragement I could get. We did another one of my tunes. Then I sang "Crazy" for Maureen. When I dedicated it to her, the crowd burst into spontaneous applause. When it was over, a line of funlovers at the bar began chanting, "Maureen, Maureen, Maureen." As far as they were concerned I could have kept singing all night. But three was enough. I was content with that.

Back at the bar another shot of Wild Turkey waited for me, a gift from Maureen, I thought at first, for singing her song. But she said, "No, it is an offering, from an admirer who shall remain forever nameless. I hope."

Nameless admirers seldom stay nameless for long, of course. This one turned out to be a fat guy in a cowboy hat who said he had heard me sing once at another club in another town. I told him I had never set foot inside that club. I had to tell him twice. He backed off about two feet and said, "Well, hell! I just wasted two dollars on the wrong goddam soprano!"

"Alto," I said, which got a good laugh up and down the bar.

I drank his drink anyhow, the way you can down your fourth or fifth or sixth or seventh. Too fast. I began to lose track of details. Little moments disappeared completely, while others seemed rich with meaning. I remember some guy leaning across the bar to tell Maureen a joke. "Did you hear about the Texas wino?" he said. "I have known a lot of Texas winos," she replied. And he said, "Well, somebody asked this particular Texas wino how much he drank every day. A fifth? A quart? And the Texas wino grinned and said, 'Shee-it—I *spill* that much!' "

The next thing I knew Eddie was sitting there asking if I wanted to move to a table where we could talk. He had something to show me.

"It was great to hear you, Holly," he said as we sat down. "Your singing always knocks me out."

"You're a sweetheart to say that. It's been a long time."

"Whenever you want to sit in, just let me know."

"I may take you up on that. Sure feels good."

I didn't know who provided them, but more drinks appeared from somewhere. Eddie raised one glass and pushed one toward me for another toast. Far far in the back of my mind a voice was saying, "This is the one that will do you in." A very soft voice. And quickly forgotten. As we sipped, he unrolled some notation charts and spread them out on the table.

"I started tinkering with this right after we worked together the last time," he said. "Been carrying it around in my car ever since."

It was an arrangement for "Honky Tonk Angels," featuring female voice and pedal steel. Eddie knew I liked that song. The fact is, it described the way I was starting to feel that night, killing time in the half-dark of The Last Roundup, with my face turning numb. I remember that the music in the room, on the between-sets tape loop, was Emmylou singing "Queen of the Silver Dollar." I remember that, but I don't remember what I said about Eddie's arrangement. I couldn't concentrate on it. The table's candle lamp was tinted such a deep orange I couldn't see the charts. We talked awhile, then I heard him asking if I thought tonight might be a good night to start working on it.

"You mean without rehearsing?"

"I was thinking maybe over at my place. Just working with acoustic guitar and voice. We could work through some of the changes."

I think I smiled. I have to admit it was flattering to be propositioned that way. It gave me a lift. But I was disappointed too, disappointed that he did not have . . . more tact, more patience.

I leaned forward and looked into his eyes. "I thought you considered yourself Grover's friend."

"I do. I love Grover. We have had a lot of fine times."

"Do you think you ought to be hitting on his wife her first night out of the house?"

"Hey, Holly. I'm not hitting on you. I mean, I am not just another guy who saw you across the dance floor. We go back a ways, don't we? You want to know the gospel truth, I have admired you for a long long time. As a woman. For a long long long time. And don't act like you didn't know it either, because a lot has passed between us. I have seen you looking at me in a certain way."

That made me giggle. "What certain way was that, Eddie?"

"The way a woman looks when she's interested."

"I am interested in a lot of people. As people. You know what I mean? What makes you think I'd want to single you out of all the people I am interested in?"

"Because I am right here. And tonight is tonight. And because

I appreciate you for who you are. You know, you are a lot better-looking now than you were five years ago. You are more worldly now. And, well . . . you know damn well I am crazy about you and been crazy about you. That song you just sang, you were singing what I was feeling, 'crazy for trying, crazy for crying . . .' "

"Ah, Eddie, that's sweet. But don't overdo it."

He was moving toward me. I knew I should have moved away, or turned my head. I delayed, and his face was next to mine, his Wild Turkey breath, his lips touching mine, brushing. I was not kissing back. Neither was I refusing to kiss. He could kindle desire in me. He had done it before, though I would never have told him so, at least not that night, not stroke him with the confession that the pedal steel itself, the plaintive rise and quiver he could send through the notes, had worked on me many times. Soft on musicians all my life. But in my muddled way I was thinking that if we were going to do something, this was a pisspoor time to start necking, since he had two more sets to play. His timing was bad. It was just too soon, too fast. There was too much else pulling at me, in spite of the whiskey. I pulled back and looked away.

He said, "What's the matter, baby?"

"You're a good-looking man, Eddie, and a good guitar player. Maybe even a great guitar player. But there is too much hustler in you, did you know that? You're rushing me. I don't like to be rushed."

"Sometimes," he said—and he was suddenly desperate, I could tell— "sometimes it's a way to ease the pain."

"Oh shit, Eddie. You've been listening to country music too long. Why'd you have to say a thing like that?"

This defused him. His eyes pinched up. "You sure know how to make a guy feel wanted."

I took his hand. I was drunk. He was getting there. But something had just cut a wide hole through the drunkenness, a tunnel of clarity through the great cloud of whiskey vision. I said, "I guess I just don't want everything to change on me all at once."

It was a one-way tunnel. Eddie's end was closed off. I could see him down there. I knew he did not know what I was talking about. He was looking at me, but he was peering into fog. I didn't mind. It was not a moment for sharing. It was a moment for *seeing*. I could see every pore in his face, every hair follicle. I could see every black hair in his beard and across the top of his forehead where he combed it back, the hairs close together yet separate, as if I were gazing into a forest. His face was not a mask, it was a perfect replica of a human face, which I had this rare opportunity to study at close range. I had never before observed anything in such detail. I was putting my full concentration on it, and suddenly Eddie's face rose up. I was gazing at the mother-of-pearl buttons on his rodeo shirt.

I heard Grover's voice saying something like "Get your goddam hands off my wife!"

I did not know how long he had been in the club or how much of this scene he had witnessed. But there he was. Later I learned he had been driving all over town and this was his final stop. He was boiling with frustration, in the mood to hurt somebody, and poor Eddie McQuaid, his favorite guitar player, was the first to get in his way.

Grover had him by the shoulders, literally lifted him out of the chair and spun him around with a fury that was new to me. He could carry a lot of anger, but most of it went unexpressed. Later I would come to appreciate what happened that night. Joking, I would be able to say, "If it weren't for Sarah teaching you how to express your deepest feelings, I would never have known how beautiful you are when you're angry."

That night, of course, I wasn't seeing it that way. They say Wild Turkey does things to you like no other brand of whiskey. I believe it. Grover decked Eddie there in The Last Roundup, just laid him out cold. Then he came for me, and I did something that took us both by surprise. I swung on him. In my paranoia I saw him as The Enemy Incarnate. I caught him on the jaw. It stunned him. He dropped back and fell into a chair at the next table.

Triumphantly I shouted, "And happy fucking birthday to you, Grover Doyle!"

He wouldn't look at me. I began to cry. Maureen came out

from behind the car carrying a white rag, just like the bartenders do in bad westerns after the fight is over. The next day I told her we were all acting like those people you hear about on the jukebox. No matter how hard you try, sooner or later you end up somewhere inside a country-and-western song.

6

The Reckless Edge

I did not want him to take me home. I protested loudly. I yelled at him the way you only yell when you are that drunk. It was an embarrassment, Maureen told me later, and yet, before many hours had passed, it had become a fine scene to describe over drinks at the bar. We two, or three, if you want to include Eddie, became the very thing I had hoped to avoid by going to Maureen's instead of Eleanor's—a tasty item of local conversation.

They tell me I passed out before we left the club. I don't remember it. I remember waking the next morning in my own bed and so hungover I could not see. Pain itself kept my eyelids glued together. There is a spot just above my right eye that will throb on such mornings. Though I have never been kicked by a mule, I imagine this narrow stripe of a searing throb is what it would feel like if a mule had caught me on the forehead with one edge of its hoof. The throb itself is not so bad. I can bear that quite easily, in isolation. But there are times when it sends reverberations through my body, ripples that make my stomach churn, broad waves of stupefying nausea. I try then to put my full attention on that mule-shoe gash. If I can only isolate that—so goes my heart-sick logic—if I lie still and slowly gather all the poison upward toward my eyebrow, I can keep the nausea under control. Some-times it takes several hours to accomplish this, and the effort makes me sweat and groan like a kid with scarlet fever.

That morning I had almost made it when the telephone rang. Though the phone was in the kitchen, down the hall and three rooms away, I felt its jangle in every suture of my skull. I told my-self to lie still and not think and not count the rings. It rang eight times. Only when it stopped did I realize something was missing. I had been waiting for someone to answer it. I had been waiting to hear the clatter of footsteps that meant Buddy and Karen were racing toward the receiver. Buddy had never cared much about talking on the phone until Karen discovered its mysteries. Now it was their battleground. They had already destroyed one extension cord, ripped it from the wall. That in turn had led to a little lesson in rewiring for Buddy. The immense silence that followed the eighth ring made me open my eyes and open my ears. The house was empty. I was alone.

I looked around the bedroom. It was unfamiliar to me. Out-side, steady rain was falling again. The light through my curtains was muted and strange, making things I had shopped for and hung on the wall look unreal, like cutouts. I was looking into a museum of dream objects, all sealed off and preserved. Framed photos on top of my piano had been propped there for centuries. The com-position book with a page flopped open to some half-finished song had been tilted like that since World War One. When the phone rang again, moments later, I almost cried out. It was the same person, I knew, redialing. I did not want to talk to anyone, but I could not bear the sound. Climbing out of bed, I stumbled toward the kitchen, slumped into a chair and picked up the re-ceiver, and heard my thick, oddly sultry, whiskey-graveled voice say, "Hello?"

I heard a click, then an empty line.

I shouted hello again, looked at the perforated mouthpiece in disgust, and hung up. I looked around the kitchen, at the fridge, at the stove, at the copper-bottomed pans above the stove, and the plants next to the window, and the window frame we had rebuilt together, and painted. It was a two-dimensional scene, a cartoon kitchen in this empty and silent stage set of a house, and into it burst Grover, the strangest fixture of them all. He came bounding up the back-porch stairs and through the door, obviously rushing toward the ring. When he saw me sitting there he tried to downplay his eagerness.

He said, "Was that the phone?"

"Were you expecting a call?"

"I heard it ringing. I didn't know you were awake."

"She hung up."

"Who hung up?"

"Whoever called. She heard my voice and hung up."

"How do you know it was a she?"

"I'm psychic."

He seemed to have a very thin line drawn around his head and body, which set him apart from the cupboard backdrop. I saw him the way I had seen Eddie, each reddish bristle on his chin and cheek, each tiny freckle. They are so close-set, he seems always to have a light tan, even in winter. That morning I saw them singly. His freckled skin was like a photo so enlarged you see the grain and lose the image. Was this my husband? My lover? My man to share a life with? How could he live two lives and only share one of them with me? And what was I doing here with this strange man in a strange house enclosed in skull-shattering silence?

There was only one thing about him I recognized or understood—a faint bruise across his jaw where I had slugged him. I focused on that, wondering if he would bring it up. My attention, I think, caused him to touch it absently as he said, "I took the kids to my folks' place. For the weekend. They always have a good time out there. Montrose built them a swing, in the big oak behind the house. And at night they get the full winter fire in the fireplace. . . ."

The matter-of-fact way he said this annoyed me. It was like yesterday, which had seemed to start like a normal Saturday. Now we were to embark upon another normal Sunday.

"Out behind the garage," he said, "there was a lot of debris building up in that culvert. I had to clear it. Keep the runoff flowing. Otherwise it could flood the vegetables."

"Christ, Grover! You talk like it's going to be business as usual."

"You want your vegetable patch to get flooded?"

"I don't give a damn about the vegetables."

"Well then, I won't worry about the culvert."

"That's right. The culvert can go fuck itself, for all I care. How many times has she dialed this number?"

"Who?"

"You know who."

"Hey. How do we know who called?"

"Now that I think of it, we have been getting calls like that for weeks."

"I'll ask the phone company to rig up a monitor."

"I have a headache, Grover. I am hungover. I don't have time for clever remarks."

He went to the stove and turned on a burner under the coffeepot and sat down across the table from me.

"Why did you take off like that yesterday?"

"If you want to know the truth, I could not stand to be near you."

"You still feel that way?"

I was poised at the reckless edge of nausea, with no taste for pretense or false drama. I said, "Right now it would be real easy to walk out of here for good. What would you think if I did? Would that make it easier? Would you like to get a divorce? I don't mind talking about divorce."

"I don't want a divorce. That is not what's going on."

"Then tell me what is going on. You said you're in love with somebody else. People who love each other used to get married."

"I don't want to split up with you, Holly. Don't you know that?"

"Maybe I'm the one who wants to split up. Did that ever occur to you?"

"Why can't we talk about this in a normal voice? If you love me and care about me, you'll try to understand what I am getting at. I have met someone who happens to be very important to me. That doesn't mean you are any less important. No one person can be everything to another person. You know this is true. Different people call out different things. Sometimes you have to surrender to a situation, you have to give yourself completely in order to learn from it and grow from it."

I was trying to concentrate on his words. One part of me wanted to calm down and cut through the hangover and understand whatever he was struggling with. I said, "Give me an example of what you are learning."

"There is a male within the female, Holly, and there is a female within the male. Until you are in touch with that, you are only living half a life."

He spoke these words so carefully, I listened hard, as if this might be the key to something. What he said was, of course, true. Everything he had said, that morning and the previous day, carried its measure of truth. I mean, you hear these ideas all the time nowadays, from people who seem to believe them and act upon them and take comfort in them. They are in the air. Much of the time I believe them myself. It was not what he was saying, it was the way he said it that repulsed me. It sounded rehearsed. Worse than that, I saw in his manner an uncharacteristic mushiness. His eyes were too soft, his voice too pleading. Ordinarily—I should say, before meeting Sarah—his remarks, even when spoken quietly, with utter gentleness, came with a vigorous edge. That had gone out of him, or perhaps been taken from him. His vigor was gone, or buried. In some way, Sarah was the culprit. This is how it seemed me then, although I did not yet know why. On that Sunday morning I only felt the loss of what once had been there, some loosening in his character. It sharpened my tongue, made it easier to say the things I said, do the things I did.

"Shall I fix up a room, then? Will she be moving in?"

"What is that supposed to mean?"

"If we are going to be sharing you, will we be sharing all the rest of it as well? Will she be helping with the dishes and keeping an eye on the kids and weeding the tomatoes . . ."

"Goddammit, Holly!"

"Or will she just get to share your inner life, while the rest of us take care of the outer life and the day-to-day trivial shit?"

"Will you shut up and listen to what I am trying to tell you!"

"I know what you're trying to tell me! You're trying to tell me you want two women at the same time. I'm telling you I am not built that way. So let's just get a divorce, and then you're free to roam."

"It's not that simple."

"It's real simple, Grover. All you have to do is make a choice. The sooner you face up to that, the quicker we will all know where we stand."

He wasn't ready for this. Neither was I. But at the time I didn't know that. I was still punching, and this one worked on him like a blow to the temple. This was in fact the very thing he had for weeks been avoiding. That brimming look came into his eyes again. Then the tears began to flow, forced to the surface by the pressures of an unsolvable dilemma. I should have taken pity on him. He was torn. He truly did not know which way to turn. I felt no pity. I felt only scorn.

I said, "Cut it out, Grover."

He looked at me, startled.

I know a lot about crying. The worst kind is crying alone. In the presence of someone else there are times when you cry with a double purpose. The upwell of emotion genuinely moves you to tears, and you are also aware of the effect of the crying. From the look on his face I knew he could not believe this show of tears had failed to change my view of him.

He was wiping his eyes when the smell of burning coffee turned him toward the stove. He switched off the flame. "You want any of this?"

"I'll have half a cup."

As he poured I said, "I need my car. I want you to drive me back into town to pick up my car."

He sipped the scalding coffee and thought about this. Finally he said, as if one favor deserved another, "Maybe later you can go pick up the kids."

I shook my head. "I don't want to pick up the kids. I don't want to drive all the way out there. I am not ready to deal with your folks."

"There's nothing to deal with. As far as they are concerned, the kids are with them for the weekend. That's all they know."

"Leona sniffs things out. She knows everything before it happens."

"You haven't said anything to her about this."

"Why would I?"

"You talk to her about everything else."

"I haven't had time, Grover, and even if I had time I don't have the energy to get into it with Leona. If you're worried about that, don't ask me to drive out there. I'm too confused. She'll take one look at my face and want to know what's going on."

"Well, you *have* to pick up the kids."

"Why can't you?"

"I'm going to talk to Sarah."

That stopped me. My eyes filled so suddenly with water, they stung.

"She's hurting too, you know," he said. "She needs to know how things stand."

"*She* needs to know!"

He looked away.

I shouted, "What about me?"

"I need time to think," he said.

"What do you have to think about?"

"Everything!" Now he was shouting. "I need some time!"

"How much time?"

"I don't know!"

"An hour? A day? A month? Give me a goddam clue!"

"I said I don't know!"

I was trying to control my rising panic. I could not control what now came into my voice, a sound I despised even as I heard it. I was begging him. "Don't do this to me, Grover. Why do you have to see her? Why can't you do your thinking here? Call her on the phone. But don't go see her. Please don't do that. Not now."

This show of weakness made him bolder. "I am going to go over and talk to her, and explain the whole situation. That's all. I owe her that."

"And then what?"

"Then . . . I guess . . . I can go pick up the kids, and I'll . . . we can meet someplace. Where will you be?"

I looked out the window at a limb of bay leaves slick with drizzle, silver-patched where sunlight leaked through the higher treetops beyond the creek. I knew he would go, and I knew I could not stop him, and I could not bear the thought of him having one more moment alone with her. I did not trust him. He had lost his will. And she, in my imagination, had some dark magnetism unavailable to me. The thought of them together filled me with a feverish dread. It made me mean.

I said, "Maybe I know what you're going through."

He looked over at me in surprise.

"I was in love with somebody else," I said, "for a while."

His face squeezed into a grimace. "What are you talking about?"

"I'm talking about having a lover."

"When?"

"A while ago. A few years ago."

"After we were married? Who was it?"

"There's no need for you to know who it was. I just want you to know that I loved him very deeply, and he loved me, and I had to make a choice, and it was a hard choice, but I made it."

"Goddammit, Holly, that is a hell of a thing to tell me at a time like this! Was it somebody from around here? It had to be."

"That's not important now."

"It was Eddie, wasn't it."

"No, it wasn't Eddie."

"You were kissing him last night. He was all over you, for Christ's sake."

"Maybe he was."

"How could you fall in love with an asshole like Eddie?"

"I said it wasn't Eddie!"

"Who was it? I have to know!"

"Well, you're not going to know."

"Then why did you tell me this?"

"I want you to think about me being in bed with somebody else. Think of somebody I love very much. Think of all the things I would do."

A look of such fierce rage came into his eyes, I stopped. His mind was running wild, as mine had. I expected him to hit me. That is, I would not have been surprised if he tried it again. At the same time I was glad to see that look. Even though fear of the immediate future was consuming me, these eyes told me that whatever she had stolen from him, or whatever he had let her steal, he had not yet given everything to her. He was not gone.

His eyes were blazing. He turned them, blue embers, toward the window, trapped in the furious cage of his own devising. A cage of mirrors. There was nothing he could say that would not reflect back upon his own behavior. He took it out on the cup he was holding, hurled it at the floor, sending shards and strings of black coffee across the tiles.

I was glad to see that too.

7

Regret Vanishes

The driveway gate would not close again, after he opened it to let the pickup through. With the earth so soggy, the gatepost had been leaning. Today was the day its bottom edge hit muddy gravel. I sat in the cab and watched him go drag a board from under the house to prop up the post so he could close the gate so the animals would not get out.

"We've had too damn much rain this year," he said as he slid behind the wheel. "I've never seen anything like it. The ground is saturated. Pretty soon we're going to have water standing in the yard and in the driveway. Every post in the fence will have to be reset."

I was filled with too much sadness to reply. As we started down the grade toward the road, I was thinking of the day we had hung the gate, when we first moved out of the A-frame he had built before we were married. During the A-frame period we were so far back in the hills, it had not been unusual for a day to pass when we saw no one but each other, until Buddy came along. Then there had been two dry years in a row. The well level dropped so low, all the plants and vegetables were suffering.

About that time we had decided we would have a second child, and figured we would sooner or later need a bigger place. This house happened to come on the market at a giveaway price, a few miles nearer town, and close to a creek that ran year-round, flowing down out of the county's watershed. A high slope protected its northern side, and all the fencing had been kept up. The timing itself seemed to be a sign that this was a move we were destined to make. Money was looming too. He had just gone into partnership, and solar paneling, so we told ourselves, would be the energy source of the future. Everyone said so. We looked for other signs. We consulted the *I Ching*. The coins led us to a hexagram entitled REVOLUTION. By chance the house we were looking at stood on Revolution Road, and the road followed Revolution Creek, named by early settlers who had moved there soon after the Civil War to found a utopian community. In the commentary beneath the hexagram we read, "Determination in a righteous course brings reward: regret vanishes!"

Such high hopes we had back then. Now here was Grover, who had set in motion the downfall of our household, and still he was the householder worrying over the gatepost he himself had implanted in concrete so it would stand and keep the gate swinging throughout eternity. And the road we had hoped to shorten was longer than ever, on such a day as this. With the air between us loaded, any road to town would be too long.

Neither of us spoke until we reached the first bridge. When we had crossed he said, "You're lying about that, aren't you. You made it up."

"Made what up?"

"About that other guy."

"If you say so," I said. "Sure. It's all made up."

That was it until we reached The Last Roundup, where my Chevy waited, gleaming by itself in the empty parking lot behind the club. It was then eleven a.m. We agreed that he would call me at Maureen's. When I tried to pin him down about the time of the call, he got vague.

"This afternoon," he said.

"I want a time."

"I have a lot of things to work out."

"Will you call me at one-thirty?"

He seemed stumped by this, at a loss for how to reply.

"Just check in, Grover. Please. This is one of the worst days of my life. Can you understand that?"

He agreed reluctantly and drove away, his face a mask of no-feeling, giving me nothing. It passed through my mind, as I watched the pickup disappear, that I would never see him again. A voice within me was shouting, "Wouldn't that be a blessing! Good riddance! Drive away and keep driving and leave me alone with my life and my thoughts!" Yet anxiety was jangling my veins, in long currents of cold electricity. I felt electrified ants crawling through my hair. Then my stomach began to growl and gurgle. It struck me that I had eaten nothing since the previous morning. I unlocked my car and fired it up.

Thinking of food for the first time in twenty-four hours, I drove to a highway restaurant outside town where they served huge three-egg omelettes. Years earlier it had been a truck stop. A freeway bypass changed the trucking routes, but this place had survived, through the sheer abundance of food they piled on your plate, the kind of place you went to when you wanted more than you knew you should eat for less than it ought to cost.

Ordinarily you had to wait fifteen or twenty minutes for a seat on Sunday, but my timing was good. The breakfast crowd was thinning, the lunch crowd was yet to arrive. I found a place and tried to read the paper someone had left behind. I couldn't concentrate. The accumulated disasters of the world meant nothing. My eyes jumped from story to story. More words. I detested words. You couldn't trust them. I ordered coffee, half a grapefruit, a large orange juice, then asked for Polish sausage to accompany the mushroom omelette covered with grated Monterey Jack and surrounded by thumb-size panfries, the house specialty.

I tried to take my time. As long as I was eating, I didn't have to think. But I couldn't take my time. I was shoveling it in, halfway through the omelette before I realized I had forgotten salt and pepper and forgotten to decorate my fries with a gob of ketchup.

When I raised my head to look for shakers I noticed a young fellow at the next table watching me wolf down the food. He was transfixed. He had a blond mustache and sideburns and hungry eyes. He too had a Sunday paper open in front of him. With a little smile he passed me the salt and pepper and ketchup from his table. I nodded and kept eating. He folded his paper and said, "I had the mushroom too," as if this were some club we now both belonged to.

I knew that if I gave him one word or look of encouragement he would be sitting across from me ordering another cup of coffee and telling me the story of his life. I said nothing. I hunched over my plate gobbling like a savage. I was the cavewoman at the start of a long cold winter, Cro-Magnon Holly, alone with my mushrooms and my scrap of roasted flesh.

At quarter past one I appeared outside Maureen's apartment. She did not know I was coming. I had neglected to let her know. As I waited, the appalling stupidity of this plan turned my stomach, made me queasy again. Suppose she were gone. Suppose her phone began to ring while I stood in the corridor. Then what would I do? When I heard the latch chain rattle I almost wept with relief. She came to the door in a T-shirt and shorts and acted as if she had been expecting me. She was floating. She had been out somewhere until four a.m. and was just getting up. From her half-size fridge she pulled two bottles of Heineken's, offering one to me.

I said, "I don't feel like a beer."

"Sure you do."

"I just ate."

"Think of your forehead," she said.

"My forehead's okay."

"Doesn't it feel like a very thin fried egg is drying on your forehead?"

I tried to visualize this.

She was grinning. "Am I right?"

"Yes."

"That is last night still talking to you. Whispering things. Last night is still whispering to me. One of these cold ones will take care of that feeling."

"Have you ever thought about tending bar?" I said. "You can make runaway drinking sound like truly noble work."

With a languid eye she said, "I don't start every morning this way, mind you. Only Sundays."

She lifted her bottle in a toast to recovery. I took a courtesy sip. "Sit down," she said. "Relax. I am going to shower."

"I can't relax, Maureen. Please forgive me if I just stand here and scream."

She had been studying my face, waiting, I suppose, for me to reveal what was on my mind, in my heart.

"You look scared," she said.

"I'm scared to death. What am I scared of?"

"You tell me."

I told her where he was and why I had come to her apartment.

"And now you're afraid he won't call."

"I guess so."

"What makes you think he won't?"

"I told him some things."

"What kinds of things?"

"Things I swore to myself I would never mention to anyone under any circumstances."

She sat down on the sofa. This was better than a shower.

I couldn't sit. Pacing, I described our conversations, the long one in the kitchen, the short one in the pickup. When she had heard it all I said, "It was a mistake, Maureen. A dumb mistake. I overreacted. There is no telling what is running through his head right now. He's frantic too. He could be talked into anything. That girl can do something to him. I don't know what it is, but I can see it in his face. What time is it?"

She turned to look at the bedside clock. It was already one forty-five.

"Oh shit, Maureen. Shit, shit, shit, shit, shit."

"Was it true, what you told him?"

I thought of telling her I had made it all up, just to hurt and torture him. But now I was eager to unburden myself. I have always envied Catholics the weekly ritual of confession. A five-year secret can eat away at you. When I told her the story was true, a kind of admiration came into her eyes, a shining warmth. She looked ready to embrace me.

She said, "How long did it last?"

"A couple of months."

"Who was it? Do I know him? What kind of a guy was he? Old? Young? Was he good-looking?"

"I have never talked about this. I made a vow to myself."

She sipped her beer and looked away, just as she would do at the bar, with someone on the verge of baring his soul. Available. But not demanding anything.

"He was about thirty at the time," I said. "It was crazy how we met. We were both standing in the same line at the Bank of America. He was married too. But the marriage wasn't right for him. He didn't quite know how to get out of it. It just wasn't working. He was getting ready to leave town. A job transfer. He wanted me to go with him. We were going to run away. We talked about it a lot, how we would manage it."

"Why didn't you?"

"There were so many things to think about. You know, you *want* to be a romantic and move on impulse and gallop through life . . ."

"But you said you loved him."

"I did. I guess I did. No. Yes. Of course I did. I mean, you know the song that goes, 'I told him that I loved him 'cause I loved him at the time.' Grover and I had just moved into the new house. Buddy was turning three. Can you just take off and leave a three-year-old behind? It was mad. It was exciting as hell, Maureen, but I was going out of my mind trying to juggle it all. That was when I joined the co-op, to have a place to leave Buddy during the day and all this extra driving around that came with it. That was my cover, you see."

She liked that. She said, "You were really into it."

"He's in New York City now. Somewhere. I haven't seen him since he left town."

"Is he still married?"

"I don't know. I'd be surprised if he is."

"Have you ever thought about him? I mean, about seeing him?"

The phone rang then, and my heart lurched. My body jumped. I lunged for the phone. She grabbed my arm and said coolly, "Let it ring a few times."

We waited, looking at each other. Finally she picked up the receiver and said, in a mellower, throatier telephone voice, "Hello?" After a pause she said, "You are calling who?" with a long-suffering face in my direction. Another pause and, "No, I'm sorry."

It was for someone who had lived in this apartment three years back.

When she hung up I was slumped into the sofa. "What time is it now?" I muttered.

She said, "Quarter after two."

The anxiety was running again, ice-cold air blowing through my arms and legs. It actually made me shiver. My elbows ached with cold. "Even if I wanted to go looking for him," I said, "I wouldn't know where to start. I don't know where she lives. I don't have a phone number. I feel so goddam inept, Maureen. How can things get so fucked up so fast?"

She was standing over me with her second Heineken's in hand.

"Will you take a look at what you're doing, Holl? Sitting here with your shoulders scrunched in. What are you—some kind of high-school girl waiting for Mr. Right to invite you to the prom? Suppose he doesn't call. What does that mean? What is the worst possible scenario?"

"It means that . . . she . . . I told you, he could be talked into something. He . . ."

"Are you really afraid he is going to split?"

I didn't know how to say what I was feeling. I groped for words. "It's not just that. It's losing . . ."

She was leaning forward, like an inquisitor, and gazing hard into my eyes.

"Now hold it, Holly. Let me suggest another way to look at this. Don't think about what you're afraid of losing. Think about what you want. I don't mean what you ought to want. But what you want. Look right at it. What is the first thing that comes into your head?"

I had a vision then. It appeared so suddenly and vividly, I blurted it out. "I want to go to New York City and spend some time with Howard."

That delighted her. She laughed. "Good for you!"

"I don't know why I said that. I haven't thought of him in months."

In this vision I had flown there, somehow, and we were both in his apartment, in each other's arms again.

"Maybe I'll go with you," she said. "I'll be your chaperone. What do you say? Shall we start packing?"

"If I had the cash, I think I'd do it."

"Put it on a credit card. That's what they're for. Don't you have a couple of cards?"

"Grover would go through the roof."

"Tough shit for Grover. He brought it on himself. This could be an important message, Holl."

"What do you mean?"

"Men understand things that cost them money."

Her eyes were so full of mischief, it infected me. She laughed again. This time I laughed with her. We clinked bottles in another little toast, and with that gesture something let go. I felt loose, and full of gratitude. I stood up and put my arms around Maureen, my big sister, my refuge. In her embrace I felt strong and safe. But the embrace did not last long enough, or I would not let it last. That day nothing could last, no single emotion. I was feeling them all, bouncing from one to another.

Next came a pang of maternal guilt. Grover's mom, Leona, had often praised my dedication to the task of raising kids. Now I saw her standing with them out there on her own front porch, watching the driveway. It was a black-and-white photograph, taken at dusk, and they all looked as if they had been standing there a long long time. Leona is a small woman, small and buxom and wise. At home she will wear faded jeans and her hair pulled back in a bun. She started life in Oklahoma, and this picture in my mind had that look about it, something from James Agee's *Let Us Now Praise Famous Men*—two little kids and a worried grandma waiting in the dust bowl for some long-gone loved one to return.

I stepped back from Maureen and said, "I should give my kids a call. They are like little barometers, you know. Even if they don't understand what is going on, they feel every change in the atmosphere."

Her eyes blinked away a quick and poignant glance at me. She had never had kids, and we had never talked much about it, except for her to say she had tried to avoid anything that would tie her down. Now she was thirty-four, and in that glance I could see the wistful query of a woman who knows her childbearing years are numbered. These are the fleeting glances that stay with you for a lifetime. There was Holly, overwhelmed by the UFO complexities of two-kid family life, her marriage pushed to the flashpoint, torn up inside by the wanderings of a man who himself was ready to bust. And there was Maureen, single again, without issue, spending as few hours as possible each night in her two-poster apartment, saying with her eyes that maybe there remains a great space in her life she may never fill. Just a glance is all it was, a flick in the air between two women sizing up their histories.

She looked down and said, lightly, "Where are they?"

"Up in the hills, with his folks."

"Well hell," she said, like some cowboy standing at her bar, "it's the best place in the world for 'em both. You may be missing them. But I'll bet they haven't given you a five-second thought since they got there. And what possible good are you going to be

to them anyhow, in your present frame of mind? C'mon. Let's
you and me get into the car and go somewhere. It's Sunday, for
God's sake. Let's go out for a Sunday drive. I can't stand this place
in the afternoon."

I saw that she was right. If I sat there five more minutes I
would be picking her sofa to pieces, shredding magazines. And
thanks to her question, I was already feeling loose again. How
long had it been since I had truly asked it of myself? You get
buried in duty, and for a while you tell yourself this must be what
you want or you wouldn't be doing it. Now that question, so long
unasked, came as a new idea. *What do you want?* It had triggered
something. As I thought of it again, it made me bold. It made
me impulsive. I thought of vengeance. I thought of freedom. I
thought of taking Maureen to see the Mothers of Us All. That
came into my mind as I watched her changing clothes. I half-
expected to find Grover and Sarah sitting in the auditorium again,
the criminals returning to the scene of the crime. It both frightened and appealed to me. If she was there I would simply confront
her, right at the podium, for all to see. Some high drama for a
Sunday afternoon. This was my fantasy. If those two were not
around, well, so be it. The conference was something I felt com-
pelled to share with Maureen, sister to sister. She did not ordinarily attend such gatherings. But I valued her opinion.

8

A Sunday Drive

We took my car. Our first stop was two blocks away, a 7-Eleven where I picked up some corn chips and a six-pack of San Miguel. I asked the clerk for a couple of small brown bags. We used these to hold the bottles, after we'd twisted tops off the first two, for highway sipping. The police had been riding herd on road drinkers, which is of course a commendable job for the police to be doing. But by the time we walked out of the 7-Eleven we were both in the mood for adventure. Just knowing twice as many cops were looking to catch us with these open bottles in hand gave a nice edge to the first few miles of our outing.

Maureen said Roy Acuff had recorded a song on this subject many years earlier. As we pulled out into traffic she began to sing:

> "There was whiskey and blood run together
> There in the pool where they lay.
> I heard the groans of the dying,
> But I didn't hear nobody pray."

She wanted me to sing along. I could have. I knew most of the words. But they spooked me. I said, "It doesn't feel right."

"Why not?"

"It could be a prophecy. You can bring things on yourself, make things happen. A song can be a foreshadowing."

"Okay," she said, approving of this idea, "let's think of a song that will make things come our way and turn out for the best. Maybe there'll be a tune on the radio we can hum along with."

She reached for the dial. Willie Nelson came in, singing "On the Road Again."

After we had listened awhile she said, "Is that a prophecy?"

"It's a synchronicity," I said. "Doesn't that happen to you all the time? You turn on the radio and the song is about what you're actually doing or something you just thought of?"

She said, "You're feeling better now, aren't you."

"I don't know."

"Sure you know. Tell me what you're thinking about."

I looked at her. She was watching me over the top of her paper bag. It was odd, being in my car with Maureen in the middle of that afternoon, when we both could have been doing just about anything else. The sudden sense of liberty made us accomplices. Her look was intimate, taking me in. It sharpened my mood. I was thinking again of Howard, in his apartment. He was just standing there with his collar open and hands on his hips. There was a view behind him—city buildings—through a plate-glass window. I was giddy with a kind of anticipation I had not felt in many years. Eager. And illicit.

She must have read my mind. She said, "Why don't you call him?"

"Call who?"

"Howard."

"He's in New York."

"You told me that. He's probably home right now. It's Sunday. You can get the weekend discount. Let's go back to my place and dial direct and see what happens. You have his number, don't you? I'll bet you have it memorized."

My body quivered with a tiny spasm, a mix of yearning and terror. I said, "I don't want to call him from here."

"Why not? What can you lose?"

"If I call him, I should already be there. It would be more effective to be there, as if I were, sort of, you know, passing through. It would be more spontaneous."

"It isn't impossible. I can drive you to the airport right now. I have the time."

"I can't just get on a plane and fly to New York."

"But you want to."

She waited, while the sweet west-Texas voice of Willie Nelson came through the speaker singing about the pleasures of travel for its own sake, and while we each took a surreptitious sip of the San Miguel. I knew she was still watching me. I kept my eyes on the road.

She said, "You want to, don't you."

She said this so seductively it made my blood race. In the next moment I was thinking again about Buddy and Karen. I suppose I had to, in order to put them out of my mind. I had not seen them since the previous morning. The truth was, I did not want to see them. I couldn't have said so at the time. Even now, it is hard to admit. But it was true. I wanted out. I wanted loose. I wanted space and I wanted time and no one's schedule but my own, and everything Maureen was saying seemed designed to justify what I was about to do. Her words fed me, fed my rush of tangled feeling, my anger and my longing. She had become the voice of some shadow person who lived deep within me, crying to get out. Either that, or she was reading my mind again.

"If I were you," she said, "I'd let Grover worry about the kids. You have done your share of worrying for a while. You think the kids are on *his* mind right now? I get so goddam tired of the deals women have to make at times like this. Grover tells you he has to spend one more afternoon with his girlfriend, and he expects you to sit around wringing your hands until he calls back. What do you think he would do if you told him you had to spend one more afternoon with your boyfriend to work out a few things you overlooked the last time you were together? He is the one running around, right? Not you. He is the one who has something going on the side these last three or four months or however long he is admitting to. And then when you find out about it, you are supposed to be filled with the milk of human kindness and have compassion for all he is going through. Your nurturing instincts are supposed to be wide open and flowing. But just let him catch you in the bar with your face up close to Eddie's, and what happens? Whammo! Fist city! Get your grubby hands off my personal private property, you cheap gigolo, you honky-tonk hustler! Doesn't it make you sick? I was proud of you last night, Holl, when you punched him out. Has he said anything about that?"

"Not a word."

"You can bet it's on his mind. He'll never forget it. If I'd had the nerve to do that to Charlie, I might not be where I am today."

"What happened with Charlie?"

"I let him walk all over me. Imagine a doormat with big letters across it that spell MAUREEN."

"I can't imagine anybody walking all over you."

"That is because I finally learned my lesson. But it took me a while, you see. I was a slow learner. We are all such slow learners. Sometimes I weep for the time it takes to see what is really going on."

We had reached the campus exit. When I turned she said, "Where we headed? I've got myself programmed for a trip to the airport."

"It's a little detour. I want to show you something."

I gave her a quick account of what I had seen there. As we entered the parking lot I began to search the rows, although I didn't really expect to see Grover's pickup. I already knew he wasn't anywhere near this place, and I knew the chance of his being here had almost nothing to do with my return.

We passed some women walking toward their cars. I stopped and said, "Is it over?"

The one who answered carried a chocolate-brown umbrella, color-coded to match her beige pantsuit. With a matronly frown she said, "As far as I'm concerned, it is."

That whetted our curiosity. We finished the beers and stuffed the empty bottles under the front seat. I parked in a space that had opened up near the stairs. From that far away, as soon as the engine died, we could hear the commotion, many urgent voices, and in the midst of the voices a rising howl, like a wolf, or a woman giving birth.

In the lobby the sign-up table had been abandoned. Both pairs of double doors were open. Inside we stood against the back wall. The hall seemed to be about half full. On the brightly lit stage six women who had apparently been sitting in front of a bank of microphones were now standing and staring at a woman in the second row, a red-haired woman, also standing, with rigid arms outstretched and head thrown back, howling at the ceiling.

Around her, dozens of others had gathered, the nearest offering hands to support her when she tipped backward or too far forward. Directly in front of her stood a woman wearing a black velvet cape, black skirt, and very black glasses. She had her hands on the stomach of the ecstatic woman and she was saying, like a chant, "Yes, yes, let it all out. Let it *all* out." In a second rank stood a semicircle of gypsy women, their eyes wide with wonder and their hands held at their waists, palms open, pushing at the air, pushing energy toward this woman who was howling with what could have been unbearably delicious pleasure, or terrible pain, or both.

Everyone in the room was straining to see. No one made a move to calm her or to interrupt her outburst. It was, I learned later, the unforeseen conclusion to the two-day conference, which had as its final scheduled event a panel discussion called "The Goddess in Our Midst." These six panelists had been responding to testimony from members of the audience when this woman stood up to unleash her wordless cry. Now the moderator, the same speaker I had heard on Saturday, stepped to a mike and said, in her academic voice, "Don't be alarmed. She is in a trance. Give her room. Let her move about. Let her take it wherever it has to go."

The woman screamed, she wailed, she laughed hysterically. In the half-light I tried to see her face. She was about forty, I figured, with a European look, a seasoned look. The wild laughter made her arms go stiff again, turned her hands to claws.

The nearest women were reaching toward her shoulders again, not to support her now but to make closer contact with the explosive release. Their reaching troubled me. It was distasteful. It was wrong, though I could not yet say why, any more than I could take my eyes off this woman. Her hair, short and close to the head, reminded me of my mother, who had been about this same age when my father disappeared the second time. Late one night he walked out of the house and we did not hear from him for six months. She didn't howl. Not out loud. But I know she carried this kind of hysteria inside. This is how my mother felt, and this is the way she would have acted if she had thought she could get away with it, if she had not been so ruled by how she might look and what others might think.

The witch lady in the black velvet cape drew back. She removed her black glasses to reveal eyes rimmed with black liner. With both hands pushing invisible waves forward from her black waist she repeated her soft and soothing incantation, "Let it out, let it out, let it all come out."

The speaker at the mike said, "Does anyone have some of those clinkers? Something to make a little noise or . . ."

She did not have to finish the request. Immediately they appeared, in all parts of the room, out from under shawls and pullovers—the tambourines and tiny drums, castanets and rattles, going tonka tonka tonka tonka, chinka chinka chinka chink. A few young women began to sway to the beat. Soon small groups were dancing their own ecstatic dances, belly dances, tribal dances. Skirts and scarves were twirling, while the red-haired woman who had ignited this display wailed and laughed and writhed and went stiff, thrust her arms wide with fingers taut as lightning rods.

It was going on too long, and I understood the reason. They were using her, feeding on her. I wanted to be appalled. But I was not. I too felt the urge to dance, to squirm. I wanted my hands to be quivering with that atmospheric charge. Her arms were my arms, her voice my voice. Without words, she spoke to me, even as I wished that I did not have to listen.

That was why I did not like the look of all those dancing, touchy-feely women. I knew too well what they were doing. I was doing it with them. I felt sleazy watching her, because she was so naked down there, so exposed. Though I wanted not to be watching this, I couldn't stop. I was the voyeur peeking through undrawn curtains. Covert. Greedy.

I glanced at Maureen and saw her eyes shining with a look I had not seen there before, so close to lust it made me uneasy. It could be the beer, I thought. She'd had three.

I said, "What do you think?"

"It's almost like sex, isn't it. Like watching sex."

It was uncanny, that her response came so close to mine. I wondered if my eyes resembled hers.

"Have you ever done that?" she said, as she turned those eyes upon me.

"Done what?"

"Watched sex."

I had to resist the urge to step away. She was reading me too closely. I was beginning to feel the way Eddie made me feel. She was getting in too close. I didn't want her to, although it would have been easy to let her, as easy as letting Eddie. Where do these signals come from, the one that shines green for go, red for stop, amber for proceed with caution? I still don't know. But at that moment I knew I had to get away from Maureen. I had to get away from everything. I was on the move, and wherever I was moving, it was going to be a solo trip.

9

Legends of Undying Love

I lied. I told her seeing that woman had freaked me out. She wanted to know what I intended to do. I said I didn't know. I wasn't sure. After witnessing such a scene, I told her, I just wanted to be by myself, which, up to a point, was true. I told her this several times. Eventually she got the message. She smiled her wistful smile and said maybe it was just as well, because Wally, the guy who owned The Last Roundup, had asked her to come in early and she could use the money, although she would happily forgo it and drive me somewhere if I needed—what was the word she used—*reinforcement?*

I dropped Maureen outside the Sunburst. When we hugged again, at parting, I held back, did not give myself completely. She felt that. I could see the question in her eyes. I looked past the eyes, telling myself I would explain everything later.

When I was two blocks away it occurred to me that I had forgotten to tell her what to tell Grover, if and when he called. I let it go. I had three San Miguels left and nothing but four-lane roads and freeway from there to San Francisco.

At the airport I left my car in long-term parking. I didn't know how long I'd be gone and didn't care, hadn't thought it through and didn't want to. I had a checkbook and two credit cards. I could buy some clothes, if I needed them. I could find a hotel, if I had to. If I went over the limit on the cards, well, Maureen had been right. No matter how it turned out, the whole experience would be good for Grover. He still had not learned one of the basic lessons of the modern world: When in doubt, borrow. The more you owe, the more you are worth. The person we care about most is the one who owes the most money and is farthest behind in his payments. Grover likes to pay his bills on time and hold debt to a minimum. In that respect he is almost unpatriotic. I told myself that a spending spree in New York City could be a way to help him move a little deeper into the mainstream of American life.

At the United counter, with a shoulder bag to carry and nothing to check through, I bought a one-way ticket to La Guardia. My timing was perfect. A price war was going on. For two weeks only, the late flight east was ninety-nine dollars. It was another sign, a confirmation that my path was the right one.

I stopped at the bar and ordered a Jack Daniel's over. The bartender asked me if I'd like a double.

"Why? Do I look like I need a double?"

"Lot of people come in here before a flight, they order a double."

"They don't like to fly?"

"They're petrified. I have seen people hold on to the edge of this bar like it was the edge of a steep cliff. I have seen knuckles turning white."

"Not me," said I. "I just go into deep meditation and concentrate on the pilot. I make direct contact with his subconscious. Holly to Pilot, I think, Holly to Pilot. I am with you in body and in spirit. We are all with you. This plane is blessed and everything is going to be okay."

Later, on board, after I had devoted my full inner attention to a safe and uneventful takeoff, I was able to relax, for the first time in days. For the first time in months, I was alone. The plane was only half full. I had a window seat, with no one else in my row. I was entirely alone and at my ease for what seemed like the first time in several years. When the flight attendant asked me what I wanted, I ordered another Jack Daniel's and a set of earphones. The whiskey came in a miniature bottle with a miniature black label. Slowly I poured it over the ice and slowly sipped as I listened to Channel Four, the country-and-western channel. I heard Conway Twitty sing "I've Never Been This Far Before." It made my veins buzz with inspiration, the lonesome passion in what could just as easily have been the best church-choir voice in Waco, Texas, or in San Bernardino, the combination of innocence and small-town masculinity and desire.

It started me thinking about Howard. Not because he himself ever listened to country music. He didn't. He listened to recent jazz. In that respect—in several—he was not like Grover. You could almost say he was the opposite of Grover. There was something brutal about Howard that used to stir me. A mean streak. Grover is never mean. His anger does not take that shape. It is not in his nature. Even in skin they are different. Grover's has always been athlete-smooth, his arms, his belly, his back. Howard was covered with hair. When we made love he would roar and thrash. We would have to find isolated places to meet so he could feel free to roar. On the plane I tried to remember the many sounds of Howard's voice. I began to imagine what I would say when I called him in New York, and then what he would say, what I would say when we met again face to face and what he would say, how he would say it, and how he would look. In my mind's eye he had not changed.

Sitting in my tipped-back seat with the unbuckled belt ends loose across my thighs and the last sip of the Daniel's mixing with melting airplane ice in my plastic airplane glass, as we cut through the night sky above North America at six hundred miles per hour, I relived our entire affair, day by day, right up to the moment he left, the way he had said goodbye, the sharp ache of that memory thankfully dulled by whiskey, the whole reconstruction anesthetized by my melancholy glow and the hum of the plane.

"I'll always love you" is what he said. I wanted to believe he meant it. How many times in your life do you get to hear that said to you, after all, with what appears to be deep sincerity? I can count on two fingers the men I have heard say it. Grover is the other one, and I remember the day, or series of days.

It was the spring before we got married. We had been living together over a year, and I just had to go off by myself for a while. The fact is, I left him twice before we were married. The second time I was gone a week. When I came back we spent three consecutive days in bed. Though I had not heard him say it since, he must have said it fifty times in those three days, "I'll always love you, Holly."

When men tell you such things, what do they mean? I can hear Maureen's answer. "When a man says that, he has reached the point where he will say just about anything to get into your pants." But when Grover said it, he was already into my pants. When Howard said it, he was on his way out of my life. It is not what someone else means, it is what you want the words to mean, or expect them to mean, that leads to so much disappointment.

What did I expect that phrase to mean? How about fidelity? Is that the key? Years and years of unswerving fidelity? That old idea still hovers around the words. But is it possible in this day and age? Was it ever realistic? God knows, I did not make it. Could I really have expected Grover to? Or anyone else? Perhaps you want the words to mean a place in his heart forever. That is closer. But not close enough. You want them to mean *the* place in his heart. Yes. You want the words to mean that you are the one he cares about most, no matter what else happens, no matter who he may encounter as he moves through the world.

If that is what "I'll always love you" means, it might explain something I began to glimpse as I sat there with my memories and my battered feelings coated and desensitized by drink. Down below the anger and the rage and the ego damage and the sexual doubt and the fear of aging, right at the bottom, there was a basic disappointment about the way Grover had managed things, or failed to manage them. A carelessness. I had known the buzz of high risk. I had arranged meetings with Howard, covering my tracks. I understood the line Grover had crossed, through sloppiness. Thoughtlessness. I resented that I had been forced to deal head-on with the situation, and I carried this resentment around for quite some time, thinking a more considerate or sophisticated man would have known how to avoid that, how to protect me. Eventually I saw that he could not have done things any other way, being who he is. I saw that he could never have protected me in that manner, simply because he is incapable of deceiving anyone for long. He is, as I said, a Puritan at heart, and a true Puritan soon breaks under the pressure of double-mindedness and deceit.

I didn't understand this yet. Months would have to pass. On the plane I was right back where I'd been the night before, drunk again, and listening to country music, where the words "I'll always love you" are sung so often they keep that old promise smoldering forever in the heart. I have never mentioned this aloud to anyone, but I think country music is our New Mythology. Maybe it is the only mythology we have left—legends of undying love, legends of that love betrayed, legends of motherhood, legends of home.

When the booze caught up with me I was carrying on a silent and somewhat incoherent dialogue with Howard. Then my eyes closed and I slept fitfully until the plane touched down.

The big clock said six forty-five when I stepped into the terminal. I looked at my watch. It said three forty-five. I looked at the clock again, stared for a long time, as if the staring could somehow recover the three hours that had just disappeared. It was like walking into Long's Drugs in the middle of the day. I was disoriented, and I wanted to be disoriented. It released me. I was free to float.

I stared at the clock until I blinked and discovered my eyes were raw. Someone had filled my sockets with sand. I could not blink it away. My whole head was packed with sand and gravel. I needed more sleep. It was too late for sleep. In the short-order shop I had an English muffin, pear halves, coffee. Gazing into the dark pool of the coffee cup seemed to rest my eyes, clear my head.

I might have been into my third cup, sipping and gazing, when I realized someone had joined me at the table. I looked up to see a young man dressed all in white—long-sleeve white shirt with white Nehru collar against the very pale skin of his slender neck, and around his neck white beads. I had no idea how long he had been sitting there gazing at me gazing into my coffee. His eyes were green, accented by a tiny green jewel on the lobe of one ear. As his eyes caught mine he smiled a priestly smile. Why, I thought to myself, is it so difficult for a woman to have a meal by herself?

"Are you alone?" he said.

"I was."

"I have just walked through the entire airport, and of all the people in this very big building I find myself drawn most powerfully to you."

I just looked at him, the way you look at a flickering fireplace late at night, lacking the will to turn away. He must have taken this as a sign of interest.

"I know you are waiting for a plane," he said. "So am I. We are both, as they say, en route. I don't live here. I am flying to New Mexico. For the light. That's all we have, you know. The rest is, well, really only a matter of time."

I glanced at the clock. Seven-fifteen. Still too early to call.

He went on, his voice in the low range, baritone, resonant and precise, a radio voice. He would have made a good talk-show host.

"I know it is hard to think about the weapons we have now. But with maniacs in control of the world, on their own self-destruction trip, any weapons they have, they are going to use. I am convinced of it. All you have to do is study the history of technology to see that those weapons are going to be used. There is nothing anyone can do to stop it. What we have to do is stop looking at it with fear and see it as another step in the evolution of life on this planet. All you can do is move yourself to a higher plane of consciousness. Become a Light Steward. Join those who will survive the apocalypse. They will be the seed people for a new beginning in a purer environment. The way you ward off evil, and I am talking about things as basic as attackers at street level, such as you find the moment you step out of this airport, is to surround yourself with an aura more powerful than theirs. I think this is also the way to survive the nuclear holocaust. You make yourself as pure as you can. You purify your life. You get on that path with the other Light Stewards and you begin to partici- pate in the evolutionary life of the planet. After the apocalypse, which is simply the inevitable climax of the industrial imperial technological thrust of the last several hundred years with its built-in self-hate and self-destruction, there will be a new begin- ning, and I intend to participate in that."

I drained my cup and pushed back my chair. He stood up quickly, as if to detain me. I saw that his white muslin trousers matched his shirt, held up by a broad paisley waist sash looped with beads.

"Did I say the wrong thing?"

"I have to make a call," I said. "Excuse me."

He placed his palms flat together in front of his chest and bowed from the waist like a Hindu, as I headed for the line of phone booths in the lobby.

Too early to call Howard, it was not too early to call the other person I knew in that city, my old roommate, Barbara. The year before I moved in with Grover, she and I had lived together for two semesters in Berkeley, in those days a town filled with people like the Light Steward. I had been one of them, in a way. That had been the last time, I realized as I began to dial, when I could come and go as I pleased. When Barbara left for the East Coast, a few months after graduation, I had said, "Don't be surprised if I ap- pear one morning on your doorstep."

"Holly," she had said, "at this point, nothing you do would surprise me."

We had been renegades together, organic girls and part-time revolutionaries. We had faced police helmets at the People's Park showdown in 1969 when Governor Ronald Reagan sent helicopters armed with tear-gas canisters into the skies over Berkeley. We were the first in our apartment building to successfully sprout marijuana seedlings in a window box.

"Barbara," I said, when I heard her voice on the other end, "if you can identify the speaker, you win a free weekend in Parsons, Kansas."

"Holly!" she cried. "I can't believe it! Where are you?"

"I'm in New York."

"My God, it's so good to hear your voice! You're here in town?"

"I'm at La Guardia. I just landed. Is this too early to call?"

"Not at all. I'm up. I'm dressed. What's going on? How long are you staying?"

"It's just a little trip. An adventure. You know. Sometimes you have to do it."

"I know exactly what you mean."

"I'll explain when I see you. I mean, I *hope* I can see you. You're probably on your way out of the house right now."

"As a matter of fact, I am not on my way out of the house. This happens to be the one morning for months and months that I do *not* have to be at work by nine a.m. The exterminator is coming at nine-thirty, and I want to be sure I'm here. He is the best one in the neighborhood. We've been trying to get him literally for months. Once I have an appointment, I want to make sure I establish a good relationship right at the beginning. You know what I mean?"

I didn't know what she meant, but I grunted something, and she plunged on. "Anyway, what I'm getting at is, I *know* you can't be meeting anybody else this early in the morning, so why don't you grab a cab and come on over now. That may sound strange, but then nothing we ever did was normal, was it, Holl. It would give us a couple of hours to talk. I can't wait to see you. My God, you can *stay* here if you want. Did you tell me where you're staying?"

"I'll tell you everything when I get there."

She gave me directions and her address in Brooklyn Heights. Five minutes later I was cruising down a wide boulevard with the Manhattan skyline on my right, bright and sharp-edged as a mountain range in the cold, muted rays of a rising winter sun.

10

Her Sense of Destiny

Barbara lived in a walk-up on a block of narrow three-story build-ings pressed side by side and all about a hundred years old. From her window she had seen the cab and now appeared at the front door. She couldn't wait until I climbed the stairs. "Let me get the cab!" she cried, as she rushed down to greet me at the curb.

"I got it," said I. "I already got it. He's gone." I was waving him on his way.

Toward the departing cab she yelled, "Hey wait! What about your bags? Don't let him drive away with your bags!"

"I don't have any bags," I said, then watched uncertainty flicker in her eyes.

Seeing that, I knew I had to cover myself. I also knew this was all wrong. I had made the wrong move, at the wrong time. It was stupid. It was doomed. Barbara looked terrific, dressed for work, ready to head off to her job—she was a design consultant, I found out later—here in the richest city in the world. The air's hard chill put color in her face, made her features sharp. Her eyes were bright, and her clothes were new. They seemed to glow with perfect taste and high fashion. And there I was, in my Emmylou Harris outfit, jeans and suede jacket and sweater, red-eyed from the red-eye special, disheveled and standing at her curb without luggage.

"There was a mix-up back in San Francisco," I said. "They put the bags on the wrong plane."

"We should call right now."

"I've taken care of it. Really. They'll be in this afternoon."

"You're sure."

"Absolutely. It's just a nuisance. But no problem."

Her eyes examined mine. Another moment of doubt. It quickly passed. She wanted to be as loose as we had been in the old days, although everything about her suggested the opposite. Barbara was shorter than me by about five inches, short and pert and trim. Her look, her stance, her clothes all declared there was no margin for error in her life. Next to her, on that particular morning, I felt like error personified.

"Well, come on up, then. I've got some coffee on the stove. I can't tell you how great it is to see you! Here. I'd better explain this right now, just in case you have to let yourself out."

She was referring to the security inside her front door—a doorknob lock, a deadbolt, a heavy chain on a bronze latch.

"I'll give you the keys before I go. All you have to remember is, you open this one first. Then this one. And when you let yourself back in, it's the reverse. The building has never been broken into. The people across the street say there is a curse on it."

She said this with a devilish grin that reassured me. It was the playful, youthful roommate's grin.

"What kind of curse?"

We were climbing a flight of wooden stairs, and she spoke softly, with a nod toward the landlord's apartment. He occupied floor one.

"They say every building has its allotment of misfortune. It is better for a building to get broken into from time to time by inept and petty thieves. That way each individual theft is small, and you can absorb each loss as it hits you. Otherwise the time will come when the house will be ravaged in a major way. A gang of professionals will move through like locusts and walk away with everything and leave behind nothing but an empty shell. It is the karma of the house that seems immune to crime."

"Something tells me you are making this up."

With a laugh she said, "That was just a test, Holly, just a test. Here is the upstairs door. One key this time. When you're letting yourself out, don't turn it too far to the left or it unlocks itself again. Isn't that ridiculous? Barry is having it changed. Meanwhile the thing to remember is, always check it."

She ushered me into a long room that ran the length of the building, front window to back window. My first glance took in dark floors, highly polished, and woven rugs and crushed velvet upholstery, oil paintings and leafy plants—all things I myself might have chosen, in another reincarnation. I was on the defensive again. I felt outclassed.

I said, "I love your place, Barbara."

"We're still working on it. There is so much moisture in the walls, we may have to have the whole thing repainted. Just sit down anywhere. I'll bring in the coffee. I want to hear *every*thing."

I followed her into the kitchen and leaned against the doorframe while she set out two porcelain cups and saucers. This room was so small you couldn't do much to it, and she hadn't tried. Just the basics. It felt better there. You always feel more at ease in the kitchen. Barbara was still talking.

"If it were just the two of us, we wouldn't have a place this size. God knows, we can't afford it. But with David coming in, we needed the second bedroom, which is the one you can use, by the way, if you want. It's upstairs. I'll show it to you."

"David is?"

"Barry's son. Didn't I write you about this? His first wife? They met each other at Columbia, and they lasted about three years. So he has, we have—get ready for this—a thirteen-year-old who calls me Mom. He stays here every other weekend."

"A thirteen-year-old. Do you trust yourself around him?"

"A couple of years from now I could be in trouble. He is already gorgeous. He left this morning with Barry and won't be back for a couple of weeks, so the timing is perfect. He lives with his mother most of the time and goes to high school in Manhattan. At this moment on a usual Monday we would all be taking the subway together. When we do, I have to make a special effort to be nice to David and not reveal my true resentment, because the morning subway ride is sometimes the *only* time Barry and I have to ourselves. I'm kidding, you understand. It's just that we hardly ever see each other. If you and I stay up late enough he may make a daring pre-midnight appearance."

A little sadness was creeping into her voice, a little cynicism. I needed to convince myself it had nothing to do with my arrival. I said, "Please don't feel like you have to put me up, Barb. I really just called to say hello. If you've had David staying for the weekend, I know you don't want somebody else barging in on you right away. Showing up at this ungodly hour to make a social call is already pushing my luck."

"I *want* you to stay here, Holly. This is the greatest thing that has happened in years. Mi casa es su casa. Right? The only problem is, you could get lonely in a place like this. Most of the time you'll have it to yourself. I tend to work late. Barry works later. He is ambitious. The original workaholic. He just turned thirty-five. If everything goes his way, three or four months from now he will be national sales director for this publishing house he is with. Right now it means literally living at the office. Unless, of course, he is living with somebody else on a part-time basis. You can never rule it out, you know. You can never really know what is going on. You hear the wildest stories. So he and I, we see each other from time to time. Ships that pass in the night."

She had been standing at the counter with the coffeepot in hand. Now she paused to pour. When the cups were filled, she waited. I knew she wanted some equivalent information from me. If I provided it, we could begin to peel back the layers, tell all, confess and purge. I was tempted. We had done a lot of that. I considered asking if it troubled her that Barry could have something going on the side, or did she just take this for granted. It occurred to me that everyone took it for granted, and I was among the last to confront the most obvious fact of married life. I was interested to know how deep her cynicism went. But I held back. I was not in the mood for that kind of talking, at least not at six a.m. Pacific Standard Time. I could feel fatigue working at the edge of my throat. Whatever I had left to bring to the subject of my love life, whatever remained of my voice or my self, I would save for Howard. I guess I was craving the male point of view.

"Am I talking too much?" Barbara said. "Please take all this with a grain of salt. I don't know why I'm going into it. Seeing you again, I suppose. It's like no time at all has passed. We can just pick right up again, as if it's been a couple of days instead of ten whole years."

"Has it been that long? I can't believe it."

"Nine and a half."

"I don't even want to think about it."

"You haven't changed, Holly. Not a bit. Now don't make a face when I say that. I'm serious."

"You're the one who hasn't changed. Except your hair is so much shorter. When did you cut it?"

"Ages ago. It was time for a change. But c'mon now. You still haven't told me what you're doing in New York."

"Let's call it a little outing, Barb, an open-ended trip."

This time the doubt in her eyes was more than a flicker. She almost smiled a knowing and suspicious smile. I would either have to tell her everything or lie again, start lying like a teenager.

"Does Grover approve of things like that?" she said. "I mean, are you and he . . . ?"

"You remember the fiddler in that band he was playing with when I first met him?"

"That guy you slept with on the night you were supposed to move in with Grover?"

"I didn't sleep with him, Barbara. When are we going to put that legend to rest?"

"It's all water under the bridge. You never would tell me what he was like."

"There was nothing to tell. Our relationship has always been . . . purely professional."

Her eyes brightened. She liked the lascivious double edge.

"This guy has stayed with it," I said, "and now he is here in New York. He has a group and some kind of recording setup where he is cutting demos, and he called me up one day. He said he always remembered my songs and wanted to know what I was working on. I sang a couple for him over the phone and he got so excited he said he wanted to use them. The next day I started to put them on a little cassette and then thought to myself, Dammit to hell, these cassettes never get the quality you want and you haven't gone anywhere in a long time or done anything much. I talked about it with Grover. We bargained, actually. Sometime during the next six months he will get to take the solo trip of his choice. Meanwhile he is now back home minding the place and the kids. Buddy is almost eight, you know. He can handle himself most of the time, and help keep an eye on Karen. So Holly Belle, mother of two, had an irresistible urge, and here she stands, ready once again to make it big in show business."

As I spoke I watched Barbara weighing all this. By the time I finished I knew she had decided to believe it. She wanted to believe it. Her eyes filled with approval.

"That is so much like you, Holl."

"It's a long shot," I said, with what I thought was an appropriately humble shrug.

"The free spirit," she said. "Doing things your own way. I could never in the world do a thing like that. I don't think Barry would mind much. But I would mind. I'd have to plan for months."

Something about the two of us came clear to me then. I understood how we had been able to get along at all. Sometimes ten years have to go by before you can grasp these things. We had been opposites. That was the key. For her I had been a kind of mentor in unpredictable behavior. We had been the long and short of it, the east and the west, the efficient and the impulsive, and Barbara still saw us—saw me—in these terms. Was there any harm in letting this continue? It would make it very easy for the two of us to continue to get along. With luck it would explain away the look of my clothes. There is no doubt I preferred to see myself that way, spontaneous, living on the ragged edge. Not a woman trapped by circumstances. Maybe that's what I was doing there, putting myself in the company of someone who saw me as I chose to be seen. Maybe Barbara could remind me who I had been, who I could become, or be again.

"C'mere," she said. "I want to show you something."

We were holding cups and saucers, sipping at the coffee, which was French roast, dark and rich, with a bit of chicory to scent the air and bite the tongue. Guiding me back into the long room, she said, "Barry waited around to the last possible second. I'm sorry you missed him. After looking at your picture for so long, he wanted to meet you. You probably passed him about the time he and David turned the corner."

"Looking at what picture?"

"Why do you have to desecrate the walls of this fine and historic building, he says, with photographs of Berkeley hippies? We weren't hippies, I tell him. We were explorers, we were pioneers. If you want my opinion, I think it's jealousy. I think he has been jealous of Grover ever since I had this picture framed."

At the far end of the room a writing desk stood well positioned for receiving window light. Among the gallery of snapshots and portraits hanging on the wall above this desk there was an eight-by-ten of Barbara and Grover and me walking arm and arm along Telegraph Avenue, the kind of photo that captures perfectly the spirit of the time and reminds you how long ago it was and how quickly every moment you have cherished rushes past. Barbara is wearing a T-shirt with no bra—we were both going braless in those days—and across her chest a slogan, LEGALIZE CLEAN AIR. The slogan across my chest reads, EVOLUTION IS A STYLE OF LIFE. My hair is down below my shoulders, hanging loose. From my ears hang gaudy bangles, on my forehead a Hindu beauty spot. My skirt is sewn from recycled flour sacks and on my feet are the old sandals made by Earthshoe.

Grover walks between us in this photo, grinning his gap-toothed grin. He has a mustache, blond and scraggly. He wears a blue workshirt, as he always did, with floral embroidery across the front, and the turquoise belt he later gave away when he decided that all Indian jewelry and metalwork looks false on anyone except a bona fide Native American, and below the belt, against the front pocket of his jeans, a large round badge saying DUMP NIXON.

Barbara said, "Do you remember what we were doing that day?"

I remembered. Grover and I had just decided we would move in together, or rather that I would move in with him. We were on our way to a barbershop. One of my conditions was that he shave off his mustache. It made him look like everybody else, I had told him, and it bothered me when we made love. His willingness to do this became a symbol of something. "Clearing the decks" is how he described it. The shaving became a kind of celebration, and in the middle of the party, just as the barber laid a hot scented towel across Grover's eyes, calling forth an erotic groan of pleasure, I had walked out of the shop and disappeared for two days. Barbara still believed I had gone for one final fling with the fiddler before settling down. Why not let her continue to think so? It suited the memory we both preferred.

Though the photo resurrected every detail of that day, I did not want to talk about it. At that moment I could not speak— Holly the Impulsive, so trapped and fenced in by the shape of her life that even here, on the opposite side of the continent, she heads directly for the one room in the city of New York that would display a photo of the husband she has traveled this far to avoid.

Finally I said, "We were such children, Barbara. Innocents in the midst of absolute depravity and sin. When I think of what used to go on along Telegraph Avenue. Look. In the background there. Next to the storefront. Somebody is folded over on the sidewalk. He looks like a pile of rags. It's like Calcutta. How could we be looking so well scrubbed and wholesome?"

She turned from the photo and leaned against the long window frame, gazing down into the yard behind the building. Winter sunshine across the fine tweed of her tailored suit made a picture like one of those old Dutch paintings, the slant of light, the woman thoughtful, her clothing correct, her eyes averted, her complexion flawless. Barbara had a knack for doing this. It was always mysterious to me, the way she could frame herself against the light and become a tableau. Some time fell away. My heart swarmed with old affection.

She said, "Let me ask you something, Holly. Do you ever think about the Sixties? As a special period?"

"I do, yes. Now that you mention it."

"You ever have the feeling that the Seventies never got here?"

"What do you mean?"

"As a decade. As an era."

"I hadn't thought about it quite that way."

"When we started at Berkeley in 'sixty-eight people had the feeling that the world was on the brink of something . . . I don't know . . . huge. You didn't know what it was going to be. But you had this feeling of something on the rise, and you were in the middle of a great anticipation. Do you know what I'm trying to say?"

"I think so. You are saying it was supposed to be The Seventies. And it never happened."

"Exactly."

"But look at you, Barb. *Some*thing has happened. You look great. You're making it in New York City. I mean, you are, aren't you?"

"That's not what I'm talking about. It's different. It's hard to feel like I'm part of anything. Do you ever feel like you're part of anything? That was what the Sixties had. Then it just dissolved. It broke up into ten million little pieces. And that was the Seventies. See, I have a theory that those years with a seventy in them, they came and went, but the Seventies, as a decade, just never arrived. I think we went directly from the Sixties to the Eighties."

My fatigue had lifted. I felt light, almost giddy with the strangeness of this conversation, its strange timing and setting. I had forgotten how her mind worked. This was typical. She had a theory, and the theory itself could stimulate her, make her hands fly around. This in turn could stimulate me, whether or not I had ever given her theory a previous thought.

"Maybe you have explained something to me, Barbara. It is incredible that you should bring this up and that we should be talking about it at this hour of the morning here by your backyard window after all these years, because I have had this vague feeling for I don't know how long that something was missing or had slipped past me. I didn't know what it was. Maybe that was it. Maybe it was the Seventies, the great promise of the Seventies. They just never made it through."

Her voice was rising now. "I'll tell you what *I've* been feeling, Holl. I am not getting any younger. I am going to be thirty-three pretty soon, and I am really glad we're talking about this because I see now that part of me has been on hold waiting for some kind of fireworks to start. Isn't that crazy? It just came clear to me. I don't care what anybody else says about the Eighties. It is my time to make something happen in the world!"

"Oh Jesus, Barb! As you say that, it goes through me like a bolt of lightning!"

We were holding each other with eyes full of fire and expectation. She had been right when she said we could pick things up ten years later without missing a beat. This was how it used to be, early in the morning, late at night. For a few moments we were back in our three-room apartment over Durant Street, we were girls again, roommates scheming.

Then the doorbell rang and broke the spell.

She glanced at her watch.

"He's early."

"Who's early?"

"The exterminator."

"Oh yes."

"I'll be right back. Help yourself to more coffee."

She went rushing down toward the lower door. I followed her as far as the middle of the room and stopped to wait, to take a closer look at her possessions, still thinking about the decade that had disappeared, the years of mothering and shopping and cooking and trading baby-sitters and driving back and forth, the gardening, the repairs and renovations on two houses so many miles from town, while Barbara's apartment reminded me of all the things you can do when you have a little more money and no children underfoot. She had achieved a sculptured elegance that I imagined might come to me one day. Sometime. Later on. Because I envied it and couldn't have it yet, her long room overwhelmed me, so fixed and stable, secure in its tastes, whereas my life, at that moment, was a blur of disorder and confusion and time wasted and time lost.

Secretly, in a place so secret, months would pass before I would be able to acknowledge it, I wanted to drop something on her transparent coffee table and send a crack across the glass. I wanted to spill dark coffee on the creamy crushed velvet of her sleek Italianate sofa with matching easy chair. How could anyone who owned such a sofa feel time had passed her by? It wasn't fair. And yet . . . well . . . I suppose it was all connected. Her major had been art history. She knew where to shop for things like that. She knew styles and periods. Ten years back she had been able to talk of different centuries and the character that went with a certain block of time. Her mind worked that way. Did this mean she was right about the Seventies? It seemed so, as I waited in her living room. I did not have a better theory to explain the recent past. It was not a subject I had ever needed a theory for, even though decade-time had been a very fashionable topic of conversation during our undergraduate days. "This is the last decade," the prophets would announce. "These are the final years." Sometimes they meant Jesus was returning to earth. Sometimes they meant The Big Bomb was going to fall and obliterate humankind. Sometimes they meant you could now do whatever you wanted whenever you chose because this would all be over soon, one way or another, and what difference did it make.

Loud voices were still making all those same predictions, the Light Stewards of the world. Nothing much had changed, except for the fact that everything had changed. Like Barbara, I was going on thirty-three. Time was running out. Though the prospects for the 1980s weren't very bright, I saw that they were all I had to work with. Something about the previous decade, its lack of character, had given the current one more . . . what? More urgency? Yes. It would have to be seized. There could be no turning back, as I had watched others of my generation turn back, toward the 1940s or the 1920s or the 1890s or the Civil War.

Perhaps it was the rich coffee she had served. Perhaps the hasty madness of this foolhardy trip had finally caught up with me and brought me to the edge of wild laughter. As I heard footsteps on the stairway below and the muttering of two voices, I was filled with a sense of destiny, a sense that the Eighties, whatever remained of them, would be the decade of my fate. That was what a decade had become, after all. In America. It was no longer merely a ten-year span. It was a feeling in the air and in your heart. Whoever I was, whatever I was to become, at this late date in the history of the nation and the race, it would be worked out during the 1980s, and it would start now, today, this morning, with whatever the next moment might present to me.

11

The Ghost of Something

Barbara stepped into the room, followed by Ray of Ray's Pest Control. He was there to get the layout and to look carefully at those dark places where mice and cockroaches lurk. When she introduced us I found myself the object of his full and nonprofessional attention. He appraised me up and down, with an old-time machismo that took me by surprise. It surprised Barbara too. She looked offended, or neglected. I took some pleasure in this bold glance from the man in coveralls neither of us knew. Was she jealous? Even though she owned that fabulous sofa, had I won a few points by simply standing here and being my disheveled and unsightly self?

"This is Holly Doyle," she said, "an old friend of mine who just flew in from San Francisco."

"Pleased to meet you," Ray said. "What do you do in San Francisco?"

"I use the airport. I live a couple of hours away."

His smile revealed straight white teeth. "What brings you to New York?"

"Business and pleasure," I said.

"Business and pleasure," he repeated, as if this idea was new and amusing. "Sounds like a great combination."

He had a celebrity's smile and intelligent eyes, while my eyes still shone—at least they felt shiny—with that newfound sense of destiny. His glance held me a moment more, before he turned to Barbara, as she began to share with him her sad tale of pest intrusion, the mice, the roaches, the occasional rat, the nameless insects driven indoors by cold weather only to be squashed inadvertently as soon as the hardwood floors had been waxed.

She was all efficiency now, and Ray was full of sympathy and understanding. He knew exactly what to do. He named the day of each month he would be able to return. As they wandered toward the front window, and as he squatted to examine a crack in the baseboard, it occurred to me that he was too handsome to be in pest control. Then it occurred to me that the money must be very very good.

He was going to apply the first treatment this morning. While he trotted outside to his truck, Barbara prepared to leave. Pulling a topcoat from the hallway closet, she said, "I hate to do this, Holly. There is so much more we have to talk about. But duty calls. I have a ten-thirty meeting I can't miss. I want you to make yourself at home. That spare bedroom is just sitting there. Here's my number at work. Here are the keys to both doors. Come and go as you please. Ray will be here for half an hour or so, he says. After that you'll have the place to yourself. I'll be back no later than six. Barry won't be home until eight, or later. Maybe we can go out somewhere for a bite to eat. We'll just play it be ear."

"And if I want to make a call?"

"There are two extensions, a wall phone in the kitchen, and one in the main bedroom upstairs. You'll see it. That's more comfortable. There's a padded chair right by my table."

She was talking fast, moving faster. A quick hug, and off she went. I listened to her footsteps on the varnished stairs, heard her pause to exchange a few last words with Ray, whose footsteps replaced hers, climbing.

This time he wore two narrow metal tanks strapped to his

back. In his right hand he carried the spraying wand. A white face mask hung at his throat.

"Holly," he said, "I am going to spray the downstairs first."

The way he said Holly was like the way he first looked at me. Overly familiar. Possessive.

I said, "What is that stuff?"

"It's completely safe."

I must have looked skeptical. He felt obliged to elaborate.

"It's been tested. It zaps the little buggies, but it is not harmful to humans in any way. I just spray along the moldings like this, see, and then along the baseboards. The only thing that might bother you is the smell. It tends to hang in the air. You might want to go upstairs while I'm working on these rooms here."

"Yes, I think I'll do that. I have to make some calls anyway."

"I'll let you know when I'm finished," he said, as he covered his nose and mouth with the mask. He was watching me. The flesh around his eyes crinkled, as if he were smiling, perhaps laughing at himself in this outfit. I couldn't see his mouth, so I couldn't be sure.

The upstairs phone sat on an antique table next to her king-size bed. Maybe it was bigger than king-size. It seemed twice the width of our bed at home, which was queen-size. I wondered where you found sheets for a mattress like that and what it would take to wash them. Two would make a load. The spread was brocade. Near the table stood a stuffed chair covered with the same material, flowery brocade. The room was painted white. The chair and bed, against the solid white, were springtime bouquets of green and yellow flowers. There was a gold-framed notepad on the table, with matching gold-barreled pen. For several minutes, maybe longer, I sat in the chair doodling on the pad, trying to compose myself.

Maureen had been right. Years back I had memorized Howard's office number. When I finally dialed, his receptionist answered. I gave her my name.

"He's in a meeting right now. Is this call in connection with . . . ?"

"It's personal. I'm an old friend."

I was searching for any sign of hope. When she said, "Just a moment," my heart leaped. Perhaps, years ago, he had left instructions to be interrupted anytime someone named Holly Doyle called. I tried to go to my center and stay calm, so that I would sound calm. When Howard came on the line his voice was full of confidence.

"Hello?"

"Hello, Howard. It's Holly."

"Holly. This is quite a surprise."

"How are you? I mean, how have you been?"

"I'm fine, Holly. Never better."

"It's so odd to hear your voice. It's been such a long time."

"It *has* been a long time. But tell me where you're calling from. You sound very near."

"I am. I'm here. I'm in New York. That's why I called. Just on the chance . . ."

"Now that *is* a surprise. What's the occasion? Is Grover with you?"

"Actually I'm traveling on my own. Passing through, as they say."

"But you and Grover are still . . ."

"It's a long story, Howard. Maybe you are the only one who would understand."

"Is it something we should talk about over lunch?"

"I'd like that. If you have the time. I'd like that very much."

"Certainly I have the time, although this morning—and please don't think I'm cutting you short—I did have to step out of a rather crucial meeting to take this call, and I really must get back in there. But what about today? Are you free?"

"It depends on what time."

"Twelve-thirty?"

"How about one?"

"One it is," he said. "Why don't you meet me here. We're

right downtown. There's a new French place around the corner I've heard is superb. You still like French food, don't you? I'll call now and reserve a table. Please don't think I'm cutting you short. It really is marvelous to hear from you. This is splendid news."

He gave me his address, and I told him I would see him there. When he hung up I was sick at heart. It was not what I had expected, what I had fantasized. I guess I wanted time to disappear. I wanted it to be the way it had been five years ago. I wanted to hear what I had heard on the day he said goodbye. There had been a high charge in his voice and in his eyes. His body had been charged with grief and pain and loss and passion. He was ready to explode. I wanted to hear some of that. I wanted to know it still lived somewhere inside him. All I heard was caution and restraint. Formality. Even his vocabulary had changed. Five years back he would never have used words like *splendid* or *occasion* or *rather crucial*.

I told myself, as I sat staring into the street below, as a car pulled away from the curb, that you cannot always tell by what a person says on the phone. You cannot see the eyes, the face, the little gestures that enliven speech. The wires connecting you to the other person are so long and thin, certain feelings never make it through. Sometimes only the words make it, and the most unreliable words of all are those disembodied telephone words with five years between you and the last ones heard.

A knock on the bedroom door interrupted my reverie. A little tap, and the door swung halfway open. Ray's head appeared. "Sorry to bother you, Holly. Just letting you know I have finished downstairs, and I'll be doing the upstairs now."

"Does that mean I have to go downstairs?"

"It's your decision. You can sit right there, and I can spray around you, if you'd like. As I said, it's harmless to humans. Thirty minutes from now you won't even know I've been here."

"If it's so safe, how come you're using a face mask?"

"A precaution. One slice of pumpkin pie can't hurt you. If you ate four pumpkin pies every day of the week for forty-eight weeks, you might begin to feel the effect."

He had stepped into the room, the twin cylinders strapped to his back, the face mask bulging at his throat again. Just below the mask, over his left pec, the company logo was embroidered on his white coveralls. I had not looked at this before. A cartoon insect was falling backward, the eyelids drooping and tiny black feeler-arms thrown wide in defeat. Underneath it the red stitching said,

RAY'S PEST CONTROL

WE DO THE JOB

I think I stared at this for quite some time, without moving.

Eventually Ray said, "You look sad. Bad news?"

"Not the news I expected."

"Nothing serious, I hope."

"Everything is serious, don't you think?"

"I guess it is," he said, with a friendly grin.

He wasn't moving. He stood watching me, the spraying wand loose in his hand, like a fencer's foil between matches. Our eyes met, and held. He saw that I was not in a rush to go downstairs. I saw that he was very sure of himself, but not arrogant. Suddenly the world fell quiet. No noise from the floor below. No noise from the street. No movement out there. Somewhere in the distance traffic was moving. A faraway horn beeped, accentuating the silence in the apartment, a tent of silence that surrounded and enclosed the two of us in Barbara's floral bedroom.

They say there are moments when time stands still. If such a thing is possible, this was one of them. I felt completely detached from everything outside that room, and this released the first warm trickle of desire. As it rose through my body, I considered Ray. My intuition was that he knew what he wanted but was not a taker. Not merely a taker. He looked about thirty. His hair was black and thick, his eyebrows full, and his lashes, black too, long and almost feminine. His face was very white, a healthy white. He was bursting with health. From his neck I could tell he was muscular, though not in the weight-lifting way.

He said, "Would you like to smoke a joint?"

"I guess I wouldn't mind."

"I know it's early," he said, with a broad smile, "but I am about ready to take a break. One of the advantages of working for yourself is you can take a break whenever you want."

"It's all right. I could use something. I'm three hours ahead of myself. Or three hours behind. Which is it?"

"You mean flying back and forth? I can never remember. I haven't flown around that much."

"Is Brooklyn where you're from?"

"Born and raised."

He unzipped a patch pocket on his trouser leg and pulled out a flat tin box. Inside, half a dozen thinly rolled cigarettes lay in a row under a metal clip. He lit one and passed it to me, saying matter-of-factly, "This is Colombian." I took a long pull, passed it back, and watched him draw in what seemed like half the available air in the room. He held it for quite a while, looking directly into my eyes. It was strong and heady stuff. One hit would be plenty. As the smoke finally came drifting from between his lips he said, "And you are an old friend of Barbara's."

"We went to college together."

"Was that out on the Coast?"

"Yes, way out there on the Coast."

"I read a book once about redwood trees and how they are impervious to termites and almost every other form of insect."

"Is that your main interest in life?"

"What?"

"Insects."

"I don't know much about incest."

"I didn't say incest."

"Maybe you meant incest," he said. "Would you like to talk about that?"

The silliness was already rising in me. "I said insects."

"Don't laugh. You can learn a lot from insects."

"For instance."

"Take New York. Some guy did a study. There are around eight million people here, and he figures for every human being in

New York City there are one hundred and sixty-four cockroaches. And he asks the question, Who is in charge, us or them?"

"Sounds like them."

"Sometimes people scoff when I describe my line of work. They don't stop to think that there are no layoffs in pest control. It is a growth industry."

He pulled again on the joint and said, through the smoker's breath-held, raspy throat, "Do you believe in reincarnation?"

This made me laugh. He started laughing. We doubled over for about sixty seconds of sudden hilarious laughter. When he could speak again he said, "What's so funny?"

"This is all new to me. Those tanks. You look like a deep-sea diver."

"You didn't answer my question."

"Sure, I believe in reincarnation."

"That's good. A lot of people don't. Just the other day I had a vision of myself in ancient Athens."

"What were you?"

"I was a roofer."

"You weren't Socrates or anybody like that?"

"It was after the Golden Age. Around 200 B.C. Athens was finished. I was just this guy wandering around roofing houses."

"You *look* Greek. You could pass for Greek."

"On my mother's side. What about you?"

"Danish," I said. "Some French. Some Scots."

"That's where you get your height." He passed the joint back to me. "Hang on to this. I want to slip out of these tanks."

He turned around. "Here, give me a hand."

With the joint between my lips, its potent smoke curling, I lifted the shoulder straps while he wriggled free. I watched him unzip his coveralls and step out of those. He was wearing a workshirt and Levi's. The way he placed his coveralls outside the door touched me. It was a gesture, sweet and modest. When he turned and looked at me again, his lovely black-browed eyes were lidded for seduction. I guess mine were too. With the coveralls gone I could see his pectorals curving against the heavy-duty cotton. I thought about my own breasts, how they might look to him. They felt swollen. My period was due any day. Another sign, I thought. Lucky timing. If anything happened, I would be safe.

The way he relieved me of the tanks, gently lifting them from my hands and placing these too in the hallway, out of sight, seemed to be a final stripping away of whatever might still have stood between us. He stepped close and said, "Tall women really turn me on, I want you to know that."

A scent came floating toward me, so subtle I could barely catch it, underneath the pungent smell of dope. It seemed to drift out from the open collar of his shirt, a hint of Old Spice or Royal Copenhagen cologne for men.

I said, "Don't say anything, Ray. You don't have to talk."

He drew the cigarette from between my lips and said, "I'd like to kiss you."

I waited to see if he would, and he took me then. I took him. Our bodies met. The clothes came off. The clothes were strewn around the room. My memory of that interlude is a blur of eager flesh, a naked flurry in the deep pile of Barbara's bedroom rug. He was not rough. But he was insistent, insatiable. He wanted certain things, gave orders with his body, and I followed them. It didn't last long, not long enough for him. When I started to come he tried to stop it. He wanted more of everything, wanted it to go on all day, I suppose. But I felt something rising, my whole history ready to burst, and I wanted to let it. I am not necessarily talking about a burst of pleasure. It could have been an epileptic fit. I went into high spasm. I might have screamed. I know I called out. I was in total darkness, calling down the long dark tunnel of my life.

When it was finished, the room was quieter than it had been before we started. I immediately thought of the red-haired woman at the conference, howling at the auditorium ceiling. Now I knew her. She was me. We were one. I opened my eyes and saw Ray staring at me. His hands were flat on the floor on either

side of my shoulders, his arms stiff, his face right over mine, staring with fear-filled eyes.

"You all right?"

When I didn't answer, he said, "Say something."

I said, "Thank you."

This did not allay his fear. "Jesus Christ. I never had a woman
do that before."

"You should feel good about it, Ray."

"Jesus Christ," he said again, as he lay down next to me, and
reached his arm across my belly in a soft and affectionate caress.

Moments later he was up on one elbow, his eyes wide again,
his head jerking back and forth as if he expected voyeurs at the
window and at the door, as if waiting for the landlord to appear
with an arrest warrant for disturbing the peace. I liked Ray then. I
began to see into his character. If the time were right he would
have been a thoughtful lover. Part of him wanted to lie close and
exchange a few aftermath nuzzles, while another part of him
wanted to get out of there as soon as possible, to put space between himself and this itinerant hysteric, Mad Holly.

Within minutes he was on his feet, back into his coveralls,
tightening the canister straps and ready to go. As much as he
wanted to be rid of me, the worried gentleman in him could not
simply abandon a woman in a strange bedroom three thousand
miles from home. Almost as a conditioned response he said, from
the doorway, "You need a ride anywhere?"

I asked which way he was headed. I did not know one end of
New York City from the other, but as soon as he spoke I realized I
too wanted to get going. If I stayed much longer at Barbara's she
would figure out that I had no bags, no clothes, no plan. She
would see that the free spirit she so much admired was merely desperate, merely groping. She would respond with compassion, of
course. She would be a good friend. But it was too much to deal
with. I did not want to go into it all with her. Not yet. Nor did I
want to go out to lunch with Howard. Whatever had flamed between us had long since flickered and died. That is what I had

heard in his voice, a ghost of something that once had lived. Who wants to go have lunch with a ghost?

When Ray, in answer to my question, said he was heading toward Atlantic Avenue, I asked if that was near the airport. Evasively, against his better judgment, he said it was in that general direction.

While he finished spraying the upstairs rooms, I showered, dressed, straightened the furniture, and scribbled a fast note to Barbara on her golden pad, using her golden pen. Ten minutes later I was sitting in the cab of Ray's van. He dropped me at a subway station the size of a cathedral and explained how I could connect with the shuttle to La Guardia. I called ahead and found out there was a United flight leaving for the Coast at two with space available. I put it on the credit card.

12

You Must Always Speak Your Heart

On this flight every seat was filled. I was jammed in between a snoring Air Force sergeant and a young woman who began to chatter before I sat down. She had set her coat on the seat assigned to me and apologized profusely when I appeared, though no apology was needed, since all she had to do was fold it into the overhead rack.

I suggested this, and she apologized again, for not thinking of it. Once the seat was clear, I discovered one end of my seat belt was missing. She was sitting on it. As she raised up to free the belt, she apologized and explained that this was only her second time aloft. Her eyes were bright with terror. As her rapid-fire talk continued, I first cursed my luck, then saw that perhaps this was a blessing in disguise. Her chatter might save me from thought. The life story she wanted to share might for a while take the inner spotlight off my own.

She was twenty-five. Her parents were Cuban. She had been born in Miami and now lived somewhere near San Francisco. There had recently been a death in the family, and she had just left the funeral or was cutting some trip short to fly back to the funeral. I never did get that part clear. The death is what she most wanted to describe. It took her a while to reach it, but that was what she needed to talk through, the circumstances surrounding the death.

"It was my brother," she said. "I have two brothers. He was older, thirty-seven years old, and so good-looking, one of the handsomest men I have ever seen. Like a film star. I think he could have become a film star, if he had wanted to. He had so many talents. But diving was his passion, diving deep into the ocean after shells and curious exotic fish. Why does a man find passion in such a thing? It always mystifies me. Twice a year, sometimes three times a year, he would make these expeditions. Last month he traveled into Baja California with his new wife, who was much too young for him, in my opinion, but I suppose he loved her, and he wanted to show off for her, show her how daring and manly he was. Before they left, my father warned him to be careful. 'You are taking too many risks,' my father said, 'and you cannot keep this up forever. You are thirty-seven, and you are still behaving like a sixteen-year-old.' My father did not approve of his wife, you see. Neither he nor my mother thought she was good enough for him. So they disapproved of this trip, which was in some ways an extension of their honeymoon. They had just come back from the honeymoon, and there had been a lot of yelling in the family. So my brother grew angry and off they went again. He had to prove something, you see. He had to prove to his wife how manly he could be, and he had to prove to my father that he was still youthful and strong, and he had to prove to both my father and my mother that this girl somehow was good for him. He spent the last money he had on this trip to La Paz at the lower end of Baja. He rented a boat and out they went toward the deep water. The second day there, he made a dive and he did not come back up. The partner he had hired, a Mexican man from La Paz who I am told was very skillful in the water, went down and found him dead and brought the body back to the boat. . . ."

Her voice broke, and she stopped. She had taken my hand, squeezing it. Her voice was very soft, but intent. She spoke with an eagerness that held me, as if in the midst of this multitude hurtling through the sky, we alone had a rare kinship and a precious secret to share. Her eyes were wet. I too was on the verge of tears.

"Have you ever had a brother?" she asked. It was almost a whisper.

"Yes," I said. "Like you, I have two brothers."

"Then perhaps you can imagine how I must feel."

"I think I know how you feel, yes."

"I cannot describe for you what a shock this has been for my family. My father had to fly down to have the body shipped back to the U.S.—you know—all the arrangements that must be made. This girl my brother married, she was helpless, she is even younger than I, and yet now she is going to inherit all my brother's belongings, his property, this and that, unless my mother can put a stop to it. But that was not the most upsetting part. When my father was in La Paz, staying in the hotel there, after he had spent this terrible day, he was lying on the bed in the heat trying to go to sleep, when he heard a knocking on the door that separated his room from the next. He sat up in bed and listened, and again he heard the knocking. He said, 'What is it? Who is there?' No one answered. For a while it was quiet. Then the knocking came again, and again he called out, and again there was no reply. After that there was silence. The next morning he mentioned this to the desk clerk, who looked at the room chart and said, 'This is very strange, because it is not a room we rent out. It is a storage room. It is always locked, and no one uses it at night because the maintenance and cleaning people never work at night.' When my father told us this story he began to weep uncontrollably. 'It was my son,' he cried, 'trying to reach me. Don't you understand? Trying to reach out to me even after death.' It filled my father with anguish because of the things he had failed to communicate to the son who was gone forever. There had been a wide space be-

tween them, and now he is filled with sorrow that he did not tr
hard enough to bridge that space. I saw my father fall down ont
his knees weeping. Watching him, I felt even worse than I fel
about the death of my brother. He was inconsolable. Next to hin
stood my mother, with her arms at her side and crying like I hav
never seen a woman cry. 'My baby,' she wailed, 'my baby boy i
dead!' "

She had taken both my hands, and she was turned toward me
Her cheeks were wet, her eyes wide and glistening. They seeme
to be saint's eyes, filled with an emotion so deep and pure it wa
beyond grief. It was impossible for me to look into those eyes an
not break into tears, weeping for the man who died, and for thi
woman who had lost her brother, and weeping for me, Los
Holly, who was the mother, and the father too, weeping for th
child who would never return, for the messages never sent.

I saw myself at age eleven the morning my mother came int
my room while I was dressing and sat down on the bed and tol
me my father had taken "another trip." From the ache in he
voice I knew it would be a long one. I stood in front of her, search
ing for words, for soothing words. I knew what she wanted t
hear, and yet my heart was with him at that moment, wherever h
had gone, rather than with my mother who had put arms aroun
me for her own consolation. Somehow the devastated Cuban fa
ther on his knees was my father grieving in a distant town. Then
saw Buddy and Karen lying in their beds the way they looked a
night when I would peek in to make sure they had fallen asleep.
thought of things I would sometimes be moved to say and the
forget to say, thought of the call I could have made before I lef
and did not make. I saw Karen's face the day she fell into th
creek, six months back, and landed head first on a slick rock. I
had been the sudden, fearful silence that sent me running dow
the path from the yard, and I found her lying in the water with
ray of sunlight shining on her face, her eyes closed, looking dead.
had talked to her then. "Karen," I had said, thinking I must sta
calm and not raise my voice and my very calmness would restor
her. "Karen, open your eyes. C'mon, honey, open them now

Please do it, Karen. Mommy loves you. Please don't be dead. Please don't be dead. Oh dear God. Please open your sweet eyes and look at me."

On the plane I felt again that same panic, felt the same cold water fill my veins. I saw the plane's nose dip, going into a dive. Suppose we crashed and I died in the crash, and those things I had yet to communicate to Buddy and Karen, with my voice and with my eyes, would go forever unsaid. I could not quell the panic or erase the vision of Karen in the creek or the vision of the plane going down in flames. In my mind I began to speak to them, hoping they might hear or feel the message I was sending.

To the woman from Miami I said, "I have a son, and a daughter too, and it is a terrible thing to think that I might never have the chance to tell them all the things I carry in my heart."

"You must always speak your heart," she said. "This I know. When we fail to do so, we fill up with regret. My father may never overcome the deep pain of his regret. How old are your children?"

"The girl is three, the boy nearly eight."

A beatific smile lit her face. "Oh, you are very fortunate," she said, squeezing my hands again. "What a blessing. Do you have any pictures I can see?"

"No, I don't."

"You should always carry pictures."

I felt a dampness between my legs and knew I had to get to the restroom. Excusing myself, pushing past the inert sergeant, I eased along the aisle and then stood for quite some time looking at all the little latch-triggered signs that said OCCUPIED, thinking there must be some cryptic law of body function that sends people toward the same set of cubicles at the same moment no matter where you are in the world. At last a door opened and a woman stepped out, and I stepped in and discovered, as I had suspected, that my period had started, the first time it had started on a plane. Early, it seemed, though I wasn't certain. I thought of Ray. I wondered if the altitude had some effect.

A few moments after I returned to my seat the flight attendant appeared with trays of food. This stirred to life the sergeant, who since takeoff had been snoring at my left. Soon we were hunched forward forking in veal cutlets and miniature salads. The young woman and I were both very hungry. The conversation turned to food. Then the food and the trays were gone, and the movie came on.

It was *Kramer vs. Kramer*, starring Dustin Hoffman and Meryl Streep. In this movie he is an up-and-coming ad man in New York. She is his young and beautiful wife. They have a six-year-old son, and early in the movie Meryl decides she has had it with Dustin and his career and their life together. She walks out and leaves him alone with his job and the kid to care for. A year and a half later she returns. She has had a change of view. She sees herself more clearly now, as a woman, as a mother. She no longer wants Dustin, but she wants the son. She believes her mother's rights transcend all other rights. Dustin takes her to court, on the grounds that disappearing for a year and a half was an irresponsible act, whereas he stuck with the son, made sacrifices, in fact lost a high-paying job because his attention was so scattered, but nonetheless did his fatherly duty, making it clear that he is more fit than Meryl to have custody. At the end, she wins the court case, which is a crushing blow to Dustin. But in the very last scene she bites the bullet and decides to let him keep the kid.

What a final scene that is, what a heart-wrencher. I could barely watch it. I was Meryl Streep, yearning to hold and mother my only son. If I'd had any tears left, I would have been weeping again. But I had already wept all my tears for the day, listening to the young woman's story of her brother's death. I was drained. I was wasted. I had not had anything close to true sleep for days. Exhausted and grainy-eyed, I sat there trying to imagine what it would be like to let Grover take the kids. I was filled with hopeless despair. A black void yawned, and I was not sure what created it—the thought of going home, of having only home to return to now, or the thought of my children cut off from me. Meryl had roamed for a year and a half, while I, after two days gone, was crippled with guilt and sorrow, and longing to see them and hold them again, to nurture them. No. To be nurtured by them.

We were thirty minutes from San Francisco when the pilot came on the intercom and told us to fasten our seat belts. "We might get a little turbulence just before we prepare for the final approach" was the way he put it, in the deep and soothing cockpit voice, like a network newscaster, the voice of authority that is supposed to assure you nothing unusual is happening.

We passed from steel-blue sky into heavy cloud cover. The first time the plane lurched, the woman from Miami clutched my hand. I began to pray. The plane lurched again, then dropped like an elevator. Again I saw the nose-dive, the flaming crash that would bring to an untimely end this pilgrimage of mine. I closed my eyes and thought, Holly to Pilot. Holly to Pilot. Heavy weather is a test of character. You can handle it. You can handle it. Be strong. Be alert. Remember your training. Rise above your fears. We all love you very much. We love you, and we are behind you one hundred percent.

13

Holly the Homing Pigeon

The pilot brought the plane in so smoothly some of the passengers applauded when the wheels touched down. I said goodbye to the woman from Miami. We exchanged addresses and hugged as if we had truly rescued each other from some harrowing ordeal.

As I left the airport, into a blur of rain, I could not see the highway signs, did not have the leisure to look at them, nor could I see very far ahead, on the road, or in my mind. Leaning forward to peer through the sweep of the windshield wipers, I was driving on automatic pilot, Holly the Homing Pigeon trying not to think, although *trying* is the wrong word. With my double dose of jet lag it was easy not to think. The semiconscious miles sped past. I was nearly through town and thirty minutes from the house when I saw red lights coming at me through the rain.

A vehicle was stopping on the road. As I neared, I saw a big Winnebago camper with Arizona plates. Ahead of it stood other vehicles, five or six cars and pickups, and beyond them a man directing traffic, perhaps a patrolman. It was hard to tell. Several minutes passed. I stopped craning to see around the Winnebago and stared at the stickers pasted across the back door. They had been to the Petrified Forest, the Grand Canyon, Death Valley, Disneyland, Knott's Berry Farm, Hearst Castle. A bumper sticker said, "America: Handle with Prayer."

I turned on my radio, to bring in some country music, thinking I must really be out of it to have driven all that way without remembering to flip on the radio. My favorite station was buried in static. I switched off my wipers, then I switched my engine off, and still it was hard to hear the music. I gave it up, turned off the radio, and sat back waiting for the Winnebago to move.

Gradually I began to hear the rain. Though I had been looking at it, and driving through it, I had not been able to listen to it. There were no trees or wires overhead. It fell straight onto my roof with a clatter like hail. But it wasn't hail. Something was wrong. Something about the sound of it. I rolled my window down and looked again at the needles of gray water falling, millions and millions of long straight needles. Was that it? The air was still. Nothing in the air gave an angle to this rain, no wind, not a breath, nor had there been a thunderclap or punctuating flash of light across the sky. Somewhere in the midst of all this clatter, there was an uncanny stillness. I wondered how long it had been coming down. It had the relentless look of eternal rain, a deluge that had begun centuries ago. The broad puddles spreading back along both sides of the road, they had the look of ancient breeding ponds, lined with ferns, where tiny amphibians swam and multiplied.

When the Winnebago finally moved, I could see what had stalled traffic. An intersection was flooded. Cars were inching across, one at a time, with water splashing at the hubcaps. The man seeming to direct traffic was not a cop. He was a volunteer standing in his hip boots to show drivers how deep the water was.

I watched a car push out into it a few feet, then pause, and back up. The car backed right past me, the driver craning and squinting, searching for a place to turn around. The camper rig moved again. I was next. I turned my ignition key and heard the starter grind. Everything was damp. It whined and moaned, as if ready to expire. I cursed myself for switching off the engine, thinking, Oh shit, this is the payoff. This is it. But suddenly she caught. I pumped the pedal till the engine roared, sending white exhaust fumes billowing into the rain.

Halfway across the intersection the camper stopped. The water must have risen by three or four inches in as many minutes. The man in hip boots was waving his arms, while the camper just waited there like a stunned elephant. It had stalled. I decided to try what the previous driver had tried. I knew where I was now. I knew another route that would be nearly as fast and would take me over higher ground. I turned around, speeding back the way I had come, feeling that this was no ordinary rain and somehow I had to get through as quickly as I could, thinking again of Buddy and Karen. Were they there? Had they ever made it home? Or were they still up at the ranch with Montrose and Leona? In my mind's eye I saw the creek, the bend of it that swings beyond our yard, saw water rising, cutting at the banks.

I reached the two-lane road that follows the river inland, swerving to avoid branches fallen from the high trees that arch and gather overhead. It was like a slalom run. I had just skirted a broad-branched limb that blocked one lane when I heard a crack above me, and then a groan that could have been a loud and mournful human groan. I glanced left and saw a tree move, lean down toward the asphalt. Its fall was slowed by the tangle of limbs. When the foliage broke free, it fell with a crash. In my rearview I saw its thick trunk and claw of muddy roots make a barricade across both lanes.

On one inside curve I skidded through a pond of mud and loose debris that had flowed out from a steep gully. I had been driving in second. I shifted down. In some places dark cones of mud were creeping toward the divider line. Where Revolution Creek meets the river road I turned right, onto the bridge. The water was chocolate-brown, roaring along a foot or so beneath the underside. I had never seen it so high or looking so ferocious.

Limbs and stumps were being hurled at the abutments like battering rams. A small log jam was building at the center. I did not see how the bridge could take much more of that. When I made it across, I had the feeling I would be the last. It occurred to me that in the midst of this interminable downpour, perhaps I had been the only one to try that bridge, the only one foolish enough to be out and driving around a river valley in this kind of weather.

It was nearly dark, an early dark, even for midwinter. Revolution Road was deserted. The creek, like the river, was ready to jump its channel. In several spots the brown rush was eating at the roadbed. Chunks of blacktop were gone. When I reached the one-lane bridge I almost backed away. It was wobbling. I was sure it was going to go. The water had risen right up to the timbers. If there had been anywhere to retreat to, I probably would not have attempted the bridge. But I had no choice. I could not go back. I stepped on the gas and sped across. If I had hesitated for thirty seconds, I would have been marooned. Moments after I crossed, a piling gave way. One splintered corner of planking dipped toward the chocolate foam.

I pushed on, not daring to interpret these signs. By the time I reached the house, night had fallen. From the road our window lights were square beacons in this otherwise puddled and drowning landscape. The effect, as I first glimpsed the windows, was confusing, as if I had seen a lighthouse, a place of refuge, but so far offshore I could not get to it. Then I was pulling into the driveway. The front door flew open. I saw Grover silhouetted in the frame, with bright light behind him. He was holding Karen. Beyond him I saw someone else. Not Buddy. A figure moved across the room, or toward the door. Something in the movement told me it was a woman. That was all I could tell from the yard.

As I stepped out of the car, ducking against the rain, the house disappeared. It turned black. I heard Karen call, "Mommy," just as all the lights in the world went out.

P A R T I I

Her temperament was more sentimental
than artistic. She sought emotions
and not landscapes.
    —from *Madame Bovary* (1857)
        by Gustave Flaubert

14

A Death in the Family

You hardly ever understand these things at the time. You react to what is right in front of you. The reasons come out later. Sometimes much later. Although *reasons* is the wrong word. Eventually, if you are lucky, you see the patterns that escape you in the heat or in the damp of the moment. I won't go so far as to say I believe in predestination. But looking back on those days now, I can see a kind of plan in everything that happened. That camper truck, for instance. Who placed it in front of me? Of all the vehicles on earth, why was it the one to push out into that muddy intersection and stall? Were it not for the Winnebago I too might have tried to cross, and stalled, or been delayed, and thus have reached the second bridge five minutes later and been cut off, since the river road was so littered with limbs and fallen trees it stayed closed for twenty-four hours, completely blocking traffic into town.

That would have made me another refugee-guest at the river road fire station, which some said had the feeling of a bomb shelter in a combat zone, there were so many army blankets and shellshocked people wandering in from their abandoned cars and broken houses. But no, my timing was perfect—if getting across the bridge qualifies as something to be desired. And you could call it a blessing, the appearance of that camper rig with the Arizona plates. Or you could call it a curse. I probably won't know for certain which it was until the day I die and the whole drama and soap opera of my life is complete.

In the short time it took me to reach the porch, I was drenched. I looked as if I had swum fully clothed across the creek, though I did not notice this at the time. My mind was on the house. I was sure the woman I had seen was Sarah. In those few seconds of rushing through the darkness and the rain my exhaustion turned to fury. I was outraged that he could have the gall to bring her there, expose the children to her. She had probably spent the night, slept in our bed. It frightens me now to think how quickly my hate rose, how close it lay beneath the surface, hate for both of them, but first for her. Much later I saw that I had learned something very basic. In five seconds I had learned what they mean when they say you see red. It was the first time I truly wanted blood, wanted to injure someone so badly blood would flow. I think I could have killed her, would have tried to, with my hands, if she had been there. But she wasn't.

Despite the dark and the slick stairs I leaped onto the porch and had one hand on Grover's arm, pushing him aside, when a light flashed from somewhere beyond him, as if a television set had been switched on. It filled the living room with ghostly furniture. It caught the woman in midstride, seemed to stop and hold her with the face in midstride too, the smile saying Welcome, the brow creased with worry and alarm.

It was Leona, his mother, who had already heard or felt the kind of energy I was bringing toward the house, before she saw it in my eyes. She is like a radar screen. And I was suddenly the killer with no one to kill.

I turned on Grover, whose eyes were wide, as if he had never expected to see me again, though they could have been widened by the first show of light. He stepped back, bumped into the door. If he had been standing there alone, it could have been bad. My mind was so full of the two of them in our bed and the fact that he had allowed it, I was ready to lunge. My fists were balled so tight I dug crescents into my palms. That was the only blood I drew that night. I now have three little crescent scars to remind me that these feelings we call *deep* are actually just a millimeter beneath the surface and never more than half a second out of reach.

Lucky for Grover he had Karen in his arms. She was his shield, his bulletproof vest. Perhaps she was his little ventriloquist too, when she said, "Mommy, what happened to your face?"

The sound of that voice, the innocence, worked like a faucet, shutting off my hate as quickly as it had begun to flow. The shift made me queasy. I could not speak. Looking into her puzzled eyes, I tried to change the face she saw. I tried to smile my mother's smile.

"Where did you go?" she said.

As I reached out, she drew back, the way a cat will when it does not yet trust your hand. Karen had never done this before. I had to find some words.

I said, "C'mere and I'll tell you," reaching again, touching her shoulders.

She came to me this time. Grover took it as a signal of release. He welcomed it. Letting Karen go, he turned, shouting at Buddy, who was the bearer of the square-beamed ready-light and Grover's one-man crew. "Find some candles, Bud. I'm going down to check the pump. We'll just let that leak in the kitchen drip awhile. Maybe somebody else can fire up the kerosene lamps."

I watched his face as he became the captain of this besieged ship. In the beam it looked theatrical—half in direct light, half in shadow, his neck corded, his eyes squinting now. I had last seen him, we had last seen each other, thirty hours ago. It seemed like thirty days. Or thirty years. He was not the same. I was not the same. The word *Grover* passed through my mind like something from a foreign language, a name you would have to practice to pronounce. *Gro. Ver. Gro . . . Ver.* A word with no content. We were strangers meeting as if for the first time, because everything had changed. And yet nothing had changed. He stepped back into the house, avoiding my eyes, and said, "Welcome home," with a martyr's edge, as if to say, "I hope you've had your fun. Now you'll get a taste of what we've been putting up with around here while you were gone wherever it is you went."

I was weary again, wet and chilled and too weary to respond. Karen seemed impossibly heavy. I started to set her down. She resisted the move, not clinging, but holding on, looking at me like an inquisitor. "You didn't tell me yet."

"Tell you what?"

"Daddy told us you were taking a trip."

"That's just what I did, sweetheart. I took a little trip."

"How come you didn't tell us where you were going?"

I put my lips next to her ear, whispering through the soft and silky hair. "It's a long long story. I want you to sleep in my bed with me tonight. I'll tell you all about it then."

"Tell me now."

I breathed deep and waited and found some more words.

"I went to visit some friends and we talked and . . . we listened to music and . . . as soon as the rain started I came straight home because I knew you would be worried about me."

Her arms went around my neck in a hug of affirmation. She kissed me on the cheek. Buddy came up to me with the big lantern hanging from his arm.

"You're all wet, Mom."

"Yes. I'd better get these clothes off."

"I didn't have to go to school today."

"Why? What happened?"

"The cafeteria got flooded. They told everybody to go back home."

"How did the cafeteria get flooded?"

"Everything got flooded. The soccer field too. The parking

lot. Mr. Rawlins, the janitor, put these big high boots on that
came all the way up to his belt. He had to give Grandma a shove
so she could get out of the parking lot. Are you okay, Mom? Do
you feel okay?"

His eyes were very serious looking up at me. He was like a
little family doctor trying to decide where to examine first. With
my free hand I pulled him to me and said, "I think I could use
some rest. I want you to sleep with me too. Will you do that,
Buddy? Help me get a good night's sleep?"

"Sure, Mom. Where did you go?"

"I'll tell you later. Right now you get some candles lit. You
remember how to drip a little wax down first, so they'll stand up
straight?"

"Anybody knows how to do that," he said, heading for the
kitchen drawer where all the candles and holders and old stubs
were stored.

The back door slammed—Grover in his slicker and his knee
boots sloshing out to check the well pump and the generator.
With Buddy's ready-lamp bobbing, two rooms away, we were
standing in the near-dark, and Leona started talking.

"Thought I'd be back up at the ranch long before this, hon."

"You're better off here, Lee. You wouldn't make it through."

"I've never seen such rain. Makes you wonder what it
means."

"Means?"

"Makes you wonder how long things can last, with the
weather changing around the way it does, and volcanoes going off
every time you read the papers. Mount St. Helens. Hawaii. All
that stuff in the air. Now they say the Pacific Ocean is heating up.
They say weather might never be the same again. Things like *this*
are going to be normal from now on, they say. I hope they're
wrong, you understand."

I told her about the roads and bridges. She told me how they
had tried to call Montrose just minutes before the lights went.

"We had finally decided to tell him it might be safer if I stayed the night down here, and when Monty picked up the receiver the signal got funny. I barely had time to tell him where I was and the line went dead."

"Whose line?"

"This line. *The* line. Dead. Not even a dial tone."

I did not yet know how I felt about Leona being there. She did not know either. We were both in a state of semishock. I had once told her I considered her my closest friend. She had laughed and said, "Holly, don't you know you can't have a mother-in-law for a friend? Don't you follow the cartoons and the situation comedies? We are not supposed to get along at *all!*" Ordinarily we could talk about anything, and did, from Mount St. Helens to Buddy's erections. Now I was dripping onto my living-room rug, wondering how much she had heard, or been told, and she was standing there as if we had run into each other by chance on the sidewalk. She did not know quite what to say. I knew she was getting ready to apologize. It would be a mother-in-law's apology. That role still made her self-conscious after all these years. Sometimes I wished we had met under other circumstances, just woman to woman, in a theater lobby or at a party, so that we did not have the blood ties to contend with. But then if we had not shared some common interest in Grover, we would probably never have met at all.

"I was going to drop Buddy off at school this morning, and bring Karen out here and drive on back into town to do some shopping. Grover called me yesterday, you see, and asked if the kids could stay one more night, and I said, 'My goodness, they can live here forever if they want' "—stroking Karen's leg—" 'they are getting to be so well behaved.' By the time we got there, the principal was out under the overhang telling people driving their kids to school to go back home, there wasn't going to be any school today, maybe not for a couple of days. Poor old Mr. Rawlins had to shove my Land Cruiser through this big lake or we'd still be sitting there. So I did my shopping and came out with Buddy and Karen, figuring to drop them off, and the rain started coming down by the tubs and buckets. Grover was here, of course, up to his elbows in mud, trying to keep that culvert cleared. He said I ought to wait until it let up before I tried to start back."

"So you've been stuck inside all day with the kids?"

"You know how it is in the morning when it's pouring down rain. Sometimes it's kind of cozy. I had a cup of coffee, and I read them a story, and the rain didn't let up. Then lunchtime came, so we fixed lunch. And still it didn't let up. We sat here and the afternoon went passing by, and I swear the rain did not slack off for one single second."

I heard no self-pity in her voice, no hint of the long-suffering relative, nor was there a finger of accusation pointed toward me, the prodigal daughter-in-law. But as she told this story, in her level way, I pointed the finger at myself. It is crazy how you can interpret things, or misinterpret them. I found myself taking responsibility for her day of baby-sitting exile. I was guilty of neglect and thus I would have to make amends.

After I had changed clothes and dried my hair and wrapped it in a dry towel, I moved into the kitchen, as I did most evenings when the world turned dark, to pull vegetables out of the fridge, the boxes of this and that. In spite of my fatigue, or rather because huge effort was required to overcome my fatigue, I felt that any effort would qualify as the kind of sacrifice required to redeem myself. It was all up to me, of course. The guilt. And the redemption.

Crazy. Like I said.

In the lamplight I groped toward putting dinner on the table. Lee had the wisdom not to say much, one way or another, but to look for helpful things to do, making moves either one of us could have made blindfolded, so many hours had we logged around the cutlery and the cooking pots.

It was the kind of busywork church women will plunge into when there has been a death in the family, so that you have *somewhere else* to put your attention. I was ten when my granddad passed away. I remember being dazzled by the offerings placed upon my grandmother's dining-room table, the casseroles, the soups, the potato salad, the pot roasts, the breads and pies. I remember wondering how anyone could think of food when we had just that morning looked at Granddad's body in the casket. It was a child's question. The women were always thankful for what appeared to be necessary work.

15

A Lullaby

We fired up the propane stove. Warmth hung above the burners like an aura, pulling us close, me, Leona, Buddy, and Karen. We tossed a salad, grilled some hamburger patties Lee pulled out of the big bag of groceries she had bought that morning, insisting we use them, and the buns too. The kids liked all that. With the lamps hissing and rainwater dripping into coffee cans, it was as good as camping out.

While we were putting food on the table, Grover splashed into the house with news of all the fearful things he had seen outside, the fallen trees, the rush of water through his culvert, some little problem with the timer on his pump, which meant we would have to monitor the holding tank above the house, and some weak planking in the shed where his truck was parked, et cetera, et cetera. Leona appeared to take great interest in all this, the mother being attentive to her son. And so did Buddy, the son being attentive to the mysterious labors of the father. I was watching a movie, a rerun from some 1950s television series. I could not believe we were actually sitting at the table again, as if these past three days had been hallucination. *This* was the hallucination, the long-lost American family, the domestic scene, Mom and Dad, two kids and Grandma, chomping into burgers on a rainy night.

I could not eat. I wanted to tip the table over and scream in his face. *How can you sit there! Where is she now! Why didn't you call me?* What stopped me from screaming? Karen, I suppose—that little moment when she drew back from my hand like an animal sensing the wrong vibration. How far would she withdraw if she saw me scream out what was choking me? There were questions I had to ask. Yet if I asked them now, only the children and Leona would be listening. Grover would not hear. I knew that. All he could hear was the merciless rain falling on his property.

I went numb. If the rain had begun to wash the house away, with all of us inside, I might have been roused from numbness. There were things I had to know, and I saw that days could pass before I would know them. And talking about anything else seemed beside the point. So I let Leona do the talking. She had started telling the kids about a storm she remembered when she was a girl growing up in Oklahoma.

"They call them northers down there, because they come swooping across the plains from Canada, and there is nothing to stop the wind or slow it down. Just the flattest country on the whole Planet Earth, not a rock or a tree for two thousand miles, until it slammed into our house and just about lifted it right off the ground. I still remember what I was wearing that day because I had been playing outside when my momma called me in. I had on a little blue dress with short sleeves. That's how warm it was that afternoon. Two hours later, after that norther had huffed and puffed and done just about everything it could think of to get hold of our house and carry it down across Texas and into the Gulf of Mexico, it passed on by as quick as it had come. There was a foot of snow on the ground and I wouldn't be wearing that blue dress again for six or eight months."

"Were you scared?" Buddy asked.

She looked at him a moment before she said, "No, hon, I wasn't scared. My momma and daddy were there, and anytime they were both there I always knew everything was going to be all right."

Her eyes caught mine and then Grover's, in a pair of glances so quick they might have been blinks. His eyes caught mine too, with a look I still remember. It was his first true attempt at reaching out. I remember how I read it, or failed to read it. If I had been seeing things clearly, I would have seen his isolation. Imprisoned by this storm, we had both ended up in solitary confinement. But I could not yet see it that way. His eyes were defensive, searching, timid. And I did not like to see him timid. It disgusted me. His look reminded me of a dog who has misbehaved. I read it as complicity. In my absence, so it seemed, they had all talked of nothing else but me. Now Lee knew everything, and she was not here as the stranded grandmother but as Grover's blood-kin ally. Somehow the kids were in on it too. With her aid he was luring them away from me. Or, by disappearing for a while, I had pushed the kids away. Or both.

I needed reassurances. Perhaps I could win my children back with body warmth. After dinner that was all I wanted, their bodies next to mine. With Lee there, Grover and I could not begin to talk. I didn't want to talk. I was ready to collapse. I thought about the joint we had smoked in Barbara's bedroom, wondered how long those hits stay with you, in the blood, like delayed-action time capsules to bring on drowsiness. How much time had passed since then? If I closed my eyes I could see Ray squinting against the smoke that floated up toward his dark lashes. I held them closed and listened to Leona tell more survival stories to the kids, while they cleaned up the kitchen, while Grover fiddled with the battery-powered radio, trying to bring in some news.

He sat up late, like a sailor on a twelve-hour watch, listening for signals, I suppose, from the drum of rain upon the roof, sipping whiskey in the lamplight, or in the dark. Lee slept in Buddy's room, while I crawled into our queen-size with an arm around each of the kids.

I sang to them, half-humming, half-murmuring the old riddle song I had learned from my grandmother on just such a night, when I was about Buddy's age. *I gave my love a cherry that had no stone. I gave my love a chicken that had no bone. I gave my love a story that has no end.* . . . They snuggled in close and listened, holding to me, warming me, so that I was both the mother and the sibling—under the blankets, a third child.

By the final verse they were both asleep. In that warmth I felt safe, even from the creek whose roar was the last sound I heard before I myself dozed off, my thundering lullaby. I must have continued hearing it, judging by the dream I had, which began with a tumbling blur of what looked like water, a great wave perhaps, or the bursting of a dam. I had dreamed before of tidal waves, one of my recurring dreams, the wall of green or cloud-dark ocean rising up beyond the beach. In these dreams I am always paralyzed, unable to decide which way to move, whether to run inland away from the water or swim out toward it and hope to clear the top before it breaks. At the last moment I will begin to run across the sand, with the crest so close I can see veins of ragged foam, and so high it blots out the sky. These dreams are always silent. I can see my mouth open but never hear the scream. That night my dream had a sound track, and the sound seemed to slow the progress of this billow tumbling toward me. It looked like smoke, or snow, an avalanche of smoky lava tumbling in slow motion. My fear of it ran deeper because I had longer to contemplate my helplessness. I felt my chest close in upon itself, as if bunched around a wound, as if someone had driven a railroad spike through my heart. My outcry, in the dream, was a howl, a prolonged howling that startled me awake.

Had I actually howled out loud? Evidently not. I felt the kids on either side of me, their ribs rising with the slow pulse of sleep. My heart was pounding. I heard the creek again. The sound had changed, louder now, roaring like an avalanche to fill the world. I listened hard and realized the rain had stopped. The sky was silent, and that doubled the roar. It engulfed me, plunged me right back into the fear I had felt in my dream. I tried to quell it by making the roar a mantra. If I could become one with the roaring . . .

The bedroom door whispered with a tiny scraping across the floor. My eyes sprang open. I watched Grover pad in, carrying his boots, watched him unzip his Levi's and step out of them and unbutton his shirt. He knew I was awake. He sat down on the edge of the bed and said, with soft finality, as if this settled something, "It's absolutely clear outside. The sky is full of stars."

I didn't move or speak. He peeled the covers back and slid in next to Buddy.

During our ten years, Grover and I had always slept together. You could count on the fingers of one hand the nights we had spent apart, and some of those would be motel rooms with twin beds, rented late, when we were traveling and all the rooms with double beds were taken.

Many months later I asked him if this was why he had climbed into bed that night.

With a shrug he said, "I was getting cold."

"Then any warm body would have satisfied," I said.

It took him a while to answer, as if he were trying to recall the scene. "I was sitting in the living room in the dark," he said at last, "thinking about sleeping on the couch, or in Karen's bed, which is way too small. I had been sipping on the Daniel's, you understand. A little hostility was creeping in. Bullshit, I thought to myself, this is my house and that is my bed as much as it is Holly's. If she doesn't like my company, she can damn well come out here and be the one to spend a night on the couch."

"Did you really think I could?"

"That would have been worse, now that I think of it."

"Worse than what?"

"If Leona had found you sleeping there. I didn't see it until just this minute. But that is what was really on my mind."

"You mean Leona?"

"I guess I didn't want her to get the wrong idea."

16

Fathers

The next day, on the radio, we learned that it had started with a cold front moving down from Alaska, just as a warm front had crossed the ocean from Hawaii. They met, from the feel of it, in the very air above our house, at the back end of that valley. They stopped each other, like two delivery vans trying to cross our one-lane bridge at the same time, neither giving way. The fronts hung there for twenty-four hours, making the air as still as eternity, killing the wind. If the word *downpour* ever had meaning, that was the day and that was the night. It was a record-breaking and legendary rain, one that is still talked about and will long be remembered for the damage it did, swelling a hundred creeks like ours, making wide torrents that hurtled seaward to fan out in brown, log-tangled deltas. The beaches north and south for many many miles were littered with waterlogged debris. Later on, in the papers we saw photos of white septic tanks, beached and broken, in among the scraps of roofing, shattered boats. For days after the sun returned, the coastal waters were colored chocolate while tides and currents filtered the mud torn loose from creek banks like our own. It is odd to think that some chunk of grassy soil we once stood on lies ten miles south and west and under fifty feet of seawater, visited now by sand sharks and perch.

When I woke that morning, stirred from sleep a second time by the deep-throated roaring of Revolution Creek, the skies were still clear, glowing with the molten blue of sunrise. My mood was out of synch with that pristine morning light. The whole damaged world was out of synch with it, judging by the little part I could see through our bedroom window.

Trees were down, among them two of my newly rooted saplings. My winter vegetable garden was a battered swamp. Looking at it made me angry. I thought of all the hours I had invested there, the produce I had hoped to reap, the broccoli, the cauliflower, the cabbages, the kale. Now I would be lucky if a dozen scrawny turnips survived. The thought of those turnips made me seethe with anger. It welled up, consuming me. Then I forgot about the turnips. I was angry at the sky for making rain, and at the sun for having the gall to shine on such a morning, at Buddy for still sleeping, and at Grover for not being here, for rising early and sneaking out of the house the way he had sneaked into bed. I saw him driving out of sight in his pickup, heading toward town to meet Sarah, saw them meeting secretly, saw them dancing again at the party on the Fourth of July, the way she shook her shoulders when he looked at her, and how she looked at him, with her hideously painted eyes.

These images nailed me to the mattress. For several minutes I could not move. On another morning I could have lain there a long time wallowing in furious desolation. But something pulled me out of bed. I think I felt the demands of the coming day. Before I knew precisely what they would be, they pulled my feet out from under the covers and onto the floor.

My first indication was the clock, which said five fifty-two. By the sky I knew it was later. I reached for the bedlamp, to test the switch. Nothing happened. Our clock was electric, still showing the minute the power had gone out. I thought of the meat in the freezer, the milk in the fridge, the butter, some leftover stew that had already been in there at least four days. I dressed quickly, my mind on blue alert running through all the things we would have to attend to. This was not the first time our power had failed, but I could not remember a time when it was gone for twelve hours.

In the kitchen a pot of coffee stood warming on the stove. I poured a cup and sipped and reached for the telephone, thinking I might dial for the correct time. In fact, I was checking for the dial tone. I needed to hear it, and it wasn't there.

I had a vision then, of all the little things we take for granted, the daily network we get so addicted to—the lights will shine, the burner will ignite, the car will start, the market will be open, the dial tone will buzz and fill your ear with reassurance, and you will know that, even though your personal life may be in shreds and tatters, somewhere in the world someone is minding the store.

Alone in my kitchen with the dead receiver against my ear, I was listening to what the universe must sound like most of the time. It was not much comfort. I was not ready for that kind of silence. The roaring of the creek was better than silence.

I stepped out onto the porch, to listen to the water, and saw Grover and his mother standing next to the fence across the yard, looking north toward the hill behind the house. I had set out a few of my saplings there, for the long hours of light that come with the southern exposure. Now the pattern of their slender trunks against the hillside had changed. One had fallen. Two others seemed lower down and closer. At first that was all I could see, the location of the trees. As I left the porch to cross the yard, I saw that more than trees had moved toward the house. During the night some huge farmer had plowed a jagged furrow across the middle of the slope. Below that furrow, half the hillside had slipped. The bottom edge of it, wet and dark, had spread out to surround the nearest fenceposts.

I was thinking mainly of my saplings, the vision I had in mind when I planted them, of fruit trees blooming all around us, apple, plum, and peach, a feathery fireworks of springtime profusion. I had considered the site for each tree, and closed my eyes and meditated upon its place in my grand scheme, and now great holes had been gouged in that dream-field of color. I was seeing those holes as I joined Lee and Grover, but he was reading this slippage another way, looking back and forth from the hillside to the house.

He began to speak, as if he had been waiting for me to arrive. It was like a report.

"I figure the whole thing has dropped about four feet. Maybe we'll be lucky and that will be it. But the slope is soaked, you see. We'll just have to watch it and hope we don't get a lot more rain. It is about fifteen yards from here to the porch, and that's across a slight downhill grade. I should have laid drainage pipes up there last summer when I was thinking about it, to leech the runoff."

He sounded then much like his father, who had grown up in this county and who had said much the same thing the first time he came down to look at the land. "I'd think twice about that hillside, Grover," Monty had said. "You might be getting a bargain on this piece of property, but if you buy it, you'll want some pipe laid up along that slope. Whoever built this house must have figured we'd already had our share of rainfall for the rest of the twentieth century."

I think that helped Grover decide to buy the place, knowing his father had doubts about it. And I think he put off attending to the hillside precisely because Monty first suggested it. Stubborn, Lee had called them both, stubborn and single-minded.

Now she said to him, "I have heard of people laying plastic tarp to cut down on the saturation."

His head moved as if slapped, that's how tender he was on this subject.

She said, "It's not too late to do that, is it?"

"I don't have enough plastic tarp around here to cover the bed of the pickup truck!"

His voice was edged with reproach, as if Lee, by mentioning tarp, was somehow responsible for its shortage.

"Let alone a whole damn hillside," he said.

The way her eyes squeezed, watching him, she could have been on the verge of smiling. I saw something then. I knew enough about motherhood to see how she regarded him. More than once I had looked at Buddy with those same eyes.

"It was just a thought, Grover."

"There's no way to get any plastic tarp!"

"You don't have to bite my head off."

"There's no way to get anything."

This could have been the voice of the son telling the mother to leave him alone. But Lee was not going to respond to that. It was also the voice of the male telling the female, with veiled condescension, that she did not entirely grasp what was at stake in the world of soils and heavy equipment. It was the voice of the husband she had lived with for thirty-four years coming from the mouth of the son she had raised. In that moment Lee was another woman looking at a beleaguered and defensive man, and I saw that she was as far removed from him as I.

With a shovel blade he began to drive a short pole into the earth, two feet ahead of the slide's muddy edge, to measure its creep. His movement was so deliberate a shiver ran through me, a thread of chill very close to horror.

"You don't really think it can reach the house," I said.

"Hard to tell. This is pure mud, and there is nothing to hold it back but grass."

"What can we do?"

"Might have to put up a wall."

"With what? What kind of wall?"

"Some kind of retaining wall, with whatever we've got."

I looked directly into his eyes then, his blue and piercing Anglo-Saxon eyes, expecting them to be hard and cold and distant. They were hard, but they were not cold. They were warm with what could almost be called pleasure. He liked the idea that all his choices might be narrowed to this one task he could not avoid. He seemed to take it as a victory. I wanted to challenge him. Maybe I wanted to pick a quarrel. "Grover," I wanted to say, "you are callous. Your heart is made of wood." But I held my tongue. With Lee there, it was impossible, the kind of quarreling I had in mind.

Over breakfast we listened to the news. Some cable towers back in the hills had slid so far down a canyon, repair crews had not yet been able to reach them, even by helicopter. The towers carried trunk lines into the county, and there was no prediction when those lines would be hooked up again. It could be days, the reporter said, "in the remote areas, a week or more."

With no idea when I'd be back, Grover had done some shopping the previous day. Lee had shopped. There were a few things in the freezer. We figured we could make our food last a week, if we ate up the perishables first. We had water in the holding tank, with a backup pump powered by gasoline. We were low on fuel for the lamps, and low on batteries to keep the flashlights and the portable radio going. But we had three days' firewood cut, and more waiting to be cut. We had three solar panels on the roof, facing south. Half a day of sun would give a day's hot water, if we were prudent.

"People got along for several thousand years without electricity," Grover said, as he switched off the news. "We ought to be able to make it for a day or two."

The roads worried us most. After breakfast he drove out to look at the bridge. He took the kids, who saw it as a great adventure, a trip in Daddy's pickup on a blue-sky morning, with no school or day-care center to threaten the great gift of their holiday.

17

Mothers

Lee and I had a dozen things to take care of, food to protect, lamps to fill, wet clothes and wet rugs and wet shoes to dry. But we sat awhile in the suddenly empty kitchen, sipping coffee, as we had so often done. The thing I like about Lee, she is not evasive. If there is a point to be made, she goes straight to it. She herself cannot tolerate what she calls "sidesteppers," people who avoid and evade the issue to the last possible moment. She poured herself a third cup and poured me some, with the warning that we were both drinking too much coffee and had better think seriously about cutting back, then she sat down across from me with her elbows on the table and her hands out flat.

I said, "I forgot to ask how you slept last night. Did you have enough blankets? With no heat that dampness can cut right through everything."

"I slept just fine, Holly, considering."

"Considering what?"

"Considering I'd sooner be just about anyplace than stuck right here between the two of you. But it looks like that is the way it is going to be, hon. It is going to be close quarters. And I think you and I had better get something cleared up."

She waited to see if I had anything to say. I didn't, yet.

"You know what I'm talking about. I don't want you to think Grover has come to me behind your back and told me things, because he hasn't. He has not said one word that would suggest anything is wrong between the two of you. If he did I would be bowled over, because that is just not his way of doing things. Nobody has told me word one. But I know things are bad. From the way you have both been acting, and by the look on your face. My guess is, he has something going with another woman. You don't have to say yes or no to that. It's none of my business either way. Still, it is not easy to stand by and watch two people you love and care about suffer. He is my son and my firstborn, and since his brother isn't here I can tell you, Grover is the one I have taken the most pride and satisfaction in. I guess the first thing I want you to know is, I am not taking sides. Trying not to. But if you need somebody to listen, I am here. I mean, I can't be anyplace else *but* here, for the next day or two anyhow."

I could not avoid her gaze. I didn't want to avoid it. Her eyes are also blue, but softer than her son's, sky-blue, with a clean line between iris and white. In Leona's eyes there is no hidden agenda. No competition. No struggle for power. It is a great comfort to look into them because you know you cannot lie about anything. Those eyes would see right through it. They are not at all like my mother's eyes, where there has always been a hidden agenda. Lee, though about the same age, is not at all like my blood-kin mother, who is vain and ever preoccupied with appearances and who, I am sure now, drove my father away with her fussing about the lawn and the front-room furniture and the unsightly scraps of paper that would gather next to the curb in front of our house due to an accident of street design and a little wind tunnel caused by the microclimate in the neighborhood of my growing up.

Kinship works in such strange ways. You have your blood family, and you have what I call the spirit family, the people you gather as you move through life. Just as Maureen is the older sister I wish I'd had, Leona is the woman I wish had been my mother. I have often wished Grover could see her as I do. As mentor. As ally. She is not part of his spirit family. Real mothers hardly ever are. Blood itself is in the way. Yet Lee and Grover get along pretty well, compared to some sons and mothers I have seen. His younger brother, Travis, for example, will hardly speak to her. Travis spent two years in Vietnam right at the end of the war. She says he still has not recovered. She is afraid he never will. For a while he became a manic Christian, a real crusader. Though he claimed he wanted to be Christlike, he could not tolerate any point of view but his own. From Jesus he moved to Buddhism and from there to Scientology, and from there to a private detective agency, which he calls a form of "law enforcement." If you disagree with Travis, as Leona often does, his jaw muscles turn to rope, his eyes squeeze shut as if blinded by an evil light.

She blames herself for what this son has become. When I have tried to relieve her of the blame, telling her Vietnam shattered the nerves and broke the hearts of a multitude of young men like Travis, she has replied, "War just releases things that were already there to be released." I am still weighing this. You should not have to take upon your shoulders the aftereffects of something as huge and brutal as a war. But this is typical of the way Lee thinks. "What about Grover?" I have asked her. "He refused to go to Vietnam." "That was because he is the older brother," she has said, "and refused to follow in his father's footsteps and go overseas and fight. But he has been tested in other ways. Whatever you undertake releases things that were there to be released. And where do these things come from? You think the mother can be excused?"

She won't let herself off easy, particularly when it comes to family matters, and this makes lying very difficult when Lee is in the room. I had lied to Maureen, the way you can lie, I suppose, to your sister. I had lied to Barbara, the way you can lie to someone you don't expect to see for quite a while. I would soon be lying to Grover, offering him half-truths here and there, which is another form of lying, the most common form. But I could not lie to Leona. She has the kind of wisdom that forces you to be truthful in her presence, to her and to yourself. I had temporarily forgotten this, the way you can forget from one day to the next something you thought was forever imprinted in your mind. The previous night I had forgotten it completely. With no one else around, just the two of us talking, and the clear cool light of early morning adding luster to those eyes, I remembered why I had been drawn to her from the first. Aren't these the people we honor most deeply, and go back to? The ones who will not let us lie to ourselves?

I nodded yes, said she was right, that was exactly what was going on. She asked me for how long, and did I know who it was. I began to tell the story. When she heard it was a younger woman, a shadow crossed her face, a hard line along her jaw that surprised me and passed quickly.

"Has anything like this happened before?" she asked.

"Not that I know of."

She waited.

"Nothing that went this far," I said.

"You're sure."

"Are you ever sure?"

"We usually know, don't we?"

Her mouth bowed up in a grim little smile. She sipped her coffee and impulsively reached across and put her hand on mine and glanced away, as she began to speak.

"When I was a good deal younger than you are, hon, Montrose started running around with a Mexican girl who was picking for his dad. They had three times the acreage we have now, you see, and pickers would come around in the summertime looking for work, just like my own dad had done. I mean, we were pickers too, for a few years there. That is how I met Montrose, working in his family's orchard. You might say he had learned to take advantage of that little bit of power he could exercise over young women on his daddy's payroll. I haven't told many people about this. No one else, come to think of it. I guess I am telling you because Grover figures in the story, in a way.

"He was two years old at the time. Maybe he heard things. Programming starts much earlier than that. In the womb, they say. I was still pregnant with Travis and I found out about this girl, although she was more than a girl by that time. I never did confront her. She was eighteen or so and already had kids of her own, you see, along with brothers and sisters, a whole clan of them working in the orchards. Too much like my own family had been, I suppose, for me to go down there and look her in the eye. At that age, anyhow. And pregnant. It was more than I could deal with just to confront Montrose.

"He denied it, of course. He lied and he backpedaled. It was disgusting to watch. It was a mess. I probably would have left him if I hadn't been so swollen and so sick every morning I could hardly walk. I tell you, it was the very low point of my life."

"Did you ever leave him, or want to, after that?"

"Yes, ma'am."

"Which?"

"Both."

"For long?"

"Oh, I guess I did what you did. Took a trip or two."

"But you came back."

"I did. Yes."

"Even after he had done something like that."

"He begged me, hon. He wept."

"Did you still love him then? Could you?"

"Love him?"

"After that."

"You fall in and out of love, hon. In again. And out again."

"And the boys were still . . ."

"Small. Babies, really. Toddlers. It is like a snowstorm, that period of your life. A blizzard. You can't see which way you are going. I don't know where you went these past couple of days. If you went out and looked up an old flame, why, I would not fault you for it. It's what I would have done, if I'd had one. After I heard him on the telephone yesterday afternoon I knew my intuition was on track, and it made me sick at heart. I was thinking, why bother to raise sons if they are going to treat people this way. Men get their ideas about women from their mothers, and there is no backing away from that."

"What do you mean, he was on the phone? Who was on the phone?"

"Is this young woman named Sarah?"

My face answered the question. My heart froze.

"He must have been on the phone three or four times. I noticed he was being careful to be quiet about it. I am not one to eavesdrop and listen in on somebody else's private business. But still, words would come drifting down the hallway."

"Where were the kids?"

"Oh, here and there. It wasn't anything they would have taken notice of. The last time he called he thought I was resting, I guess. And I was. But not sleeping. It was then that he raised his voice, asking for her by name. It was then I figured he must have been calling the same place all along and someone had been telling him the same thing every time he called because he said, 'What do you mean she's away from her desk? She *works* at her desk!' Then whoever he was talking to said something back and he said, 'She can't be away from her desk for five hours straight,' and he banged the receiver down. I'd say that was about two-thirty yesterday afternoon."

The pickup had just pulled into the driveway. We could hear the metal doors scrape, the kids piling out while the engine stuttered to a stop.

"Sounds to me like she doesn't want to talk to him anymore," Lee said.

"But he sure as hell wants to talk to her. The bastard. I can't stand it, Leona. How do you endure something like this?"

She didn't have an answer, or if she did, she didn't have time to put it into words. She was looking at me with pure compassion when the kids came bursting into the kitchen, both jabbering at once, eager to tell us what they had seen. A dead dog had floated past while they stood by the bridge. Or perhaps it was pinned to a log somewhere on the far side. That was all I could make of the story. They were so excited they began to argue over who could tell us what. I told them to take turns. Buddy could talk first, I said, because he was oldest. That was a mistake. It set Karen off. "Buddy always goes first," she wailed. "He's always the oldest. Why can't I be the oldest?"

It was bedlam. I wanted to pick her up and throw her against the wall. I was ready to throw them both against the wall, when Grover strode in like John C. Frémont returning from his explorations of the Rockies and the whole Far West and announced that the bridge was in bad shape, with one corner dangling like a loose tooth, but repairable. Two people working half a day could get it propped up for a vehicle to cross, he said. We would just have to wait until the water level dropped another foot or two, then we'd have to wait again, until a road crew appeared, because fifty yards beyond the bridge it looked as if another hillside had come apart, burying the roadbed. Meanwhile, out toward Eleanor's place, a chunk of Revolution Road had simply dropped away, leaving a long slick embankment with live root ends poking out and water swirling where the asphalt ribbon used to lie. Before the road reached Eleanor's, it began to climb toward a back-country intersection, which meant that with a little luck they would probably have a way out. But we were cut off in both directions.

It was serious, we all agreed, very very serious. I had been looking out the window as he described these things, toward the remains of my fruit trees. I looked around the room, at my stove, at my cupboards, at my kids, at my mother-in-law, at my so-called husband, at my life. Everything was serious. Everything had to be attended to. There was not much margin for error, and once again there was no time to talk. Knowing Grover, there might never again be any time. Days could go by and in that silence my throat could burst.

All the busy work had to be done, of course.

Of course.

Of course.

The issue here was not domestic image—should I clean the drapes? It was not some nuance of consumerism—should we spend money on X or Y or Z and thus push the credit card out to the limit? We were back to daily survival. And who gives a damn about love life when survival is on the line? It is a good question. I know I had never had to consider it before. Maybe I was like Eddie. Maybe I had been listening to too much country music, where love life is the one and only subject. It may well be that if people had less spare time and more to do with their hands, they would not worry so much about who has put his peepee into whom. Maybe it was a little lesson in humility, to have a hillside creeping toward the porch and both vehicles useless and a shed full of firewood to split.

18

Screens

We sat down at the kitchen table and made a list, an agenda of sorts. Food and water. Fuel and light. The roads. The bridge. The hillside.

We all walked out together to look at the stake marker. There was no denying the mud had moved forward at least another foot. If the gash across the slope could be described as a mouth, it was no longer grinning, it was smiling at us now. At ten a.m., when the weatherman forecast more rain within the next forty-eight hours, Grover made up his mind. He enlisted Buddy. They pulled some two-by-fours out from under the parking shed, and some railroad ties he once had taken in trade for a day's work and never got around to using. He lashed these to the pickup somehow and dragged them to the fence. Then they plodded off into the nearest grove with the chain saw. We could hear its rising whine above the rush of water, like a motorcycle engine that would start and die, start again and die. They felled four young redwoods and stripped the limbs, so that by early afternoon he had six twelve-foot posts lying out there at six-foot intervals pointing toward where he planned to dig the holes. After lunch he started digging. Two feet into the first hole he sawed half the handle off a shovel so he could make a deeper scoop.

Lee and I worked outdoors most of that day, saving the inside chores until after dark. The work helped. It wore me down. It made my bones ache. For hours I stopped thinking, as I moved from chore to chore.

I was carrying a load of firewood into the house when I thought of Barbara. It seemed incredible that only yesterday I had walked into her elegant Brooklyn Heights apartment. I looked down at my arms, at the pine splinters caught in the sleeves of my jacket, at the mud on my boots, and thought what a bewildering world it is. Here I was, suddenly pioneering, while my old college roommate was feeling cut off and short on identity with nothing to console her but a crushed-velvet sofa and her husband's forthcoming promotion. I thought of where I had been exactly twenty-four hours earlier, in a 747 somewhere over Nebraska, listening to a woman from Miami talk about her brother who had drowned in the Sea of Cortez.

My picture of those hours on the plane, in the foam-cushioned seat, with a buckle across my lap, the crumpled trousers of the snoring sergeant, and the young woman's saintly eyes as she described what she had lost—all that sharpened the scene before me, caused me to *see* it, as if a laser stencil had outlined each clump of matted weeds, each dark redwood, each liquidambar, stripped of leaves, the spider limbs edged by winter sun knifing through the clouds. A double vision is what I had. Though I was grounded in that place, rooted, bound, imprisoned, the memory of another time and place so different made this one seem exotic, a field I had just dropped into by parachute. And there across the yard stood a man I knew yet did not know, up to his waist in a hole, lifting out a shovelful of wet dirt. I was seeing this man at his very best. And at his very worst. He was glad to be doing what he had to do. If left alone, he would not talk about anything else until the task was done. I once had a vision of twenty fruit trees in full bloom. He had a vision of a retaining wall rising up at such and such an angle between the hillside and the house. He saw how all its pieces fit and he by God would make it work and hold. It gave him focus, to be out there protecting his house, gave his life meaning, justified his very nature, and thus—the task itself seemed to announce to the world—there will be no need to go into the details of past behavior.

In the set of his shoulders as he lifted the shovel there was a message, and it went like this: "Don't you see the nobility of character? Don't you see how productive and competent I can be?"

It was necessary for the wall to be built. I knew that. We had all accepted that. But he was using it, as we can so easily use things to screen ourselves from the pain of deeper truth.

I remember seeing a physician once, in a hospital. This was when my grandfather passed away. Unable to look at the dying man, this physician looked instead at the charts, at the I.V. tube, at the plasma bottle and all the paraphernalia surrounding the bed. The equipment was there for a good reason, to serve the needs of the dying man. They also served the needs of this poor physician who could not afford to expose himself, who would not attempt eye-to-eye contact with death.

So it was with Grover, as he slaved away until the last shred of dusk faded above the western hills. Working to hold back the flow of saturated soil, he was screening himself with time and labor. I could not have described it quite that way then. I only see it now, both of us caught in the hormonal drama, Grover gathering about himself layers of silence, and Holly building up a head of steam.

What I saw at the time was the stubbornness and his retreat into a fourteen-year-old's gloomy sulk. By dinner I was again ready to kill. In my mind's ear I could hear what Maureen would be saying, if the phones had been working so that I could have called to describe this day. "You can count on it, Holly. A man will build a big fence and go hide behind it every time."

Yes, Maureen—I could hear myself shout—you are right! You

are right! Men do this, and men do that, and if it weren't for the insufferable way men are . . . !

This was how my mind was running. It took a while for me to see the kinds of screens I too was building. Lee is the one who finally put me straight. "Men build screens of work," she said. "And it may well be important work too, but a man will tend to overemphasize the importance and use it as a way to bully you around. Women build screens of blame. We are always blaming men for certain things that have happened or failed to happen. Up to a point, you know, it is true. Don't get me wrong. It has been my experience that men are about half the problem in any woman's life. I guess everybody is about fifty percent right."

19

The Yin and the Yang

The silence was intolerable. We were both taking off our clothes. My back was to him, and I was trying to keep my attention on which nightgown to wear, which was heaviest and would keep me warmest, thinking of the dampness that would come in the pre-dawn hours. Though I wanted to shout, I could not speak. Though speeches and accusations had been alive in my mind for hours, I could not now find the word to start with, the one word that would cut the deepest.

I had unsnapped my bra when I felt his hands upon my shoulders, rough and warm. They made the rest of my body more aware of the cold. I could not move. I was appalled. He wanted sex. He had no idea what was on my mind or in my heart. He actually imagined it was a possibility.

I knew his every gesture. When his hands slid down my arms, I knew he wanted to take my breasts, and in that same instant I wanted him to. I could not believe it. How could he touch me at a time like this? And how could I even think of allowing it? Where could desire come from? I felt its loathsome tickle in my loins when he murmured, "Holly."

"Don't touch me, Grover."

His hands moved again. I crossed my arms, shrugging him away. "Don't even try to begin touching me."

I heard an intake of breath. "I just thought . . ."

"You can forget that thought. My period started."

"When?"

I had to think. It seemed so long ago.

"Yesterday."

"I didn't know that."

"Well, now you know it."

My voice was like a whip with a sharp flick. It backed him away. He stepped to the window and looked out as if examining the sky for weather signs. He waited until I had climbed into bed, then he climbed in and drew the covers up to his chin, and closed his eyes with his head and shoulders half turned toward the wall.

I was in turmoil. My chest, my throat were on fire. Something had to give, had to move, or I would break into a thousand pieces, or I would break the world into a thousand pieces. I said his name, like a question. I was not surprised when he didn't answer, but his silence fed my desperation.

The lamp was on my side of the bed. I had not yet blown it out. I sat up and turned the wick to a high flame. "Look at me," I said.

"That's wasting fuel." His voice was thick, as if already groggy with sleep.

"I said look at me."

"I'm exhausted. I can hardly move."

"I have to ask you something."

"Can't it wait?"

"No. It can't wait."

"It's too late."

"It isn't late. It's just dark outside."

"Jesus Christ, Holly. After a day like this?"

"Look at me."

"My eyes hurt."

"My eyes hurt too. My mouth hurts. My head hurts."

"I need some sleep. Really. Tomorrow morning, when we've had some rest . . . I can't even think."

"Tomorrow will be just like today. You'll avoid and avoid and avoid . . ." I heard my voice rising, getting shrill. I didn't care.

"Avoid what?"

"You know what."

He turned slightly, in anticipation, as if waiting for specifics.

"Me!" I shouted. "It! Us! Them! Life!"

This stirred him, stirred his sense of righteousness.

"There are a million things to take care of, you know that. More rain coming. If I don't get those postholes sunk . . ."

"Postholes is not what I'm talking about."

"You want the house to fill up with mud?"

"It's already filled up with mud! I'm choking on mud!"

"Not so loud. My mother is right down the hall. The kids."

"I know where the kids are."

"You don't want them hearing this."

"Why not? It might do them some good to find out how their daddy spends his spare time."

"You really want to mix it up, don't you. Okay, Holly, let's talk about avoiding, then. Who disappeared for two days? What do you call that? There was a lot of time when I was dying to talk. But there was nobody here."

"The last I heard, you were talking to Sarah."

"I told you why I had to talk to Sarah."

"Why didn't you call me when you said you'd call?"

"I did."

"When?"

"That afternoon."

"Bullshit."

"I called a bunch of times. Nobody answered. I finally got Maureen, and . . ."

"And what?"

"I said where's Holly and she said I am not at liberty to say. She told me I had blown it. I said what do you mean by that and she said you'll find out soon enough. Great friend you have there, Holl. A real heart of gold. Where did you go?"

"It's none of your business."

"Of course it's my business. You take off and leave me here with the kids in the middle of a fucking rainstorm."

"I hope that didn't spoil your plans for the weekend."

"Where did you go?"

"I took a trip."

"The kids don't believe that any more than I do."

"Well, it's true."

"You were with Eddie, weren't you."

"How did you guess?"

"If it was Eddie, I'll kill the sonofabitch."

"Don't get so dramatic. Do you think I give a damn about Eddie McQuaid?"

"Who was it, then? Who were you with? You went to see that guy, didn't you?"

"Which guy?"

"That guy you said you were in love with."

"If I did, I wouldn't tell you."

"You're probably still in love with him. It's no wonder I never get a reaction from you."

"What is that supposed to mean?"

"You're tired, you're distracted, you're busy, your back hurts, you're talking on the telephone, you never even smile. It's like living with a zombie half the time."

"Damn you, Grover! That's not fair!"

"Who was it? Who is it?"

I thought of telling him. I was on the verge of telling him everything I had done, in complete detail, to watch the pain come into his face.

He said, "How many others have there been?"

"Others! That really takes nerve!"

"You think I don't see you look at other guys?"

"I wish I had time to look at other guys."

"Don't deny it."

"There's nothing to deny."

"Then why did you tell me that stuff?"

"It was a fairy tale. There isn't anybody. Don't turn this around on me. I want to know what time you called Maureen's."

"I told you."

"You haven't told me anything."

"I called that afternoon."

"You said you'd call at one-thirty. I was there until at least two-thirty."

"I didn't write down the minute and the hour. I called. What is this, an FBI report?"

"Did you talk to her?"

"When?"

"You know what you sound like? You sound just like a ten-year-old."

"You make me feel like a ten-year-old. What do you want, a videotape of my life?"

"You said you were going to talk to her one more time, and I want to know what happened. Is that too much to ask? If you don't want to talk about that, and be honest and open about that, then . . ."

I stopped. The thought of what I was about to say seemed, suddenly, unsayable. Tears flooded my eyes, angry tears that made the words come out like a choke. "Then it's just . . . finished."

He had closed his eyes again.

"Don't do that," I said. "Look at me."

This time he looked, and I could see remorse on his face, though I did not know if it came from what he saw or something he was remembering. His voice changed. His defensiveness seemed to fall away.

"That conference over the weekend, it wasn't what I thought it was going to be. I thought . . . we thought it would be a good idea to go. We had talked about the feminine side, you see, the need to experience that. It would be a way to go further into that part of myself, to open up to that, the yin that balances the yang."

He thought this explanation would appeal to me. I heard it as another prepared speech. He sounded like a boy carefully explaining some misdemeanor to his mother. I did not want to be Grover's mother. But there is one in each of us who gets called out when you least expect her.

I said, "How could you let her talk you into something like that?"

"Nobody *talked* me into it."

"But it was her idea."

"I guess she heard about it first."

"She has you by the throat, doesn't she."

"I don't know what you mean by that."

"A collar right around your neck. If you could have seen yourself on Saturday morning . . ."

"She was my teacher, Holly."

"Your teacher! A twenty-year-old with big tits and a part-time job?"

"Don't say that. She has . . . a lot of insight. You don't have to be a senior citizen to have insight. If you met her you wouldn't say that."

"Why did you say 'was'?"

"When?"

"You said she *was* your teacher."

He closed his eyes again. I watched his Adam's apple move. He took a deep breath through his nose, as if all his strength had to be summoned. At last he said, "Because it's over."

This stopped me.

With his eyes still closed and his words coming slowly, edged with gravel, he said, "In a way it was good you were gone. It gave me time to think things through. I told her we couldn't see each other anymore, that we just had to draw a line. I told her you and the kids were more important to me than anything else. I told her what you said about making a choice and that maybe it was like smoking cigarettes. If you really want to quit you don't cut back in stages, you just quit."

He turned toward me, his eyes open and direct. "That was why I was late calling. I can't say it was an easy day. But I told her we would just break it off completely. And that is the way we left it. I called Maureen, then I called Leona and asked her to keep the kids one more night, and I went out looking for you, like I did the night before."

"How can you look me straight in the eye and lie like that?"

"I wouldn't lie to you now, Holly, not about this."

"You are a lying bastard!"

"I swear to you . . ."

"Why did you try to call her yesterday?"

His eyelids opened like a pair of lenses pushed to the next f-stop.

I said, "Leona told me you were on the telephone all day long."

He looked away. "I can explain that."

"Don't bother. If you lied about that, you can lie about anything, the same way you lied about Lake Tahoe. Four days to get your transmission fixed. She was with you then, wasn't she."

No answer.

"Wasn't she!"

"You want to know why I called her yesterday?"

"What else have you lied about?"

"Do you want to know why I called her?"

"If it makes a good story."

"Is sarcasm your idea of talking? You are the one who wants to talk."

"What do you expect? You look at me with those sincere blue eyes I always thought I could trust and you tell me you drew the line, and the truth is you couldn't wait to get to the phone."

"Do you want to know why I called her?"

"If you have to talk about it."

"Do you want to know?"

He was shouting now. I shouted back, *"Yes!"*

His eyes drilled into mine. "Because I spent all Sunday afternoon looking for her and I couldn't find her."

As he said this a rasp of anguish came into his voice I did not think he could fake. He is skillful enough with words, with managing words, with anticipating thoughts and arranging words. He is not very skilled at managing feelings. I remembered then that if I was going to know the truth, I would have to stop listening so closely to the words.

"Why didn't you tell me that?" I said.

"I called her place, and there was no answer. I drove over there and found a note on her door that said, 'Dear Grover, It is too complicated.' That was it. One sentence. Her car was gone. I stopped at her office. It was locked up. I tried a couple of other places. She had vanished. I called Maureen's then, and you had vanished."

He was blinking back real tears.

"But she was working yesterday," I said.

"I don't know. Maybe. She wasn't taking calls. From me, anyway."

"So this is your great companion and soul mate."

"Why would she do that?"

"You're asking me?"

"I don't understand it."

"When was the last time you saw her?"

"Saturday afternoon."

"You mean at the conference?"

"Later. After I dropped the kids."

"What happened? What did you talk about?"

"She wanted to take off, said we should both go to Mexico. She knows somebody in Cuernavaca at some institute where they study dreams. Some Mexican tribe down there is supposed to be closer to their unconscious, according to her."

"Why didn't you go?"

"It was too far over the line. It was insane. She wanted to fly. She wanted to leave then, Saturday, and put it all on credit cards. Once we got there, everything would be taken care of. There would be a villa, with some kind of guest house in the back that we could have all to ourselves. We wouldn't need any clothes, because of the climate. But anything else we needed we could buy when we got there. The dollar is so strong now, she said, Americans can do anything they want. She was talking like that, a mile a minute, like somebody on speed."

"But you considered it."

He didn't respond.

"You're still in love with her, aren't you."

His moist eyes searched mine, as if searching for the correct answer.

"Look at you," I said. "Tears pouring down your face. Have you ever wept that way for me?"

"You don't know why I'm crying."

"You're crying because you don't know where she is."

"You think it's as simple as that?"

"I think it's sickening! It's stupid. It's as if, in your view, our life has been completely . . . worthless!"

"That's not true."

"How could you *be* so stupid! How could you risk everything on a little slut who bolts the minute the pressure is on! Maureen was right."

"What does Maureen have to do with it?"

"She knew exactly what was going to happen."

"Maureen is burnt out."

"Maureen saw you come into The Last Roundup one night

and hang around drinking and talking it up. You have spent a lot of nights like that. Was that opening up your feminine side?"

"I am trying to be straight with you, Holly."

"Why? Because you're afraid you lost your girlfriend?"

"Because I love you."

"You only love yourself. What is right is whatever pleases you. Your schedule. Your so-called personal growth. Your house. Way the hell out here at the end of the road. Look at us now!"

"Don't start that."

"Drowning in mud!"

"You think I invented rain?"

"Your sweetheart disappears, so it is time to come home and kiss and make up."

"This is our house," he said. "We both chose it."

"When I think of the way you dropped Buddy off and left him."

"I didn't *leave* him. He was having a hell of a good time with his pals at the Pizza Hut."

"It's so typical. I have always come second. The kids have always come second. They hardly ever see you."

"Bullshit, they never see me. How many kids even have fathers at home?"

"And that is supposed to be enough?"

"Look at the soccer team. Fifteen kids. Show me the fathers. Four. Maybe five."

"A warm body with a Daddy sign around his neck is not enough."

"Be careful, Holly."

"I know what you're going to say."

"You want to talk about the kids?"

"So you don't have to say it."

"You want to talk about the kids, tell me who *wanted* kids."

"Oh shit, Grover. Stop it."

"Was it me?"

"Stop it! Stop it! Stop it!"

"Was I the one dying . . . ?"

"You are the one who was so hot . . ."

"I remember other plans," he said. "We were going to have a band, see the country."

"Don't blame this on Buddy."

"Did I mention Buddy?"

"That's what you're thinking."

"I'm just reminding you of a few things."

"I told you I wasn't safe."

"You didn't tell me anything."

"We could have waited."

"All you did was spread your legs."

"That's so cruel, Grover."

"It's the truth."

"All my fault, then? Is that really how you see it?"

"I didn't say that."

"That is what it sounded like you said."

I watched his eyelids close again. After a long silence he said, "No. I didn't say that."

"Look at me."

He wouldn't. He said, "Why don't you blow out the lamp. I am too tired to talk."

"We have to talk."

"Blow out the lamp."

"I'm not blowing out the lamp until you look at me."

"It's getting late."

"It isn't late."

I watched his mouth, little twitches of the lips, ready to frame some more words. But they didn't come. He was actually dozing off. I watched his facial skin release. His jaw quivered.

I said, "Grover, it is not late."

No answer but the soft and steady breathing.

How could sleep come, after the things he had said, while I had to lie there playing them over and over?

I don't know how much time had passed when it occurred to me that the lamplight, soft as it was, bothered my eyes, made them sting. I should have blown it out, but in my frame of mind I saw that move as a form of obedience, some kind of giving in. I let the flame burn, and we both lay there, Grover wheezing, Holly with her eyes wide, staring at the ceiling and the strange shimmer that filled the room.

20

Daily Lessons

Certain tribes in Mexico live closer to the unconscious, he said. My Mexico is that early-morning time between sleep and waking, when the dream has faded but not the feeling of the dream. I woke the next day cursing the weather that had cut off all escape routes. I was aching to get away from him, leave everything behind, although I know now that if I had truly intended to leave, I could have. I would have. Hadn't I already tried, and returned? It was far too early in the day or in the flow of events for me to read the message and the meaning of that. I imagined myself with one of the kids, or perhaps alone, walking out, following the creek. The sky was overcast but the roaring had subsided, after thirty hours without rain. What was the worst possible scenario? A little mud? Some rocky wading? A few hours of low-grade hardship? I had the energy for that sort of exit building up inside of me. I saw myself doing it that way. I lay there imagining my furious departure, until the door squeaked open and Karen came in and said, "Where's Buddy?"

It was a veiled accusation, as if she knew he had taken off to do something he was not supposed to do. It was bitchy, and it annoyed me. I knew she had learned the sound from hearing me ask similar questions so many times. But her question had a second edge on it, a mother's worry, that cut through my mood.

"I thought you and Buddy were sleeping with Grandma."

"I did. But Grandma says maybe he came in to sleep with you. Is Daddy mad at you for taking a trip?"

"Why? Did you hear us talking last night?"

"No."

"Maybe Buddy's outside working with Daddy."

She shook her head. "His jacket's gone. His boots are gone."

I found Lee in the kitchen making coffee, wearing two pairs of trousers and Grover's parka. Her face looked worn, as if she still needed rest. Around her eyes the skin was deeply shaded.

"He got up once for a drink of water," she told me. "Seemed like it took him a while to get that drink, then he crawled back into bed. Later I heard him get up again, and that time he didn't come back. I figured he had crawled in with you."

She turned to see that Karen was out of earshot and dropped her voice. "This was after the commotion had died down."

I looked at her, and she added, "Insulation in this house isn't all it could be, Holly. Like I told you yesterday, I'd sooner be anywhere than cluttering up your life at a time like this."

"You think Buddy heard us?"

"He couldn't have heard it all, hon, or understood half of what he heard."

"Oh Lee, this is dreadful."

"I wouldn't get upset until after breakfast." She managed a courageous smile. "Boys almost always come home when they're hungry."

I wanted her to be right. Putting my anxiety on hold, I stepped out onto the porch and called his name, and saw my breath make a puff of icy fog, and heard his name echo back from the hillside, at the foot of which Grover had already started to work. I walked over there and looked down at the muddy hole he stood in, his arms streaked with mud, his cheeks red against the cold, and asked him if he had seen anything of Buddy. He said no. I said I thought he might have heard us talking and he might have run away, and Grover, muscling the shovel in deep for another scoop, not looking up, said, "It's early. Wherever he went, he'll be back."

I waited for him to say something else. I did not know what I expected, some reaction to the previous night, regret, sorrow, a change of heart. Something.

At last he said, "See this first layer of topsoil? That is soaked right through. Then it's grainy for a couple of feet and easy digging. Then it's wet again at the bottom, seeping underneath. You see? It starts to be clay. Just like the hillside. The whole thing probably slid across the clay."

I walked back to the house. While we sliced the last of the fresh fruit and boiled water for oatmeal, I listened to Leona tell a story about boys who disappear.

"Grover ran off once when he was a little older than Buddy is now. He might have been ten when this happened. Montrose was burning the weeds off that meadow behind the outbuildings. He needed some help, and Grover was hanging back, resisting, just being a brat. He didn't like the smell, is what it was, and working in the heavy smoke. Montrose started yelling at him, called him lazy and worthless and he might as well not have a son at all. A short while later Grover was gone. We looked all day for him, and he finally turned up at dinnertime acting like he hadn't done anything unusual. It was months before he would talk about it and begin to tell me how he really felt and how it stung him to hear his father say such things. He was always a sensitive boy, soft as butter inside, but with this tough face to the world, which of course he got from Montrose. A man doesn't flinch, and a man doesn't complain, a man pays his own way and carries his own weight, stands up straight and doesn't hit first but hits back when he has to and so on and so forth. See, I think Montrose always secretly liked it that Grover ran off that day, because it showed him the

boy had . . . Well, you have heard Monty say things like this
often enough—'There is only so much shit a man is expected to
take.' "

The word *shit* she mouthed silently, because Karen walked
into the kitchen at the end of this story. A moment later Grover
walked in and switched on the portable radio, for news and
weather, and that got us through breakfast, with no one mentioning the unused bowl and the unused plate. Afterward I
stepped out onto the porch again with Grover, who was sniffing
at his coffee cup and itching to get back to his posthole. With the
business-as-usual look on his face he was studying the sky, the
gathering clouds.

"Maybe you do not fully understand what has happened," I
said. "I think Buddy heard those things you said last night."

"Things I said? What about you? You're the one . . ."

"All right. Us then. He heard *us* last night."

"We don't know that. Not for sure. He could be out there
hiking."

"It's not like him to hike this early and miss breakfast. He
loves breakfast."

"He might roam around for a while, but he'll be back."

"What if he's hurt?"

"He can handle himself. He is curious, but he doesn't do
crazy things. You remember that time he climbed up on top of the
fruit ladder at my folks' place? An accident-prone kid would have
fallen in a situation like that. He has never been accident-prone. I
could tell right then he had a built-in sense of balance and that it
would serve him all his life."

"My God, Grover! You talk as if things are normal. Things
are not normal. The ground is loose. It's getitng cold again. Anything could happen."

As I said this I saw again what I had seen on the plane, the
young body lying in the stream bed, with eyes closed and face in
sunlight, saw myself hunched over the body, and saw that it had
not been memory but premonition. Icewater ran through me.

"What if he's fallen into the creek?" I cried.

"Don't panic. If he fell he probably got wet. He can swim. He can walk. It's not that deep now."

"Well, I am going to go out looking for him, and I am not going to wait."

I watched him gaze a moment longer at the hillside and at the posts he had laid out and at the holes yet to be dug. A breeze came up. In the air you could feel the threat of rain, you could smell it. I knew he was weighing priorities, and remembering himself at that age. It just added to my dread when he turned to me and nodded. "I guess we'd better both start looking."

Lee stayed close to the house, with Karen, in case he reappeared, while Grover started down the road and I moved up the road, crisscrossing it to call into the trees and peer along the paths that lead to the creek. I was maybe fifty yards from the house when I recalled a spot Buddy had used as a hideout for a year or so, at age six, a small clearing behind a thicket of manzanita, with pines rising high above the thicket. I had discovered him there one afternoon, by chance, while I was out for a stroll, and he liked that. He led me in under the branches, and it became a secret between just the two of us. Now I was certain he was waiting for me to discover him again. His disappearance, I knew, was a message to me and to me alone. I was so sure he would be there, I ran to the spot without calling, expecting to see him hunkered and waiting with a little conspiratorial smile as I ducked under the final archway.

But he was not there. By the layer of leaves and twigs and damp pine needles I could tell no one had been there for months.

It emptied me. I felt a desolate loneliness, an actual loss of faith, thinking there are no such things as premonitions, there are no patterns, there is only accident, one accident after another. This happens, and that happens, one day fog, one day drizzle, one day pouring rain, one day blazing sunshine, and we are all here like drops of rain, or falling stars, each falling a separate track that only shines once for a third of a second and blinks out.

It was more than the look of the thicket that stirred such thoughts. For a few moments I was eleven again and hearing my mother and father argue late at night in our house in Sacramento, where it was hard to sleep even when the house was quiet because summers are so sultry and you sweat and toss and wait for the cool hours before dawn. *All right, Diane, all right,* I heard. *We'll do it your way. As usual. We've always done it your way. Why stop now?* Then it was early, very early, and I was wandering through the house feeling emptied, afraid to open doors. Something terrible had happened I did not want to know about. When I finally peeked into their bedroom, she was lying under a sheet with a pillow over her eyes. I thought she was sleeping, or perhaps dead, until her mouth moved, saying, *Holly? Holly dear, is that you? Come and lie down next to me.* I turned and ran outside in my underwear and ran across the backyard to a little shed where my father kept his garden tools. As I approached the shed I thought he would be there waiting. Somehow I knew he would be.

This memory was so real, I almost called his name. Instead I heard my own name being called. It was Grover shouting, from somewhere near the house. I ran down there. He had found muddy footprints on the bridge and had come back for a two-by-four to prop one corner so we could walk across. "Buddy must have made it," he said, "but he doesn't weigh that much."

We took the pickup. He needed someone to hold a strut in place while he wedged his prop under a boulder and nailed the other end. For a few minutes we were both under the splintered beams of the bridge and close enough that I could smell the musty wool of his shirt. As he worked I watched the side of his face. Grover takes great pride in certain small details, like nailing nails. At times his concentration is so complete you wonder about his humanity. How can a warm-blooded human being exclude everything in the world but the placement of a sixteen-penny nail? I was ready to ford the stream, splash or swim, whatever it took. It was an act of the will to stand there while he drove in three.

He shook the post to test its stability, then glanced at me for the first time, with a sidelong glance that was almost sly. He almost grinned. And in return I almost gave him something, I nearly smiled. It was one of those small moments I shall never forget. Warmth rushed through me, and I did not know where it came from.

"It ought to hold," he said.

"Then let's get going. C'mon."

I scrambled ahead of him up the embankment. The bridge wobbled as we eased our way across. Below us the water was a lighter brown than it had been, and lower down. A residue of scum had grayed the highest rocks and the branches of the foliage nearest the flow.

Stepping onto the opposite bank was like entering a strange land for the first time, one we should proceed through with caution. I had no time for caution. Where the road bellies out to make a shoulder I had a long view downstream. I thought I saw something, a patch of blue cloth. I began to run. Grover yelled after me, "Take your time! Look as you go!"

"I see him!" I cried. "He's in the water!"

Where the road follows a tight bend, a cut into the hillside had given way, sending down tons of topsoil and caramel mud, a sloping blockade that covered the roadbed and spilled into the creek. Just past that bend, a waterlogged stump was lodged, a big redwood stump with its torn underside toward us. The patch of blue was a leg of Buddy's jeans seen through two gnarly limbs.

I called. There was no reply, and the leg did not move. I called again, as I started into the water. I wanted to run, but the bottom was cobbled with invisible stones. Behind me Grover yelled, "Holly! Be careful!"

A submerged branch caught me. I lost my footing and fell across the branch, onto my hands and knees. Grover went splashing past. I felt the water then, felt the burning cold on my wrists and thighs, and watched him clamber around to the far side of the stump and brace himself and bend forward, speaking words the creek rush swallowed.

I wanted to shout, "Is he alive?" but couldn't voice it, as if the question itself would pronounce him dead.

"He's all right," Grover shouted.

"Don't move him."

"No. He's . . . it's nothing. He's okay."

I saw the leg move, flexing, as Grover hunched to make the lift. Then he had Buddy in his arms, with his legs wide for balance, taking each step solidly, stone by stone. Near the stump the water was well above his knee, which meant it had been waist-deep for Buddy. From there he stepped up, as if out of a pool, his jeans dark and dripping and Buddy shivering, gangly as a calf. Grover bent to tell him something, the lips so close to Buddy's ear it could have been a kiss. The way Grover carried him, the careful tenderness of his embrace, made me think of the day Buddy was born, the first time Grover took him from me and held him and whispered to him in the hospital room, so softly I could not hear. By the time they reached me I was weeping with relief, and trying not to weep, trying to give Buddy the mother's look of concern and support, but weeping for childhood, and for fatherhood, and for the look in Buddy's eyes. He was not in shock. They were red with cold and pain.

"Buddy!" I blurted. "What were you doing way down here?"

My voice made his lips press closer. I did not want to scold him but I couldn't help myself. "How many times do we have to tell you things?"

"Don't yell at him," Grover said.

"He could have been washed away!"

"He's too cold to talk."

His left ankle was swollen. When we reached the bank, I took his shoe off. He had slipped, evidently trying to wade around the slide, and sprained an ankle. He could not go forward and could not get home, so he had clung to the stump. His face was scratched. His pants were torn where he had fallen, and the ragged tear was edged with blood. He wouldn't speak. He was like an animal caught in a trap, both scared and defiant. He too was trying not to show tears. I wanted to tell him it was okay, to let it out, whatever it was, let it all come out, but Grover's embrace was both tender and possessive. The very maleness of it said, Don't cry.

I walked ahead of them and switched the pickup engine on so the cab would be warm. Grover placed him in the middle of the seat, then hopped down the embankment for another quick look—"As long as we are right here"—at the support post and the underbelly of the bridge, already calculating the lumber he would need, and which tools. This left me alone with Buddy. I was calmer now. I had an arm around his shoulder. We were calming each other. His shivering turned to little spasms, from the sharp intake of sobbing restrained.

I said, "Is it your ankle?"

He shook his head. He was looking straight ahead at the radio speaker. Tiny tears glistened on his cheekbones.

"You want to tell me what you were doing? Did you forget how high the water was?"

"I went away because . . . then you and Daddy wouldn't fight."

"Oh Buddy, honey. You're not the reason."

He was choking on his own words, spittle in his throat. "I made you and Daddy fight."

"No you didn't. Please don't think that."

"I don't want you to . . ."

"Fight any more? I don't either."

". . . live in different houses."

"I guess we only have one house to live in, hon."

"Why did you say those things?"

"People say a lot of things they don't really mean, Buddy."

"Not you and Dad. You always say what you mean."

"Buddy, we love you. We couldn't stand it if you went away. Promise me you won't run away again."

He looked up at me, the fear and defiance receding, as he became a confused little boy again, holding to me. For one moment

his moist eyes were Grover's eyes, just as they had looked the previous night, and I sat there as confused as Buddy, caught again
between the father and the mirror-son. They seemed to be inter-
changeable. In the lamplight Grover had been this boyish and this
vulnerable, as full of pleading for some kind of resolution. Had he
regressed? Or had Buddy grown suddenly much older? Or both?
By not-crying he was his father's son. Yet by crying, he was closer
to his father. I saw then how each lives in the other, and how little
you can know about a man until you begin to know his children,
how important it is to see things paired, the young and the old,
the brother and the sister, the male and the female, and how much
is lost when generations drift too far apart, how these compari-
sons are lost to you. I thought of Montrose, whom I knew not
nearly as well as I knew Leona, wishing he were there among us. I
was certain something in his look, in the webs of flesh around his
sixty-year-old eyes, would tell me more about the man I had married and this son we had spawned, and thus about myself, since we
all turn together, teaching one another, by these tiny daily lessons,
who we are.

21

A Kind of Talking

I want to include something here about Hank Williams, who has not gone out of style since the day he cut his first hit back in 1949. Why do we still listen to him more than thirty years later? As far as I am concerned, it is the way his voice convinces you that the words he is singing, most of which he wrote, describe what he himself has lived through. It is not a melodious voice, like Sinatra's, or Paul McCartney's. It is not an inspirational voice, like Luciano Pavarotti's. Nor does it qualify as Easy Listening. You will never hear Hank on any of the senior-citizen Easy-Listening stations. You will never hear him on the Muzak loop at Long's or K Mart, because it is not the kind of voice that moves you to purchase anything, unless it be another quart of Jack Daniel's. Of all the male singers I have listened to and admired and fallen in love with, Hank comes closest to sounding like a pedal steel guitar. I would not be surprised to learn that the pedal steel was invented by someone who wanted an instrument that could penetrate the soul like the voice of Hank Williams. It just tears at you. I should say, tears at *me*.

That nasal call of his just rips the scabs right off the wounds of my life.

I have in my collection the big double-album reissue called *24 of Hank Williams' Greatest Hits*. Until we spent that week without any power coming into the house, I did not realize how much I had relied on it. Not the power. That album. It is important to have around you a wide range of LPs and cassettes, so that you can find the music to amplify your mood, whatever it may be. There were dozens of times that week I wanted to listen to Hank. I felt I had just reached a point where I understood the longing and the poignancy. "I Got a Feelin' Called the Blues." "Why Don't You Love Me Like You Used to Do." "If You Loved Me Half as Much as I Love You." "I'm So Lonesome I Could Cry."

I wanted to hear them all again. I knew it would be like hearing them for the first time. They would validate something. But I couldn't hear them. Not yet knowing how long we'd be cut off, we could not listen to the radio simply to be listening. We had to save the batteries for weather reports and more news, which had told us road crews were working their way up some of the valleys but not how close or how far away they were.

It was a week of no recorded music at all, and I suppose that accounts for why we started singing with the kids. Though we could not yet talk openly between ourselves, it was a kind of talking, and a way to tell Buddy and Karen some order was being restored in our world, which, for kids, is *the* world. We wanted it as much as the kids did, of course. Order. Can singing do that? I think it can. Maybe you feel the effect of it more when you are outside of town with no lights but lamplight and nothing through the window but darkened landscape and the great vault of heaven. Then the sound of human voices gathered around the same key, with little lines of harmony thrown in, is a calling out for order in the void.

We had pork chops that night, with applesauce. I had been saving them for a special occasion. If we didn't eat them now, they would spoil. For the kids' sake we tried to make a little party of it, mashed some potatoes, and Lee used the grease and some flour to make brown gravy. The kids loved that, since I tend to stay away from gravies. We ate in the living room, where Grover had built the kind of big fire that can organize the world for you the same way singing can, when it becomes your source of both heat and light.

I remember looking at Buddy in the firelight in his thermal underwear and two sets of pajamas and his bathrobe, with one ankle wrapped, and being thankful he was only slightly hurt, thinking of the worse things that could have happened, and had happened, in other episodes, despite what Grover said about his innate sense of balance. It was not the bodily harm that moved me when I looked at him. It was the thought that he and I had both tried to flee this household. He did not know why I moved across the room then and hugged him close. It was to hug away the return of emptiness, a sense of something missing at the very center of my life, our life, something gone that might never be replaced.

Lee was watching me. When I circled Buddy with my arms she caught my eye. Something passed between us, mother to mother. In that moment I was totally outside myself, outside my slough of Hank Williams self-pity. I saw how it must be for her, as mother of this thirty-two-year-old son, watching him ready to crash, while she was sentenced to witness it, to listen and to witness, perhaps remembering long-ago sprained ankles, with the mother's tendency to hover, wanting to nurse and guide and scold, yet too far past those times and that age. And still the mother, her face looking haggard now, after two nights of fitful sleeping and this long day of the grandson lost and found.

The singing that began soon after dinner was a sound sent out to fill all these voids, although by the time we started, my sadness had been softened some by the whiskey we got into.

Grover brought out the quart of Jack Daniel's and stood in front of the fireplace to unscrew the cap. He had finished his postholes and buried all six posts by nightfall. Later in the afternoon the looming overcast had sent down some drizzle, but no real rain. He wanted to feel good about his race against time and triumph over the weather, and about rescuing his son. He had made some sort of peace with Buddy. After we had him cleaned up and warmed up and fed, Grover sat with him for half an hour, before he started back to work. Now he was trying to make a moment out of the unscrewing of the cap, construct a celebration for himself and for the kids. It took some effort. It wasn't easy for any of us that night.

"Anybody care for a taste?" he said.

Leona spoke right up. "I might have some."

This surprised him, pleased him too. "We don't have any ice. Lots of water, but no ice."

"Half an inch will suit me just fine."

I had never seen her drink anything but wine. But I understood this kind of thirst. When Grover looked at me, with a lift of the bottle, I nodded yes, remembering what Maureen had said about the way whiskey and certain songs encourage each other. I did not want to get drunk, although I could have without much encouragement. I could feel the demon whiskey would release, like a second set of eyes peering out. I wasn't eager for those eyes or any other part of the demon to show. I just wanted the early benefits of a single shot. In a flash I understood why there are so many suicides in Norway, so many alcoholics in Alaska, or why these legends attach themselves to Norway and Alaska and other zones where too many closed-in nights can stir up secret appetites known only to the marooned.

"I'd like to propose a toast to Buddy," Grover said, when the pouring was done, "who toughed it out, there on that rotten stump in the raging waters of Revolution Creek, until reinforcements arrived."

"And remembered to take along his jacket," Lee added. "Don't forget that."

"Yes," said Grover, "the kid knows how to plan ahead. If

combat was absolutely unavoidable, I mean, if we had to go into battle and there was no way around it, Buddy is the first guy I would want in my platoon."

He raised his glass. Lee and I raised our glasses. Buddy and Karen had cups of hot cocoa. They raised their cups, and for the first time all day, Buddy smiled. Grover opened his velvet-lined guitar case then and lifted out his Martin twelve-string and hit a big chord that filled the room. The chord made his face squinch. Leaning over the sound hole, he listened to each string, bringing in a couple that were low. "It's the curse of the twelve-string guitar," he muttered. "All these wires squeezed in so close. Worse than a goddam mandolin." Every time he tuned this guitar he said the same thing. It was a private joke which tonight sounded like an obligation, something he had to tell himself, and us, to make this like any other night.

He sipped again and tried another chord. "I think I know a song we can all sing," he said. "It's about a mountain and a woman and all the things that happen when she comes to visit. And it goes something like . . .

> *"She'll be comin round the mountain when she comes.*
> *She'll be comin round the mountain when she comes."*

He had taught this to the kids. One by one we started. By the end of the first verse we had all joined in:

> *"She'll be comin round the mountain,*
> *She'll be comin round the mountain,*
> *She'll be comin round the mountain when she comes."*

"Now," said Grover, still strumming and looking at the kids, "Who remembers another verse? What are we going to have for dinner when this strange woman shows up?"

"Chicken and dumplings," Buddy called out.

And we sang that verse.

Karen remembered the one about killing the old red rooster, and we sang that verse.

"Who do we have to *sleep* with?" Grover said.

Buddy and Karen both cried, "Grandma!" and we sang that verse and then all the others: *She'll be driving six white horses . . . We'll all go out to meet her . . .*

When we had run through the standard verses, we made up some new ones: *She'll be wearing blue galoshes . . . Oh, we'll have to sweep the driveway . . . Oh, her teeth will shine like Jell-O . . . Oh, her hair will smell like varnish . . .*

This went on for an hour or so, as we sang every sing-along anyone could think of. "On Top of Old Smoky." "I Been Workin' on the Railroad." "You Are My Sunshine." "My Darling Clementine." "Deep in the Heart of Texas." "Row Row Row Your Boat." We even threw in some Christmas songs— "Santa Claus Is Coming to Town," "Jingle Bells"—though it had not been three weeks since we thought we had sung them to death.

I will say this for Grover. He can play anything on the guitar, can find the chords for any song ever written. Not that these sing-alongs were a challenge to his ear, but he does have an ear musical women fall in love with, just as I once fell in love with it. He is a natural performer too. His eyes will roam around and seek yours out and make it seem as if he is singing right to you. I watched him do this with Karen that night and make her laugh, and remembered the first time he did that to me, in the club on Telegraph Avenue, the night I met him. He found my eyes in that smoky bar and made me laugh and blush. The memory caught my heart, as I imagined how he must have used this same look on Sarah, and untold other women, his roaming performer's eyes, wishing then I had never heard of her, wishing he had found a way to keep her in a separate compartment of his life so that I could hold on . . . to what? To something I used to have. To the illusion of what that performer's look used to mean whenever it fell on me? Our singing made me yearn for lost times and took me back to that first night, which was a night much like this one, restless, a night of restlessness barely held in, when *some*thing was going to happen, had to happen, though you did not know what, and you wandered in search of it, drinking cappuccino, drinking glasses of wine, as it wandered toward you.

Twice we had stood outside the coffeehouse, Barbara and I, wondering if we should join the throng. A benefit was in progress, raising money to send an independent delegation to Southeast Asia to find out what was really going on. A dozen local bands had volunteered. The second time we stopped, acid rock was pouring out into the street, so loud and hostile I made a face, squinting as if into a heavy gale, and moved on to the bookstore next door. There, among the paperbacks, I ran into a fellow from my anthropology class, researching an assignment we both had to turn in the following day. He was a gentle and studious fellow, but athletic-looking too. A swimmer perhaps. A rock climber. We had glanced at each other a few times before and after class. I remember his eyes, hazel, and quick. He touched my forearm, held it possessively, as if to prevent me from getting away. His eyes held mine, and he seemed to me very worldly, somehow older than he looked. He mentioned coffee. I can still hear his soft voice in the bookstore saying, "You know that small place around the corner? I have these lecture notes I've been trying to unscramble . . ."

Since this offer did not include Barbara, she took it personally, as usual. It was her turn to make a face. Before I could answer him she was heading for the sidewalk. I have often wondered how my life might be different if I had lingered to talk about anthropology with this fellow who already knew that would be his chosen line of work. Would I be in the tropics somewhere, wearing shorts? Would I be living in New Guinea learning dances, collecting masks and tribal chants?

With a head tilt inviting him to come along—an invitation his friendly shrug declined—I followed Barbara back to the coffeehouse, where another band had taken the stage, a bluegrass band playing "Down by the Riverside." To appreciate what happened next, it helps to know that in bluegrass music the fiddle and the banjo get most of the attention. They lead, and the best players work out these virtuoso licks that dazzle your eyes and ears. But the true power and driving force is in the right hand of the rhythm guitar player, who is expected to provide a relentlessly steady yet syncopated beat in the style perfected by the kingdaddy of all bluegrass guitar players, Lester Flatt of the Flatt and Scruggs Band. It took about eight measures for me to single out the power source in this group, a red-haired strummer who not only drove the band along but also sang tenor, leaning toward a voice mike each time the trio came in on a chorus:

> *"Ain't gonna study war no more,*
> *Ain't gonna study war no more,*
> *Ain't gonna study . . . war . . . no . . . more."*

I was possessed with two urges that became a single urge. I wanted to be standing next to that guitar player, and I wanted him and all these other like-minded folks to hear a brand-new song I realized had been written to be introduced in that room on that night. It was called "This Won't Take Long."

I left Barbara and shoved my way forward. By the end of the next tune he had caught my eye, and I had caught his and then had him bending to listen to my request, my vision. As my foot touched the stage he hit a chord which happened to be the tonic chord of the key I wrote the song in. Since I had not yet mentioned the key to anyone, I took that as a sign. The first of many. We soon learned we had been born in the same month, we had both enrolled on the same day three years earlier, we were both fed up with the campus and the war and the town and street politics, and in an era when most of our colleagues still revered the Beatles above all other bands we were both closet Flatt and Scruggs disciples.

As I sang in the Berkeley coffeehouse, at the benefit to raise money to send a delegation to Southeast Asia, we watched each other, our eyes already making plans. Gazing at me through the smoky spotlight beam, his seemed to know more than mine, while my eyes, in memory, were as innocent as Karen's. Yes. That was what our fireside singing made me yearn for. Old innocence. The oldest kind of yearning in the world.

22

Leona

We sang until the kids wore out and lost interest in the singing. When Grover stopped strumming to stoke the fire, Lee began to tell a story, though *story* is not quite the word. She began to talk, in order to fill the house with something after the singing ended. I should explain that it had taken some getting used to for all of us, the media blackout, the night-time silence that surrounds you when the equipment is shut down. At first I thought it would be hardest on the kids, feared their addictions ran the deepest. I was wrong.

After dinner on the second night they had started whining that there wasn't anything to do, which meant no TV to plop in front of, adding that buzzfly of complaint to the general tension. Twenty-four hours later their withdrawal symptoms had dissolved. I remember my relief at seeing how quickly they could let it go, how content they were to sing two dozen songs and afterward sit back while Grandma talked, as her talking became a memory of a world such as this, in the days before twenty-inch and thirty-inch screens came on the market, before Betamax, before video games, before Walkman, before LP records, before transistor radios and tape decks and Muzak.

"Things used to be a lot quieter than they are now," she said. "Did you ever think about that? There wasn't as much to listen to and look at, and people talked slower than they do now. As I recall, they didn't talk quite as much either. A lot of people talk from nervousness, you know. There wasn't as much nervousness when I was growing up. If we be real quiet for just a minute, you'll get an idea what I mean."

She caught each of us with her eyes and brought the room to silence. For three or four minutes we sat with the only sound a crackling of logs. Something settled. This was different from the silence outside the house. It was a silence seized and shaped by Lee, by her eyes. It was hypnotic, a kind of meditation.

"There used to be more room around things," she said. "So when somebody sang a song, you remembered the words for a long long time. When somebody gave a speech or a sermon, it stayed with you for the rest of your life. I can still see a preacher we heard at a revival meeting when I was about twelve. . . . No, come to think of it, I had just turned thirteen, because it was the end of the summer and we were starting to pick apples, still moving from town to town, you see, from field to field, wherever we could get work, and we happened to hit this one town the week a revival meeting was going on.

"Do you children have any idea what a revival meeting is? I suspect not, seeing it's been a good many years since any of us has gone to church. They used to be as common as a rodeo or the stock-car races. There would be a tent set up somewhere outside of town, and the tent would be at least as big as a circus tent. There would be rows and rows and rows of folding chairs facing the stage, and sometimes there would be singers, ten or twelve of them in matching outfits. Sooner or later a preacher would be telling you about Jesus.

"In those days there wasn't much else for us to do at night after work. My dad couldn't afford to take all of us to the movies more than once every couple of months, if then, even though it only cost a dime, and I am talking about 1941 when a dime was still worth something. So we spent every night that week inside this big ol' tent. I can still see the preacher with his white sleeves rolled up and his tie loose, waving his arms and marching back and forth across the stage, and the sweat pouring off him. Later on I figured out he was just too fat and probably on the verge of a stroke, judging by the way his face would get red and shine and drip. At the time it seemed to me to be part of his holiness and the fever of his belief.

"There was no ventilation to speak of, so we were all sweating, listening to his warnings. 'Does Jesus love you?' he would shout, and then answer his own question. 'I have never heard a more ridiculous question in all my life! Does President Roosevelt love the United States? Did George Washington cross the Delaware? Does the copper penny say "In God We Trust"?'

"This fellow made a big impression on all of us kids. By the end of the week my brother Tim went forward and confessed Jesus and said he was ready to be baptized. Half an hour later we were standing on the riverbank just down the hill from the tent, singing 'We Shall Gather at the River,' the song they always sang at times like that. Then we were watching Tim get dunked, and oh, how I envied him at that moment. Not because he had found Jesus. No. It was one of those hundred-and-five-degree evenings, and he was getting himself cooled off in the river. Then afterward I watched the way everybody gathered around to shake his hand and make over him, and this had *quite* an effect on me, since he was the brother closest to me in age. He is two years older, minus a month."

She stopped and looked down at the kids, who had both fallen asleep while she talked, making this the perfect bedtime story. Buddy and Karen were out for the evening, while Grover and I, now into our third shot of bourbon, were made alert by the memory, which came to both of us as a kind of news.

He said, "I've never heard you talk about this, Ma."

"Of course you have."

"Not the part about Uncle Tim."

"I don't know what made me think of him."

"You never talk much at all about Uncle Tim."

"He is an embarrassment to the family, as you well know. Might be that Travis has been on my mind. Of all my brothers, he is the one Travis takes after most. Tim was such a rascal, growing up, the one who could always make us laugh. But when it came time to settle down, he just couldn't get the hang of it. I guess he has lost every job he ever held, and every woman too. If those people over in Visalia knew the true life story of the man standing up in front of their congregation every Sunday morning, they would be praying overtime. I don't think Tim has changed much at all since he was thirteen. That day he got baptized, he wasn't thinking about Jesus. It was high adventure. For him it was just more entertaining than sitting still. Then here came his kid sister Leona thinking, If Tim did it, maybe I better do it too.

"That happened on a Friday, you see. By the time Sunday came around I had just about talked myself into it. The meeting had already ended. The tent was rolled up and on its way to the next congregation. This was a regular Sunday-morning service in the local church. I figured if I confessed Jesus in a real church instead of in a circus tent, I would be one up on Tim. Sunday also turned out to be the hottest day of the whole summer. So when the preacher pleaded with us to come forward and confess our faith before it was too late, I found myself walking down the aisle. Next thing I knew I was out there where Tim had been, watching the preacher's hand rise over my head, while his voice boomed out, then down I went, into the cool cool water."

She paused and looked straight at me.

"It is so strange to think about those times in your life, the big ones, the times that are supposed to stand for something. What is baptism supposed to stand for, Holly?"

"Rebirth," I said. "Being born again."

She shook her head.

"I was too young to be born again. Faith in Jesus, that was how Momma and Daddy saw it. How can you possibly understand a thing like faith when you are twelve or thirteen? Maybe I began to understand it twenty years later. Maybe I finally understand it now, at fifty-three. Maybe I finally understand what Jesus was talking about, what he meant by love. But you get caught up, don't you. The ritual carries you right along. Do you understand what I am saying? We get caught in these moments that were created for us long before we ever got here, the big rituals of life, and we are hardly ever prepared. It just seems like a good idea at the time. Or maybe we don't have a better idea at the time. You go ahead and do what somebody expects you to do, usually for the wrong reasons, and years pass before you get some true understanding of what it meant and what you did."

I could tell she had not said all she had to say. But she stopped and smiled and reached for her glass, to take a sip. It was empty. She was humming, half-singing, "We shall gather at the river, the beautiful, the beautiful river," staring at her glass like the last lonesome drunk at the bar at closing time. But she wasn't drunk. Not yet. She was thinking. Humming and thinking.

When Grover poured her another inch, she nodded thanks, and I liked her more for that. It was pure Leona. She did not fake modesty, as women her age will sometimes do, whether or not they are in a mood to drink, saying, "Oh my goodness, I ought to stop right here."

Lee was in the mood. We all were.

When he had filled the glasses, Grover lugged Karen into our room and came back for Buddy. On another kind of night, with the kids stowed away, his next move would have been toward a compartment in the rolltop where he kept his baggie and his Zig-Zag papers, a small stash for what he called "certain occasions." By this he meant the arrival of friends, usually musicians, who expected dope to be served the way some people serve mixed nuts. Tonight would not be one of those occasions. Leona looked askance at dope. She had tried it, she told me, two or three times.

"But I do not honestly see what all the excitement is about," she had said. "Maybe you are already so spacey," I had said, "it can't take you anywhere you haven't already been." "Oh," she said, "there are lots of places I haven't been. I guess I'll just pick my own way of getting there."

We were all staring at the fire, sipping, when I asked her, "Do you remember being underwater?"

"I do. As clear as day."

"What was it like? Did you think you were going to choke?"

"Oh no. Nothing like that. He had one big hand behind my head and the other one pinching my nose. I felt real safe."

"Did you open your eyes?" I said.

"Yes, for just a second, while I was down there. Even now, after all this time, some mornings I will wake up and feel light coming through my eyelids before I open them, and for just a minute or so I become that little girl again looking up at a blur through water jiggling green and brown and silver."

"When you see that," I asked, "what is your feeling?"

"I want to stay there, I don't want to come up."

"You feel safe."

"I know when I come up, something will change, I'll be different, and I don't want anything to change, and it doesn't, as long as I keep my eyes closed."

"Just a minute or so."

"That's about as long as I can make it last."

"I would never have a vision like that," I said.

"Why not?"

"Water has always been fearful to me."

"Any kind of water?"

"In dreams. I guess I mean when I dream about water. Your story reminds me of a dream I had the other night."

"Your tidal-wave dream," she said.

"How did you know that?"

"It's the only one you ever talk about."

"But I haven't had it for a long time."

"Well, tell me what you make of it."

"I want to know what *you* make of it. Doesn't water stand for something?"

"Water can stand for a lot of things. You look in the dream books, they have got it all charted out. Water equals this, snakes equal that. I have quit paying so much attention to the definitions. I am more interested in what the dreamer makes of the dream. It is like a message somebody leaves on your answer-phone. Somebody else can take the message, but you are really the only one who can call back. There was a wall in there, wasn't there?"

"A wall of water."

"And every time this big wall of something or another raises up, you are filled with alarm, and then at the last minute you start to run. What do you think about that wall?"

"It could have been a premonition."

"Of what?"

"Of the hillside slipping, starting to threaten the house."

Lee and I both had recurring dreams. Hers featured an earthquake, which we had talked about so often she had wearied of the subject. Perhaps she was weary of my dream too, or perhaps it was the whiskey that allowed her to dismiss my first interpretation. In times past a good premonition could have satisfied both of us, plunged us into a long exchange of synchronicities and moments of bizarre foreknowledge. In calmer times she might have said, "Yes, Holly, you know what probably happened? You heard that movement in your sleep or felt a strong vibration coming up through the floor. At some deep level you *knew* what was happening outside before your eyes first saw it."

But not tonight. She shook her head and made a sour face. "That is so easy, Holly. That's not even interesting."

"You don't think premonitions are interesting?" I said.

"I don't think that is what this dream is about. It has been going on too long. The question is, What are you afraid of?"

As she spoke, a paralysis gripped me, stronger than any I had ever felt in that dream. In an instant, it seemed, I had grasped the deepest pattern of my life. I could not voice it. I could only look at her unblinking pale-blue eyes and listen to the next question.

"You always end up running, in the dream, but you are even afraid to run. What are you trying to run from? Do you know?"

It can take half a lifetime to discover the most obvious thing about yourself. Sometimes it comes upon you in the dead of night. Sometimes it is simply a matter of waiting until the right person asks the right question at the right moment. Then hearing the question is enough in itself. When you are ready for the lesson, the teacher will appear. When you are ready for the answer, someone will ask the question. And when you hear it, the answer can be so self-evident you feel both wise and unbearably dense.

Color transparencies went flashing across my inner screen, triggered by some automatic timer, a sequence of scenes that showed me running. Out of fear. I had run from Grover the first time on the very day we decided to move in together, wanting it, wanting him, yet fearing it and fearing him, fearing the choice, which meant not-choosing the host of other men, actual men passing through my life at the time, and the fantasy men not yet in my life, the unmet Howards and Eddies and Rays. After we had lived together for six months I drove off in my Packard in search of breathing room. "We are getting too close"—that is what I had told him and told myself—"and I am feeling smothered." I did that twice, for the distance, for some time to think. And five days ago I had run again, for reasons I did not yet fully understand. But somewhere it fit into this pattern. Impulsive Holly. Propelled by rage.

There was more. I couldn't get at it, didn't know if I wanted to. Lee's question opened a window, and already it was closing. This much would take some thinking through. I still did not have words. Only scenes. I reached for my drink.

She must have known I wasn't going to answer. She said, "I wonder if it's marriage."

I said, "Why would I be afraid of marriage?"

"A lot of people are."

She let this sink in and looked at Grover.

"Anybody here afraid of marriage? How about you? You haven't said much yet. Here I have told a story, and Holly has told a story, and you haven't told us one damn thing. And you have to, you know, because we are stuck out here with each other for Lord knows how long, and we have got to keep each other entertained. People *used* to do this all the time. What is your opinion of marriage, Grover, after the first nine years?"

Belligerence was creeping into her voice. Grover tried to ward it off. With a grin he said, "You know, Ma, when I refilled your glass, I think I made a big mistake."

"No, you didn't. I told this to Holly. I'll tell it to you. Times like these, I would rather be anywhere than here. But I must be here for a reason, and whatever it is, we have got to look it right in the eye. I am your mother, Grover, and you know I love you . . ."

His grin faded. He turned toward me, eyes burning with indignation. "What is this? What have you been telling her?"

"She hasn't told me anything," Lee said.

"Goddammit, Holly! Can't you keep your mouth shut?"

"What do you mean, *my* mouth?"

"This is none of Lee's business!"

"Don't shout like that!" I shouted. "It is everybody's business, thanks to you!"

In an instant we were all shouting, eyes burning.

Lee stood up. "Don't you go jumping on Holly!"

"Jesus Christ, Ma! This is just between the two of us!"

"Maybe it used to be!"

"It still is! We'll take care of it!"

"You expect me to keep acting like I don't know what's going on? I'm tired of pretending! I don't want to pretend!"

"I don't want to talk about this!"

"I know that!" she cried. "We all know that!"

When Grover stood up I knew he was ready to leave the room. I cried out, "You chickenshit!"

That got to him. He actually doubled his fists, flexed his knees, as if ready for a free-for-all.

Lee was not intimidated. "Grover," she said, "you are making a mess of things, and we just flat have to *look* at it."

"Fine," he said. "You two look at it to your hearts' content."

He knocked back the last half-inch in his glass and started for the hallway. With surprising speed Leona sprang up and planted herself in front of him. She had her feet spread and her arms flung wide like an opera singer. She resembled an opera singer and almost sounded like one, as her voice jumped a few keys.

"Look at you! Trying to pretend I don't know what's going on! Acting like nailing up that wall will hold something together! You think that is what holds things together? You have got to look at your*self*, Grover, or you are not going to make it through! You are going to end up just like Travis!"

"Don't bring Travis into this!"

"If that happens, I might as well go jump into the river."

"This has nothing to do with Travis!"

"You are the one I have counted on."

"Don't start that!"

"You are the one I knew had strength. Travis has never had strength. He just wanders."

Her eyes were wild, her body was weaving as if the quickness of that leap made her giddy. Against the flickering light Grover loomed above her, astonished, off balance. I don't think he had ever seen her this way. I know I never had.

Her voice fell almost to a whisper. "He will always be a drifter. But you are stable, Grover, you are like a rudder in my life."

His voice filled with regret. "Ma. It was the war that hurt Travis, you know that."

"I don't want to hear about the war!"

"He shouldn't have gone."

"The war," she cried. "The war! The war! You always say it was the war!"

"I told Dad a dozen times . . ."

"You told Dad what? You're both the same. You think war explains things. Well, war does not explain anything! Men are always talking about how the war explains this and the war explains that. And you can hardly wait for the next one to start so you will have another explanation. I am tired of it. I am sick and tired of it. You can talk about war till your tongue hangs out and never look inside your own heart. This is where the knowledge is . . ."

She held her hands against her breastbone, then moved them down onto her belly. ". . . and here."

Her voice changed again, grew lighter, nearly singing, but in an eerie way, as if someone else spoke through her. It was a younger, girlish voice.

"I know everything about you. You think you can keep anything from me? You may want to. You can't do it. Before you were born I knew you, I knew everything. You think I can bear to listen to what I had to listen to last night?"

He heaved a great sigh of impatient self-restraint.

"I'm sorry you had to be here, Ma. It was nothing any of us could help."

She began to sway. The wildness in her eyes turned glassy. She said, "Mothers always know what's going on. Don't you ever, ever . . . forget that."

"Look out, Grover!" I called. "She's losing it."

Very slowly her head turned in my direction. She smiled a mechanical smile, reached for the sofa's armrest, and missed, plunging. Without Grover she would have landed on her face, and yet, once upright again, she shrugged his hand away, stumbling for the hall.

Perhaps it was the carpet, where a frayed edge had started to curl. Something made her lurch again, and again he held her. She fell against him, helpless, and then her arms reached up groping toward his neck, her head against his shoulder. "Grover," she murmured, "Grover, Grover, Grover."

Her voice still made that haunting, distant sound. There were no tears. This was not apology or loss. It was more potent than that. Though I had not heard it before, I recognized the voice coming back from thirty years ago, the young mother murmuring to her infant son, "You're the one I love the most, you know that, don't you?"

"C'mon, Ma," he said. "Straighten up here, so we can get you into bed."

He tried to move one arm around her neck, to guide her along the hallway, but her body had gone limp, sliding. Caving in, she repeated, "You *know* that, don't you? Hmmmm? Hmmmm?" He hunched and slid one arm below her knees and lifted, the same way he had carried Buddy from the stream, carrying her into the darkness toward her child's bed.

From Karen's room I could hear their voices, his patient and yet commanding, hers complaining now. "I can take my own shoes off."

I sat there trying to remember when I had last seen her touch him, or him touch her. She loved to hold the kids. She touched me often enough, whenever we talked. Many times I had seen her embrace Montrose, and Travis too, in the past. I had seen her flirt with Travis, for the fun of it, play seductive and wait for him to play seductive back. He was her youngest, and until he stopped coming home this was their game. But I had never seen her play that game with Grover, until tonight, and this wasn't play. The way she hung on him, it was with a lover's eagerness. I was not at all surprised. It simply confirmed something about motherhood I realized I already knew. I thought how Buddy and I had sat side by side in the pickup that morning, with my arm around him, and how I understood his confusion and his grief and drew him close and kissed him. I wondered at what age you have to stop kissing, or change the way you kiss, and wondered how many of those kisses a son remembers.

I wanted to ask Grover about this, and knew I wouldn't. It is hard to get a man to talk about his mother. Some men never do. My father never did, nor did Howard, talkative as he was. It is the central relationship in any man's life, and the one he is least able to look at, let alone find the words for. Mysterious and primal are the words I would use, if Grover asked me, though he probably never will. "Of course I love my mother," a man will say. Or, if he has been to a workshop of some kind, perhaps the reverse. Whatever he says out loud, he will go ahead and buy her flowers from time to time, send cards, and call her on the phone, do any number of things that somehow "express his feelings." But none of that comes very close.

A man and his mother. I think of Buddy looking up at my face with eyes that say, "You are the only one who can tell me the world is still together." I think of Grover like a father and a bridegroom carrying Leona down the hall.

I had seen something that night, and I knew when he came back to the living room he would not want to talk about it. He would change the subject. Somehow I knew he would be sexually aroused, though at the time I did not connect this to anything that had gone before. I still do not know if there is any connection. Grover is so often aroused, in situations so incongruous and strangely timed, I have never been able to trace the sources of his sexuality to anything other than itself.

23

Wolves

I heard the back door slam. I could imagine him outside walking around in his jacket, breathing deep, clearing his head and his lungs. I could have used some night air too, but I did not trust myself to stand up.

The next thing I knew he was warming his hands in front of the fireplace, saying, "I just went out and peed on my wall."

"Good for you."

"It's a territorial thing."

"Wolves do that. You expecting wolves?"

"You pee all around something, other creatures know who's in charge."

"How's Leona?"

"Out."

"All of a sudden it caught up with her," I said.

"Whiskey will do that if you're not in practice."

Half turned, he groped along the mantel until he found the Daniel's. "One last splash?"

"Have you ever seen her drink that much?" I asked.

"It's my fault. I should have put this away."

"She would never let you say it was your fault."

"I know what she would say."

"What would she say?"

At that moment a loud snore came down the hallway, a nasal ratcheting that rose to a snort. It made us both giggle.

"Something along those lines," he said. He was pouring an inch into my glass. "Here," he said, "this is the end of it. There's nothing left, not even a can of Budweiser."

He emptied the dregs into his own glass and plopped down next to me.

"I shouldn't have brought up the war," he said. "It always sets her off."

"Do you think she was right?"

"About what?"

"About anything."

"I know I do not need to hear anybody else tell me I am the stable and dependable one, the son to be relied on. I have been hearing that all my life. I am sick of hearing it."

"You can count on me. I will never mention it again."

"I'm rather drunk, Holly. My mind is floating. I just want to tell you one more thing."

We were watching the flames dwindle, bright coals with flames so hot and orange you could not tell where coals ended and flames began, a glow surrounded by the mouth of blackened bricks in an otherwise unlit room. It had become like a first or second date. That is how it was beginning to feel to me. We were sitting on the couch after the parents had gone to bed, and somehow he was courting me again, or perhaps he was courting me for the first time, since we had never done it this way. In the early days I had no house for him to visit, only the jumble of a shared apartment. My mother, the one time I took him to meet her, had already sold her house and bought into a condo she didn't like. We had met in parked cars, in parks, on campus lawns, and so on. Now here we sat, side by side on the front-room sofa, except that this was our own front room, and our own kids were snoozing down the hall.

"The last time Travis was here," he said, "we were standing outside like that, in the dark, peeing, and looking back at the kitchen window, and you know what he said?"

"I give up."

"He said, Do you ever think about light? And I said, I think about it all the time, it is my business to think about light. And he said, I just mean in general, the way we turn something on as soon as it gets dark. Do other creatures do that? he wanted to know. What do wolves do when darkness falls, or lions, or elephant seals? Then he told me about a night when he was overseas, coming back from some kind of patrol, alone, and he saw a building with light coming through the doorway, from a fire or a lamp, and he looked at it for a long time and it started him thinking how humans are the only creatures who do this. The longer he looked, the less human he felt. He said it didn't matter who the shack belonged to, friend or foe. He had lost all feeling for either side. He became an animal looking at this light some human made, and he felt closer and closer to the animals because they understand that the natural condition of the night is darkness. Now, that is my own brother trying to tell me something about himself, and I'd like to know where an idea like that comes from."

"Acid, maybe," I said, after a while.

Grover wagged his head very slowly. "I am serious, Holly. That is how his mind has always worked, for as long as I can remember, long before he ever went to Vietnam. But where does it come from?"

When I did not respond, he waited, and then said, "I just want to ask you one more question. I would like to know if there is anything wrong with seeking light?"

The good part about alcohol is, it separates each moment from all previous moments. You don't have to think about what you said or did or thought twenty minutes ago, because that time does not exist. Grover's question hung in the air as the only question being asked anywhere on earth.

The bad part about alcohol is, it slows down your reaction time. It took me so long to think about this, I nearly forgot what he had said. I may have dozed. I think we both dozed. A log burned through and broke with a crack, alerting me, sending up new flames that threw shadowy supernatural figures across the walls.

As my eyes sprang open I said, "It is basic, Grover. All creatures are light-seekers. They roam during the day. At night they fold up and wait for sunrise. Plants too. Plants reach out toward the sun. It is the most basic thing there is."

We sipped again and stared at the fire the way any creatures would, and by this time Travis was forgotten.

"You're right," he said. "I see it now. What we do is *add* light. We are the only creatures who try to add light to what is already there. The guy with two spots on the cab of his pickup, he wants to get four. Right? The biggest city in the world is the one with the most lights shining. Right? It is said to be a sign of progress. But it is also very primitive, when you think about it. Another torch lifted into the sky."

His voice was soft, and the idea sounded interesting, and the way he offered it touched me, filled me with warmth and loneliness. It had been a while since we talked this way. Like companions. For the first time in days, or weeks—I did not know how long—I felt secure, or nearly so. The whiskey made it easy not to think, easy to believe things might stay like this. Like they used to be. As if we were almost friends again. Or friends on the edge of becoming lovers. And afraid of becoming lovers. Perhaps he had planned it that way, because his next move was a hand upon my knee, the tentative hand of a suitor.

I could feel his body waiting for some response. He seemed to think we had talked enough and drunk enough.

"I wish we had sound," he said. "I'd put some music on. Some Willie. Some early Emmylou."

It was an old signal between us, the aphrodisiac of certain songs at certain times. It was all he needed to say to tell me what was on his mind, as if I didn't already know. Perhaps my silence undermined his faith in the old signals.

Very softly he said, "I wish it wasn't your period."

Subtlety has never been one of Grover's virtues. He shouldn't have added that. He didn't have to. It disappointed me, and yet I did not hold the remark against him for long, since I was wishing the same thing. Part of me was. He probably wanted to do it right there in front of the fire. I could imagine that. I guess I could have been talked into it.

I turned and looked into his eyes. They were steady with the false steadiness whiskey brings, unblinking, glazed with tiny flames. He is a wolf, I thought, looking into those flaming eyes, wondering if mine looked the same in that light. Yes. We were both wolves, drawn to the same fire and warmth. How do wolves do it? I wondered. Like all the other dog-shaped creatures? Like spaniels and boxers and coyotes and hyenas? If we were wolves in deep wilderness coming upon a fire some light-craving humans had abandoned, would he mount me inside its circle of heat and howl at the moon? Would we both howl and then lie down and let heat creep through the fur?

I looked away and closed my eyes, glad for the little obstacle that excused me from having to comment on what should happen next. Though part of me wanted him at that soft moment, I was relieved not to have to deal with his advances.

He is not a wolf. He is goatlike. If previous behavior was any guide, his testosterone would be running at the full. It has a way of cutting through, like a laser beam, no matter how bad he feels or what misfortune has befallen him, and he will want some satisfaction. This had been going on unrelieved for years. At times I have dreaded the demands he would make. When you have talked to women whose husbands seem to ignore them consistently, I suppose you can take it as a form of flattery, that you are being desired at all. Of course, when you step back another pace and give it a good long look, you see that if he could aim his testosterone at Sarah he could aim it just about anywhere he pleased. Maybe he had. Maybe I was not the chosen object of his desire that night, or any previous night, but just another target in his shooting gallery. As my eyelids drooped again, it occurred to me that maybe I was just the nearest and the handiest, with the roads in both directions blocked—apart from his daughter and his mother, the only female for miles around.

24

Beauty

The next morning I looked at myself in the full-length mirror on our bedroom door. What I saw then I still see.

I am not beautiful. My legs are too long, and my hips are too wide for my body. So are my shoulders. And my lips are too thin. I have tried all sorts of ways to conceal this, using liner, using paint, various coatings of this and that. None of it works. My mother, for whom looks were everything, used to tell me that if I wore my hair long it would compensate for a multitude of short-comings. "You do the most with what you've got," she used to tell me. "Play up your bottom, play down your top. You have beautiful hair, Holly, so wear it long. And wear it full. There is a symmetry there. It balances other things."

I have done all that. I am still not sure any of it works. I have never had much confidence in the way I look. I have never had much confidence. Period. The dreams I'd had about who I could be, or could become, I had not believed in them. Or not believed enough. I had run from them as surely as I had run from Grover.

I have thought it all through, and I am now fairly certain this is the reason I allowed myself to get pregnant in the first place. I began to see it, get a glimmer of it the next day, which was another day of chores and busywork, as I thought about the events of the night before and the night before that. Sorting and sifting. Some people say whiskey clears the mind. I think it's true, if the hangover is mild enough. Sometime during the day that follows a night of heavy drinking, there can come a rare singleness of attention. An inner lens can slide into sharp focus and direct you straight to the center of something you have been struggling to see, or struggling not to see. What Lee said about baptism, that affected me deeply, how these key moments in your life can come along and you plunge in, with not much idea at all of the why or the wherefore. Getting married was like that. And my motherhood too.

It was so easy to let the baby grow in there, let the belly swell. The mother's body shines and glows with its own purpose, and you do not have to think much about who you are or what other calling might be yours, or look back, or look ahead. The whole of life and being who you are is self-evident. Beyond speech. Holly Belle, Mother of One. Then, Mother of Two. There was a part of me who could have lived with that indefinitely and did in fact heave a great sigh of relief knowing the future was decided. On the day Buddy was conceived it was the tiniest of voices, a whisper saying this will relieve you of having to make up your mind about what you say you want to do and who you say you want to be and how to proceed. Yes, I did exactly what Grover said I did. I opened to him, and would not let him withdraw when I felt that impulse in his muscles.

It was July, in the middle of the afternoon, we were on the floor of the A-frame he had built, and we were soon to be married. The wedding day was two weeks away, and we were wild, climbing all over each other. But he was not so wild that he lost himself completely. When he was ready to come he asked if it was safe. We had started using condoms, but he didn't like them. Neither did I, so it was easy to talk him out of using one. I told him it was okay, it was okay, and held him with my arms and legs and lips and said I always wanted us to be like this. As we rocked in the ecstasy of that climax and all its delicious aftershock, I felt light as air. I had relinquished something. It made me feel in love. I suppose I *was* in love. I had surrendered to wifehood and motherhood. Is there a line between love and surrendering? Can anyone show me where it is?

Nearly nine years had to pass before I could face all that had been in my mind that day, lurking around the edges. During those few days when we were cut off, I heard it for the first time, the long-ago voice, listened, began to admit it existed, admit that whatever Grover had of mine I had given to him, and there was not much point in hating him for having accepted it. This was the first step in getting my resentments unscrambled. I know of nothing more counterproductive than poorly aimed resentment. Hating him for going after Sarah was different from hating him for accepting whatever I had given him. If there was something I wanted back, hating and resenting would not get it. If I wanted something back, I would have to give it to myself.

"I need space," I had told him more than once. "I need space and time! I need wider orbits, Grover!" He would shout back, "We all need space!"—neither of us understanding then what we were asking for. The kids were everywhere, of course. The house and household had us surrounded. But the greater hindrances are always within, not without. If I truly felt a new opening toward more songs and more music, I could find a way to step into it. If I wanted to turn the little story I had told Barbara into precognition, I could seek out that fiddler with the studio console for cutting demos, or someone like him, perhaps closer to home. Let's go over to my place, Eddie had proposed, and work out some new arrangements. Well, there were various ways to parlay those arrangements into gigs of one kind or another. And that did not necessarily have to include going to Eddie's place, nor did it necessarily mean abandoning the domestic life. When I think of domesticity now, I have a vision of a household as an anchor point, and you are both tethered to it, and what you have to agree on and be very clear about is the length of the tether.

I say this is my vision now. That Thursday I was still thinking blame, still asking, as I had asked two nights earlier in the lamplit room, "Is it my fault, then?" as if it were an either/or situation: if not my fault, his; if not his, mine.

Toward midafternoon, I was standing alone in the yard with the remnants of my little grove of saplings, looking down at one of the bent and spindly trunks, thinking some of these thoughts, and also wondering if this young tree was gone for good, or could it be revived, when he came up behind me unannounced, and took me by surprise. I did not expect to see him anywhere near the house until after dark, assuming he would be underneath the bridge. He had moved down there, with his tools, as soon as he had nailed the final scrap of planking onto the retaining wall, which stood now like the false front of a movie set, a Walt Disney Technicolor movie that included a backyard fortress. It was a hodgepodge of timbers and ties and old wind-eaten two-by-twelves, nailed and stacked and wrapped with wire, six feet high, thirty wide, and catching three feet of wet dirt from movement triggered by a heavy predawn shower. New rain and the advancing soil added to our peril, but proved his hunches and calculations had been correct. Without a wall, our back steps might now be threatened.

How long this rickety barricade would hold, or have to hold, we didn't know. Grover had done everything he could think to do, with the tools he had. We could only wait and watch and listen, just as we listened each morning and afternoon for some signal of an approaching road crew. Because we expected them at any time, we kept postponing the long hike to the first store, to replenish our supplies, although we could not put that off much longer. Tomorrow perhaps. Saturday at the latest. One person with a pack could make it down and back in half a day. Following the creek or hiking cross-country would take the same amount of time, he figured, depending on the weather. A sudden downpour such as we'd had early that morning could swell the creek again, if it lasted very long. You would not want to get caught out in the middle of that, along the ridge or in the creek-bed canyon.

Squatting to examine the little sapling's torn-up roots, Grover said, "I'll replant this and stake it so it can't fall over."

"Where'd you come from? I didn't hear the truck."

"I ran out of gas driving back."

He looked so serious I started to laugh. "What happened to the reserve can?"

"I left it here when I loaded up this morning. I think it's a sign."

"Of what?"

"That I should quit work early."

"That'll be the day."

"I feel like taking a walk, before the sun goes down."

"Long? Short?"

"Long enough to get away from the house. Where are the kids?"

"Karen's coming down with a cold. Lee's keeping her inside. They're all inside."

"How's Lee?"

"Subdued, I would say. Taking one step at a time. She is teaching them how to make something without eggs. She calls them Dust Bowl Cookies."

"I've had those. They're terrible."

"She feels bad about last night, Grover. Says she drank too much, and made a fool of herself."

"I wouldn't say she made a fool of herself," he said. "I saw a side of her I'd never seen."

"You should tell her that. You should go talk to her."

"I will. I'm planning to. When the time is right."

We were crossing the yard, hands shoved into our jacket pockets, following a path that led toward the line of trees where he and Buddy had cut posts.

After a while he said, "Are we out of eggs?"

"We're running out of everything."

"We should have chickens."

"I despise chickens."

"Times like this they'd come in handy. Half a dozen would keep us in eggs. My folks have always had chickens."

"Lee despises them too. She has told me so. My uncle raised chickens. At one point he had over a thousand. I spent two months with him one summer. I never recovered. They are the most disgusting creatures on earth."

"I'm not talking about a thousand chickens. I'm talking about five or six. For eggs. A fryer now and then."

"I'd rather be a vegetarian than raise chickens! I'd rather be a Seventh-Day Adventist eating fake drumsticks made out of soybeans!"

The previous day and night had softened me, but I did not trust the softening. I made myself sound harsher than I felt, and this silenced him. We trudged on into the trees, pushing our boots through mulch and matted twigs, until the house was out of sight.

"I don't want to argue about chickens," he said. "That is the farthest thing from my mind. I don't want to argue about anything. I want to see if we can start to understand what is going on."

I waited.

"When you were gone," he said, "I did a lot of thinking."

"Yes."

"About us."

"Yes."

"I was afraid I had lost you."

"Maybe you did."

"I don't want to lose you, Holly, what we have."

"Why didn't you think about that a little sooner?"

"Have you ever spun out? I mean, completely?"

I looked at him, saw new darkness around his eyes, from not enough sleep and working long hours at hard labor, his body burning more than food and rest could replenish, and so something was being burned away from the flesh around his eyes. He was hurting bad, or he would not have dropped everything to take this walk, never generous with words in the best of times, not the kind we needed then. He would rather talk about weather than feelings, rather talk about guitar strings than what was in his heart. This was something else that had drawn me to Howard, who could be a rambling talker, with intimate stories to share, whether or not the Daniel's had loosened his tongue.

"Yes," I said, "I guess I've come close enough to know how it feels."

"Why did you come back?"

"I don't know yet."

"You still haven't told me where you went."

"What difference does it make?"

"It makes a lot of difference. If we're going to be honest with each other."

"Are we really going to be honest, Grover?"

"We have to try."

I thought about the credit card, the air-fare billing that would appear in our mailbox sometime soon. If I could catch it, years might pass before he would hear a word about that journey. I would have to pay the bill, of course, which meant coming up with money I did not have. Two hundred plus. Maureen would probably lend me that much if I asked her, but then I would have to pay her back as soon as possible. I could work some extra hours, yes, and pilfer dollars from the grocery budget, and thus prolong a scenario of petty deception that made me nauseous to contemplate.

"I flew to New York," I said.

When he hears something truly alarming, Grover has a way of not-reacting, of weighing all the possibilities before sharing his response with the world.

I said, "You don't believe me, do you."

"It doesn't make any sense."

"I have proof. It'll be on the next Visa billing. A round trip to La Guardia."

"Christ, Holly! How the hell are we supposed to find the cash to cover that?"

"The same place we found the cash to cover your vacation at Lake Tahoe."

This led to another silence.

I said, "She was with you then, wasn't she."

"What happened?" he said at last. "What did you do?"

"I had a cup of coffee with Barbara."

"Barbara from Berkeley?"

"That's the one."

"And then?"

"I flew back."

"I don't get this."

"Have you ever spun out? Have you ever felt like killer ants were crawling up and down your body, like you wanted to scream and shout and kick out all the windows in your truck?"

We had reached a rise above the creek. A short muddy trail led down to a glade where we had picnicked a few times. It was a quarter mile from the house. The rush of water muffled all other sound. In front of us a section of the bank had been sliced away, as if trimmed off clean with a paper cutter. A thick madrone limb curved up next to us, its red bark slick, its broad leaves glossy-slick with moisture. Though this glade was filled with light sifting through the trees on the far bank, nothing glittered. These leaves, the limb, the dark soil, the flowing water all seemed to absorb light rather than reflect it.

Watching the flow, he said, "Was there another guy?"

"You don't have any right to ask me that."

"I have to know."

"Maybe I'll tell you if you tell me the truth about Lake Tahoe."

He weighed this, then said, "There *was* another guy."

His matter-of-fact delivery told me he was willing to bargain for information. I said, "I made a call. To someone I used to know, used to care about. Nothing happened. We just talked. It wasn't very pleasant. He wasn't glad to hear from me."

"What do you mean, you used to care about him?"

"I mean it was a long time ago."

"Was it that guy from your anthropology class?"

"Nelson? I haven't seen Nelson for years."

"I always thought you had something going with him."

"Well, I don't, I never did."

"You remember that day you were supposed to move in with me and you walked out of the barbershop and disappeared for two days? I always figured you were in the sack with Nelson."

"You never told me you thought that."

"I guess I didn't really want to know."

We weren't looking at each other. We were looking at the water, and that must have settled our nerves. They say moving water releases negative ions that have a soothing effect on the whole personality. Perhaps that is why this conversation was so strangely muted. We were not shouting this time. We were like two layers in recess, dispassionate, discussing a case.

"Promise me something," I said. "Right now. Promise me you will never see Sarah again."

"I can't do that."

"Why not?"

"You don't just cut people off. She can still be a friend."

"After what she pulled? Dropping you like a hot potato?"

"She was confused. Everybody is confused. I don't hold that against her."

"You are still walking around with blinders on."

"She has been an important person in my life."

"What if I told you it was me or her?"

"I'm not saying I want to move in with Sarah."

"What if I told you, 'Promise me you will never see her again under any circumstances or it's over between us'?"

This stunned him. I was surprised myself to hear it put that way. It was not something I had planned to say. Instantly I saw how much had changed in the past few days. Though I still did not understand the hold she had on him, I had heard enough to know mere companionship would never satisfy. She was not the kind of friend you wanted a husband to cultivate. I also knew more about myself. Reckless statements didn't frighten me. Internally, something had started to shift. I had tried, a couple of times, to imagine life without him and discovered that I could.

I said, "She was up there for those four days, wasn't she."

When he didn't answer I turned and saw his head nodding.

"And there was nothing wrong with the transmission," I said.

His head wagged from side to side.

"And the two-fifty, you spent that on what? Motel rooms? Slot machines? Dining and dancing?"

His head stopped moving.

"Do you know how long it has been," I went on, "since you and I took a four-day vacation?"

His head dropped, as if waiting for an ax to strike. The guilt and resignation in that move made me ruthless.

"When I think what we could have done with that money. Have you looked around the house lately? Have you looked in the kids' closets? Do you have any idea?"

He had drawn both lips in between his teeth, biting down and blinking hard. I knew he was close to violence. I knew he would turn it inward, upon himself. That knowledge made my voice colder, cold as creek water.

"You have lied to me over and over again. You have cheated. You are standing here talking about what we have and what you don't want to lose, and yet you would steal from your own children. That is what it amounts to. Can you see that? And for what? Is it sex? Is it just sex that would make you think so little of us? What do you get from her?"

"I have been trying to tell you." His voice was tight, almost a whisper. "I have wanted to tell you . . ."

"How did she get up there? Did she ride with you and hang around while you guys played the job? Does everybody in the band know about this now?"

"Nobody knows anything. She has her own car. She met me. Later."

"Where?"

"What do you mean, where?"

"I mean, where exactly. In a bar? In a parking lot?"

"I think," he said, "it was a Burger King."

"That is so tacky, Grover."

"It's easy to spot when you first swing off the highway."

"I can't believe how tacky that is."

All week this episode had been on my mind. Obsessively I circled it, imagining the sordid details. Somehow, in my imagination, it held the key. Much later I saw why. I had long known that I myself was capable of elaborate deceit. I had never believed Grover was. My fallen prince. I wanted to punish him for this in particular, and perhaps he wanted me to. When his eyes turned toward mine again, they were wide with a disturbingly familiar expectation. It was not quite fear. They were just like Buddy's eyes at times of total vulnerability. In that moment he *was* Buddy, and I was the mother who has within her the power to emasculate the son. I had felt it more than once. A look comes into the eyes of the son, and the sadistic side of motherhood is called to the surface. It can take an act of the will to resist using that power. Here was Grover, the husband/son at his lowest point of self-disgust, and the vicious mother within me knew she could bend him and have revenge.

I was torn. I wanted more revenge. Yet I did not take it. Maybe it was the memory of that night in The Last Roundup when I had slugged him and he had fallen back defeated by his own guilt. That brought me instant revenge, but no victory. I did not want him like that. I did not yet know that I wanted him at all. But my survival instinct was taking over. Somehow I knew that whether or not we stayed together, I did not want him bent, broken, ball-cut, or in any other way weakened. He would be no good to me then or to anyone else who might inherit him. Am I talking about love right here, or pure self-interest? Is there a line between the two?

His eyes were wet, but not crying. "Holly," he said, "I know it's not easy to think about forgiveness."

I could not take his eyes. I was looking at the water again, trying to find words I had never spoken. My heart was pounding with the dread of what I was about to say.

"I have something to tell you, Grover. I don't know what it has to do with forgiving. I don't know much about that, except it sometimes takes forever. I am going to tell you where I went after I left you in the barbershop. I have never mentioned this to anyone because the whole thing always seemed so dumb and pointless. I spent so much money doing nothing when I had no money in the first place, and then I had to borrow some from the student loan office to get through the month and pay my half of your rent, since that was part of our deal, if you remember. Barbara still thinks I spent the night with the fiddler she was so hot for. She is still trying to get the details out of me, ten years later, just for the vicarious thrill. The truth is, I wasn't with anybody. I went and bought a pint of Southern Comfort and a big bag of tortilla chips and checked into a motel down on University Avenue. I was going to sit on the bed and watch TV and drink, and that is what I was doing when a show came on, a rerun of a western called *Jubal Troop* starring Glenn Ford, who around the eyes and forehead looks almost exactly like my father. I kept the picture on but turned off the sound and picked up the phone and tried to call him. I hadn't talked to my father in about two years, and I didn't have a current number. I started calling one place after another, trying to track him down. I spent about forty dollars, calling all over the country. I never did get him. I have seen him since, but that was the night I needed to talk to him and couldn't. Do you understand what I am saying? These last couple of days I have been thinking about him a lot. I always wanted him to take care of me, and he was never much good at it. When I was growing up, he was gone half the time. One day he just took off. I have told you about that, but what I didn't tell you is that when we got married, what I wanted most was for you to take care of me. And yet I didn't really believe you would. So I have always kept something back. Do you follow that? What I am trying to say is, you are not the only one who has stolen. We have both stolen things from each other. I never gave you everything I have to give. I don't know if I ever can. But I want you to know this, because I have just reached the point where I know it. I have been afraid that if I gave you everything and then you abused it or rejected it or walked away from it . . . I would have nothing left."

These last words came very slowly, each word a rasp. My voice was going. Saying that much out loud to him was one of the hardest things I have ever had to do. I could have said it to Leona with no difficulty. On the plane, to the woman from Miami, I could have said it with ease, if I had thought to, and she would have embraced me and her eyes would have glowed with acceptance. Voicing this to Grover filled my throat with phlegm, which made the words stick and come so slowly they sounded like a confession extracted by interrogators.

I had no idea where this would lead. I felt naked, standing in the forest without clothes, in the presence of a stranger whose reaction was totally unpredictable. He waited so long, I began to tremble.

At last he said, "Me too, Holly. I have held back a lot. Or let things get in the way and stay in the way. You can get buried in the busywork, can't you, get stuck there and stop seeing things."

"*Stuck*," I said, "is a very good word."

"Maybe I have been stuck for a long time."

"Maybe we have both been stuck."

"The thing about Sarah . . ."

"Yes."

"This came to me while you were talking."

"Yes."

"Because you asked."

"What about her?"

"She is not like you."

"In what way?"

"She likes . . ."

"What?"

A spasm shook his chest, as if this chilly air had made him feverish.

"She likes what, Grover?"

"Emotional danger."

"You'll have to explain that," I said, trying not to sound threatened.

"She likes to be right there at the edge of someone getting hurt. When are you going to tell Holly, she would want to know."

"And you didn't see that as a form of honesty?"

"I guess I tried to. But for her it isn't being honest. It is the danger, the thrill of waiting for the shit to hit the fan."

"And for you?" I asked, my blood racing as it had the morning I first saw his scribbled note on the program.

"There *is* a rush. I can't deny it. She was leading me out to a brink. She is the kind of woman who will stand with you on the edge of a cliff and say, O.K., if we both jump together we will both be able to fly. And by the time you are there, you are ready."

"To fly?"

"To jump."

"But you didn't."

"I was on the verge."

"What held you back?"

"Fear, I guess."

"Of what?"

"Of . . ."

"What?"

"This is tough to get at, Holly."

"I know. Just say what you're thinking."

"A couple of nights ago something very strange happened. While I was asleep I remembered a dream I have had dozens of times, a dream of falling from a high altitude. I've had it since I was a kid, and never thought of it while I was awake. I will be flying along above the earth, feeling great, not going anywhere in particular, just looking down at the fields and the towns. Then for no reason at all I lose power and I begin to fall, and I always have plenty of time to react, to think about what's happening, plenty of time for the terror to build up. At first, I am certain I will level out again. But pretty soon it's clear that nothing is going to slow me down. I watch the earth coming toward me and I imagine some lucky out like landing in a haystack or landing in a thick tree full of leaves that will break my fall and I will do some kind of tricky parachute roll when I hit the ground so that I might break a bone or two but still survive, all of that a fantasy because I am falling too far and too fast and I am terrified."

"What scares you? Death?"

"No. Not death. This is what I'm trying to tell you. Losing power. Losing control. And in the dream I want to weep at the stupidity of what I have got myself into, but down I go. And I never hit. The dream always ends before I hit."

Grover and I had often traded dreams. For a while he kept a dream journal, which was still filed away somewhere in his pigeonhole desk. I realized it had been many months since he had described one to me, and I wondered how many he had described to Sarah. In my mind's eye I saw them sitting intimately, trading dreams. This joined other scenes conjured by his words, *emotional danger* and *losing control*, scenes I did not want to dwell on, scenes of unspecified abandon that would rattle me if I let them become specific. I felt poised on the threshold of something. I wanted to stay poised there. I pushed the scenes away and held on to the dream.

"Is that your deepest fear?"

He looked at me, his features fixed.

"Losing control?" I said.

His eyes went narrow, studying the water farther downstream.

"It has come up before," I said. "Control. And surrender."

It had come up a lot. In Grover's inner landscape, this was bedrock. We had talked about it a dozen times, theoretically—how you first identify a fear, then confront and test it. We always reached the same conclusion: When the need to control something starts to overwhelm you, it is time to surrender. If your feelings have been banked, like a heap of slow-burning coals that must last through a long night, then it is wise to give away some of the heat, before you explode.

Now he said, "That's right. Maybe that's what has been going on. Maybe I surrendered to the wrong person."

"Why do you say wrong?"

He had been studying the water for quite some time. When he turned to look at me again, his eyes had relaxed.

"I am thinking about what you just told me . . . how you have held things back, afraid to give me everything you had to give."

"Yes."

"As soon as you spoke the words, I knew what you meant. Somehow I already understood that."

"About me?"

"Yes. No. About me. About us. I guess I have been afraid to give too much to you."

His eyes were very steady, watching mine. Something had come clear for him. This is how I account for what I saw next. For what we saw next. For me it was a moment of clarity and amazing double vision. I was seeing him and also seeing us, the two of us alone among the trees at sundown, while all my passions fell away. I neither hated nor loved him then, wanted nothing from him.

There are several ways to enter, or rather, to be admitted, inside another person's life. I happen to believe you can enter through the body. You can also enter through the eyes. This is what I felt was happening. Months later, when we discussed this day, he said yes, it had also felt that way to him. I believe I saw *Grover* for the first time. He was not husband or father or son, nor was he joint tenant or performer or soccer coach or breadwinner or suitor or lover. Nor was I, in his view, wife or mother or sex partner or daughter-in-law to his parents or cook or sometime singer. For this brief interval, whether or not we stayed together did not matter much to me. We were meeting there, at last, Holly and Grover, who happened by some miracle of existence to be standing next to the same tree above the same creek on the same continent at the same time in the history of this whirling globe.

All our roles fell away, and we recognized each other. That is how it seemed to me—a moment of high recognition.

It passed quickly, of course, as all such moments do. You can only stand naked for so long. Then you gather the roles around you again, like layers of clothing against the weather.

I heard the tumble of water below us, though I could not see it, and across my skin felt the riffling of air that floats above the moving water, cold air that had stiffened my fingers. As if to protect them he reached out and touched, and that brought me back into my physical body. Shocked me back. I squeezed. He squeezed and tugged, drawing me toward him. As our bodies met, the living warmth brought me close to tears. Against the cold, our body warmth itself seemed a miraculous gift.

25

Familiar Mysteries

The sun had dropped behind the ridge with a last-second brighter
wink, filtered by the trees. The air felt damper. We had to start
back. Without words we turned and sidestepped up the muddy
trail. The creek was maybe forty yards away when he reached out
and pulled me close again, and this time it was the other warmth,
the old craving. I knew what he wanted. I wanted it too, the instant he touched me. In the same way. The body itself. My arms
went around him, my head pressed into his neck, the woolly smell
across his shoulder.

He said, "It's been a long long time."

I said, "It's so cold out here."

"The house," he said, "is so damn crowded. They're all going
to be running around."

"We can wait until later. After dinner."

"That's hours, Holly. I don't know if I can wait."

"You never want to wait."

He kept his arm around my waist as we moved on, speeding
our pace. We saw a tiny square of light through the foliage—our
kitchen window.

"We'll have to go back to the house," he said.

"We'll just say we have to be alone, to talk, and it's getting cold and dark outside."

"We'll just say we're resting," he said. "It's been a long day and we have to take a good long rest before dinner."

We told them that and locked the door. Outside the bedroom window, pink and orange ember-glow hung above the hillside like one intense band from the aurora borealis, brief, and merging with the black-blue of impending night. He closed the curtains, lit the lamp.

"So I can see you," he whispered.

We were trying to be quiet. The cool damp from outside still hung on our clothes, making the flesh feel warmer when our hands touched. After we pulled the jackets off he wanted to strip and crawl under the covers. I held him close. Standing by the creek at that time of day had reminded me of the first time we made love. I think I wanted this to be like that distant afternoon, when we had started fully clothed, on an empty beach. We had hugged through down jackets, long and hard. The broad slabs across his back, smooth and layered by the jacket, worked on me like the smell of food when you are famished. We had slipped the jackets off and hugged again, to feel the bodies through thin cloth, and only then had the shirts come off and the skin touched, first for texture, the lightest kind of touching, cool fingers skittering over the warm and youthful flesh.

Ten years later the clothes fell again, in stages, as our hands began to fondle the familiar mysteries that were well known, yes, yet after this separation, new. The one possible reward for so many days and nights apart is the double pleasure of reunion, when it comes, rediscovering each caress, our chests touching, our legs, from chest to thigh the heated touching.

Was it love we were trying to feel, or beginning to feel? Is need a form of love? Or are they one and the same? Is there anyone on earth who can show me the exact line where one ends and the other begins? Deep need, and true love?

Our bodies had joined a thousand times, at least. But since the last time, I could not think how many days had passed. This was more than new. It was urgent. Was it a starting over? A rekindling of love? I can ask that now, thinking back, although I could not have asked it then. My body did the talking. At odds they were, the body and the mind. At war. Should I allow this? my mind was asking. Can I allow it *now*? Should I let him? Let him what? Take advantage? What advantage? Who needs what? Do I really need him, or want him? Or do I need to know that he still wants me? Yes.

Yes. That was getting close.

We tumbled onto the bed. I knew what he liked, or thought I knew. I used to know. But would it be the same? Would it still ignite him? That is what I needed. That knowledge. Sarah flashed on my inner screen, doing things I could not do. What kinds of things? I had to know. Several times I had almost queried him, crazed with jealousy and doubt, but never voiced the questions. I did not want to know. I did not want to look at the pictures on my screen. They undermined my passion, and I wanted my passion, wanted to know it was still there.

I erased the pictures while my fingers grabbed at his shoulders, his neck, dug into his hair, took chunks of hair in my hands and tugged and pressed my face against his and felt the blood stir within him and knew it had begun. The fire was lit. And I had lit it, or both of us together had, passing through need into the dark room of fiery passion, and the extraordinary thing was, I was watching. I was in it, a body catching fire, and I was watching myself catch fire. Something seemed possible that had not been possible before. I saw then that I could give my entire body to Grover and still be able to observe the effect. A veil fell away. A veil that had been covering my body since birth.

Every part of me went swelling toward him, my flesh warm, filling his hands wherever they touched. His lips brushed my cheek, my neck. His arms around me worked like switches. Along my spine I felt thin stripes of light. I wanted time to stop so I could savor this. I wanted each instant to last forever, but the light had sparked toward my legs and shoulders. Then it was not light. It was something else. Negatives of light. Or threads of hot darkness. They numbed my toes and fingers with a fine dark tingle. In a black rush the threads and stripes flowed together, and there was violence in it, an electric violence I had not felt in years, that youthful urgency that makes you squirm and almost hurts, the current is so intense. *Voltage* comes to mind, the word that measures the thickness of the current. The world behind my eyes went silky dark with a black electric silk that expanded until my arms and legs and trunk and head were full with pulsing, glossy black. My limbs were full to spilling. Fuller. I called out in the darkness. I think I called his name. No answer. Time unraveled into no-time. No weight. No body. Pure and weightless current waiting for the light, for the first light, which came glinting around the edges like a lining along the dusky neon tubes that were my arms and legs. Before that influx of softer light the dark pulse receded. I felt my body weight again. I felt flesh again, suffused with buoyant afterglow, and memories of silk, while all past memory came flooding in, the sense of time before, and after.

As the room returned, warm water smeared across my cheek, my lips. I touched it with my tongue and tasted salt. He was weeping, his face so close the tears from his eyes wet both our cheeks. His chest was heaving, not simply breathing deeply, as he sometimes did in the aftermath, from the effort. These were convulsings. And these were tears that had been gathering for a lifetime.

His lips moved in through my hair up next to my ear and the words were soft, a throaty whisper. "You are my woman, Holl. You are my only woman."

Then he was kissing me as we had never kissed, our lips lubricated with the salty smear, tears pouring now from my eyes too, my heart so full I could not speak, filled with joy, filled with sadness, believing in this moment, yet not believing, and the sadness came from wanting to believe it completely and knowing I might never be able to again.

His arms, his eyes, his tears were saying, "Things will still be good between us." That did not mean they would ever be the same. The kind of trust I had been carrying around was like a child's trust. At age thirty-two I had finally lost my innocence. Anytime that happens you are going to grieve for what has been lost, and for what it does to your sense of the future. It is a little like finding out about nuclear weapons. You have to do two things at once—let go of the future, and continue to believe in it. You take things one day at a time. You try to read the signs, to be on guard, and yet not guarded. You learn to gird yourself against betrayal, hoping of course it never comes.

PART III

All the suffering of humankind
is produced by attachment to
a previous condition of existence.
                    —I Ching

26

Liberation

The song "Love Life" was written right after Howard left for New York, during one of my very lowest moments. Now that it has been recorded and released, I receive these little royalty checks in the mail from time to time, causing me to ponder the strange truth of something Maureen said not long ago, while we were listening to a new country music tape. "I envy the people who write these songs," she said. "They have actually figured out a way to turn their most painful episodes into money."

I have Eddie to thank for the checks. Or perhaps Grover, for catching Eddie with his face next to mine and decking him. I suppose I could thank Sarah too, for the part she played in sending me out to the club that night, in which case I should also thank Howard, for originally inspiring the song. Months later, when most of the smoke had cleared, after Grover had apologized to Eddie and vice versa, and they had opened a bottle of whiskey and picked a couple of tunes together as a way of burying the past, Eddie and I were talking and he said, in confidence, that the whole experience had made him feel somehow "closer" to me.

When his new band landed a contract with a small label out of L.A., he included two of my songs in his first album. He insisted that I sing them too. The woman who owns the company said albums sell better if you have the same singer on every number, somebody you can headline. I wasn't ready to cut a whole album, but Eddie persuaded her that I was the only person who could do justice to these particular songs. The album has done well enough, and they are talking now about bringing out a little single, just me, entitled "Love Life." We'll see.

It is so ironic. The first version of that song was written from a man's point of view, a song about a guy who has just learned his woman has been cheating on him. He is sitting in a bar when she comes in and asks him for forgiveness. As I wrote it, I imagined Grover forgiving me. I was certain he would one day discover my secret. This is why I changed the song around—the first time I sang it aloud, I knew it could be a dead giveaway. I made it a song about a woman, and so instead of fantasy it turned out to be a kind of prophecy.

Which is not to say I had forgiven him. By the end of that long, long week I knew I could. I did not know that I would. But I knew I could. My body had already forgiven him. My mind would take a lot longer.

I had thought the song was my farewell to Howard. I can confess now that it was a good while before I truly got over him. Maybe I didn't get over him completely until my flight to New York City. Maybe that is what it was all about, and maybe the years between his trip and mine were not what I had told myself they were, not at all a return to . . . I was going to say a return to normal life. But I do not use the word *normal* anymore. I can't think of anything it describes.

While *normal* is useless to me, two words like *getting over*, from where I'm looking, seem inspired with poetic wisdom. Do they suggest someone looming in front of you, like a hill that must be climbed? That is what they suggest to me, when I think of getting over Howard. Even though his body walked onto the plane and flew away, something else remained, heaped in front of me. The burden of it, of him, the memory of him, or of us together, all of that, what we were, what we might have been if we had somehow stayed together, that fantasy was a mountain in the mind and in the heart which I had to climb and then, yes, descend and gradually return to what I thought was level ground.

Maybe all this helped me comprehend what Grover was going through, five years later. But that did not make it any easier to endure a flood of feeling poured out toward some woman other than me, a woman who, from all I have heard and seen and imagined, did not come close to deserving it. I know he has not told me everything about her, even now. I don't expect him to. He has his private history. And I have mine. You share what you can, as you can, meanwhile keeping your eyes and ears open. Information has come to me, and I have sought it out, rumors, drips and drops of fact and semi-fact about her habits, her previous and subsequent relationships. Though she left the county not long after all this happened, she preoccupied me for months. My inner telescope was constantly scanning. I was like an astronomer studying the dark star some scientists say has been circling the sun these billions of years, while the sun circles it, as much a part of the solar system as the sun itself. They identify it mainly by inference, by what you might call the gossip of the galaxy. Questions that cannot otherwise be answered are all answered if you accept the idea that a dark star is rolling around out there somewhere, an unseen mirror of the sun.

Lee understood this before I did.

"You can save yourself a lot of time," she said, with a melancholy smile, "if you go straight to her, go look her right in the eye. You will learn more, faster, and so will she. If she is only twenty there is no way she is going to know how life looks from your point of view, unless you tell her. My advice would be to call her first chance you get. Make an appointment. Force her out into the open."

"That's easier said than done."

"I know it, hon. I have always regretted I didn't have the nerve."

"What difference would it have made? She moved on. Montrose stayed with you."

She hesitated, looking for the truth of something she had never expressed.

"I was going to say what a great satisfaction getting even can be, though I don't know what I could have done to get even. Anyhow, that isn't it. Maybe I have made too much of this over the years, Holly. Maybe I have carried it around too long because I never did deal with her. Only with the idea of her. You know how a person can carry a photograph, a snapshot of an old boyfriend for years and years? It is like the opposite of that, a place in myself where that snapshot would be. Does that make any sense?"

I did not know how to respond. I didn't want to. I was afraid to imagine what Lee said I should do. I told myself I did not have time to think about it, I had too much else on my mind, I had other fish to fry.

Which was true.

It was Saturday morning when she spoke these words. We were sitting in the kitchen drinking the last of the coffee, with new assurance that more coffee and more of everything would soon be filling up the shelves. A road crew was about to push through the final mudslide and our five days of isolation was coming to an end. We were about to rejoin the rest of the world.

Grover was working on his pickup that morning, certain we'd be taking it into town before the day was out. That is why, an hour before noon, Buddy and I came to be parked by the bridge when the front edge of a scarred-up metal blade lifted the last scoop of twigs and mud and matted leaves to open a ragged track through the slide. Buddy had pestered us all through breakfast, even though Grover told him twice the road crew did not want kids around and there would not be anything to see until two big trunks were cut, which could take till after noon because they were both half buried. I finally drove him down there in my

Chevy wagon, for the outing, just to look, and our timing happened to be perfect.

Fifty yards away a yellow rig eased through the gap it had made and came rumbling toward us, reminding me of pictures I had seen, old film clips from World War Two of the liberation of European cities, with tanks cruising along cobblestone streets surrounded by smiling citizens. As we climbed out of the wagon I felt like one of those citizens, and looked like one. I could not help grinning.

A bill-capped driver chugged right up to the creek bank before he stopped. With the engine plocketing he sat awhile regarding the fragile bridge. Small letters across his canopy said CONSTRUCTION KING. When we had made our careful crossing, he switched the engine off, slowly ducked out from under the canopy, and hopped down with a grunt, as if his lower back bothered him.

A reluctant liberator, he dipped his head in a kind of bow and said, "Howdy, ma'am."

"We're sure glad to see you."

"Lots of people seem to feel that way. I guess it's been a long week."

He was husky, with a dark thick beard, neatly trimmed, and dark eyes that glittered underneath the bill of his dozer cap. The stitching on the cap said EZEFLOW PIPE AND SPRINKLER SUPPLY.

I said, "You doing this all by yourself?"

"No ma'am. I just cut the first swath. The rest of the crew will be coming along."

"Well, what's it like? What's going on?" I broke into girlish laughter. "I mean, this is a momentous occasion. You are the first person we have seen in days."

His smile was weary. "It's not as bad as it was. I spent half of Tuesday at the fire station passing out blankets, helping folks get dry and get their cars out of trouble. I have seen whole cars up to their door handles in mud. Most of 'em are back home now, digging out, or found somewhere to stay while they dig out."

"How about the road? Can we get through?"

"There's a couple of places you don't want to be leaning toward the creek, because you might fall in. And you'll want to honk real loud on the turns. A lot of the way there is only room for one vehicle. But you take your time you'll make it okay, if you've got four-wheel drive. We're clearing as we go, filling in the worst washouts."

He shoved his cap back and said, "You know, you look awful familiar to me."

"You live out this way? We might've passed each other somewhere."

"Maybe," said he. "But that isn't it. You're a singer."

"I do sing from time to time."

"You sang at a fundraiser last year. I don't even remember who the hell was running for office, but I remember seeing you sing. My name's Floyd, by the way, Floyd Pellegrini."

This was good for my confidence, I have to admit, to be recognized by a total stranger. I extended my hand. "It's a pleasure meeting you, Floyd. My name is Holly Doyle."

"That's it!" he cried, as if I had been on his mind for a year. "Holly Belle Doyle! Damn! This is great!"

Buddy had hobbled over next to the machine, running his fingers into the tire's deep tread. Floyd looked down at him. "You want to get up into the cab?"

Buddy flashed his winning smile. He leaned his crutch against the tread, while Floyd lifted.

"You're sure that's safe," I said.

"He can't hurt anything. Just a bunch of levers."

"What's that sticking up back there?" Buddy said, already kneeling on the seat, pointing at the crab claw hanging from its stanchion behind the cab.

"That is a backhoe. It's for digging long holes without a shovel." Floyd turned to me. "I'm pretty handy, if there's any trenching to do."

"We might take you up on that. We've got dirt sliding right behind our house."

"I'd be pleased to take a look at it. Of course, we'll have to shore up that bridge some to handle this much weight."

We both turned to look at the bridge, and he said, as if the time had come for us to share more intimate details, "I took fourth once in a backhoe contest over near Stockton."

"I didn't know they had contests for the backhoe."

"They're not common. I just entered for the hell of it. Quite a sight—thirty-five rigs like this all lined up on a football field, with a big crowd of people sipping Budweisers and waiting for the contest to start."

"Sounds like quite a sight."

Floyd took his cap off and rubbed his shaggy head and rubbed his eyes and looked at me and looked away.

"I suppose you're married."

"Yes, I am."

"Getting along with your husband too, I suppose."

"We have our ups and downs."

"Don't take offense. I just thought I'd ask. Please don't take it the wrong way."

"Oh, I wouldn't do that, Floyd."

"You're just a real warm and attractive woman. I just wanted to tell you that while I had the chance."

"Maybe you have been out in the wilderness too long."

"No ma'am. I'd tell you that no matter where I ran into you, or when."

He stepped closer to the embankment and looked down at the supports underneath the bridge, or perhaps at the water, his face pensive, as if we had been going together for two years and had just decided to break it off. I was looking at his profile, thinking *comrade*, thinking I wouldn't mind getting to know Floyd a little better. In our part of the world a fellow with his own backhoe is someone to stay in touch with. I could imagine having a beer with Floyd at The Last Roundup.

I said, "I feel like you have something else you want to tell me."

"I am just thinking how hard it is to find a woman you can really talk to. You know what I mean? There are so many airheads around these days. . . ."

From the way his voice was dropping and his eyes were sidling toward mine, I knew he wanted to seize these few moments we had and tell me more, perhaps begin to talk about the women in his life or no longer in his life, and I would have listened, had not Buddy found the ignition key at that very moment, causing the starter to grind and leap and my heart to leap along with it.

Floyd bellowed, "Whoa there! Look out now, son!"

He jumped up onto the platform to pull Buddy away from the controls. As the starter fell silent, the voices of the rest of the crew came drifting down the road. I saw them then, trudging out of the swath, my muddy heroes, lugging tools, shovels, chain saws. The sight filled me with gladness. Then a pang sliced right through it, a premonition that came and went. I saw how cut off we had been, and I saw what was waiting out there at the other end of Revolution Road. Along with the telephone hookups and power lines and the great benefactors who would restock our empty shelves—K Mart and Sears and Safeway, where I would pick up the lemons to make the broth for Karen's cold, and Long's, where I would pick up the Vitamin C and also the Ace bandage for wrapping Buddy's ankle—there were all the moment-to-moment signals, both blatant and covert, in the busy swirl of men and women, the lonesome Floyds and roaming Sarahs who made you wonder if domestic life was any longer possible or even probable.

Part of me wanted Floyd to turn his rig around and pile up the mud again and seal off this road for good. And there was still a part of me who wanted to be the first one through the pass, drive out and keep on driving, and not look back.

The crew scrambled around under the bridge awhile figuring what they would have to do. When I told Floyd how much loose scrap we had, he rode with us up to the house. Grover leaned out from under the pickup hood and shook his hand and showed him the lumber pile and then the hillside. For quite some time Floyd studied the retaining wall, like an archaeologist coming upon a long-forgotten temple. It bonded the two of them, I could tell, his silent admiration for Grover's monument. A mixture of wonder and amusement showed through Floyd's beard as he said, "You put this whole damn thing up by yourself?"

"Me and my boy there," Grover said, faking a cowboy accent and slipping Buddy a fraternal wink.

It did not take the two of them long to strike a deal. Grover would provide some lumber and work with the crew until they had the bridge strong enough to roll the backhoe across, then before moving on up the road toward the long washout, Floyd would make a side trip into our yard, dig some diversion trenches to relieve the pressure, and use the trenched-out dirt to build temporary embankments. The wall was already leaking. Strips of mud oozed out between the planks. As soon as the soil dried, they both agreed, a permanent wall would have to go up. Meanwhile, it was Floyd's idea to install what he called a "deadman," a thick pole buried back into the slide and attached to the wall by cable, to provide an anchor against any future flow.

"Winter's not near over," he said solemnly.

Floyd thought he could trench out the deadman's narrow tomb without starting an avalanche, which raised the question of where to get the cable he would need as soon as first thing in the morning. This led us into a husband/wife debate so delicate and highly charged, Floyd soon walked away and hid behind the far end of the wall, as if summoned to inspect a detail he had missed the first time around.

Our subject, on the surface, was getting into town and what needed to be done. There was grocery and household shopping, usually my department. And there was the hardware shopping, in this case, cable, cement sacks, plastic tarp, some mesh fencing—which was usually Grover's department. But there was also Buddy's sprain, which made it unwise to take him on a trip full of uncertainties and potential hazards. And there was Karen, who could be living hell in a supermarket, with or without a cold, and who would have no patience with the delays due to one-way traffic zones both going and coming. As for Lee, she had twice declared that she had overstayed her welcome, which I read to mean she was itchy to make her own escape, get back home to the ranch and to Montrose. One of us then would remain with the kids, and one of us would make the drive into town. But in which vehicle? And how long would it take? And where would be the optimum place to gas up? And in the event of a few more days without power, which groceries were least likely to perish? And which checkbook should be used for what?

Suddenly I was plunged into the pit of depression, thinking nothing had changed, nothing at all. The Unidentified Flying Objects of day-to-day family life were hurtling toward us from all directions, with the added burden now, the hidden agenda of doubt, our mutual and unvoiced uncertainty about what could happen when the other one reached town alone. You weren't supposed to be dwelling on this, of course. Survival was uppermost in everyone's mind. Food. Heat. Health. Shelter. Yet I knew he imagined an unidentified lover waiting somewhere around the first turn. And from my point of view there was not much to prevent Grover from going straight to Sarah, if only, as he would put it, "to talk." Maybe he knew better. But knowing better does not necessarily change things.

I give him credit for how he handled this. He must have deduced that the only way to hold on to me, if that was truly something he wanted, was to let me go again. He used groceries as the reason I should blaze the first trail. He hates to shop for groceries.

I was saying, for the second time, "I am talking about a *huge* shopping, Grover, which would take you four times as long . . ." when he reached into his Levi's and pulled out the keys to his precious pickup. He takes keys very seriously, by the way. He never leaves them in the ignition, even when he is parked right next to the house.

He saw me watching his seriousness and grinned, laughing at himself, a surprisingly worldly grin of a kind I had not seen on him before. I understand it now. It was a gambler's grin. He was gambling on a show of trust, and knew it.

"Just don't ride the brake," he said. "And use the low gears until you cross the river."

27

Flood Victims

Our mini-caravan departed right after lunch, Lee following the pickup in her red Toyota Land Cruiser. In my rearview I could see her perched behind the wheel, sitting straight with her driving glasses on. The road crew stood back from the bridge, leaning on their tools to watch us pass. It was strange, entering the gap they had cut. Serious damage is always strange. Pale moons shone on either side of us, where sawblades had sliced through fallen trunks. Around the moons, twigs and root ends were poking out of the dirt, root tendrils and hairy feelers still hoping the open air might nurture them the way deep soil had.

Beyond the slide I saw the snaggly stump where we had found Buddy. It rose from the water like a soggy sculpture. Was this how far he had run? It seemed such a short distance now. And how much farther did I think I was going to go? I knew I would be coming back to deliver my load of groceries and supplies, to store the food so that it would not spoil, to rewrap Buddy's ankle and nurse Karen's cold. Would I then remain? Could I? What happened after these things were attended to, I couldn't foresee, or didn't want to foresee. Each chore was a single act. They were not connected to one another or to anything else. This is what still confused me, the connecting tissue, and whether it was there. Love is the word that describes it best, and we all know how elusive that word is. It was too much to think about with the road slick and full of new ruts. I was taking one job, one hour, one mile at a time, as I always do when setting out into unknown territory.

The nearest house to ours stood just around that bend, a vacation cottage the owners kept locked all winter. It looked to be a total loss. The high-water mark was a pale stripe above the porch railing. A tree had sheared one corner off the roof. There was no way to cross and see what might be salvaged or protected. The middle of their wooden bridge was gone. Beam ends dangled above the flow. It teaches you humility to witness such a sight, helps you keep your own so-called calamities in perspective. I shuddered and I gave thanks.

That happened to be the worst damage on our road. The next place was set higher up, an old two-story frame house perched under soaring trees. Though these were our closest year-round neighbors, we didn't see them much. The husband was perhaps forty-five, a member of the National Rifle Association and the Libertarian Party. He kept German shepherds and drove a camper truck with a ragged and fading sticker that said WHEN GUNS ARE OUTLAWED, ONLY OUTLAWS WILL HAVE GUNS. Since he was home most of the time and had no known profession, we imagined a field of marijuana flourishing somewhere up the ridge.

This morning his camper was gone. Heading into town, I figured. The heavy chain across his driveway still carried its warning sign: KEEP OUT. I stopped at the mailbox anyway, feeling sociable. Behind the house his dogs began to bark, a fierce and deep-throated echo of the sign.

For a hundred yards we had to hug the upside of the road, where another long chunk next to the creek had been eaten away, leaving a one-lane track. There were three sections like that, one with a flagman at either end, and numerous slides large and small.

Dozens and dozens of trees were down. Where the creek finally meets the river we saw muddy debris snagged in the brush along its banks—a bedsheet, a plastic bucket, a piece of someone's fence.

The fire station stands near that intersection, set well back from the road. It's just a long shed wide enough to house two trucks, with a couple of rooms in back for cooking and sleeping, though they are seldom used. You could tell something had happened, by the heaped and overflowing garbage cans and by the pattern of wheel tracks all across the concrete pad and looping out into the muddy clearing between the shed and the river. But when we pulled up and stopped and shut our engines off, it was so quiet it seemed abandoned.

Among the many notes and notices on the door, one was signed by the volunteer fire marshal saying he would be right back. We were reading that, when two people appeared at the corner of the shed, from the sunny side, where they had been squatting and trying to keep warm waiting for a ride. They were bundled in scarves and foul-weather coats, each carrying a sack of groceries. They looked to be about twenty-five. With brave smiles they told us where they were headed and why they were on foot. They lived five miles up the river, on the banks of another creek like ours. A tree had fallen onto their van. They were hitchhiking until the county buses started running, meanwhile trying to raise the money to buy something to replace the van, which was totaled.

Upriver was Lee's direction. She soon had them installed inside the Cruiser, with the heater going full blast and some baroque music on her cassette deck. The Pachelbel Canon in D Major, as I recall. "This is wonderful for problem solving," I heard her tell them. "It soothes the spirit and clears the mind."

A pay phone hung by the station door. She walked over there and held the receiver to her ear and evidently heard something. I watched her reach up and drop coins in, her gray hair pulled back, her pullover stretching, her boot heels lifting slightly as she dialed, calling Montrose. In this small move there was a kind of loyalty that made me shiver. They had been together thirty-four years. It seemed incredible. How did anyone last that long? Was it a matter of ingenious planning? Do some people actually plan that far ahead?

She hung up and joined me on the riverbank, between the vehicles.

"How's Monty doing?" I said.

She shrugged. "No answer. He's probably out in the barn. Down in the orchard. He could be anywhere. I'll catch up with him."

"You've missed him this week, haven't you."

"It doesn't hurt to have a few days off from time to time. But sure, of course I've missed him."

"I guess you'll have to tell him about me and Grover."

"I suspect he knows. He reads Grover pretty closely."

"That's the part I hate most, Lee, all the people who have to hear the news."

"I'll try my best to play it down. It is the least I can do after all the trouble I have caused."

"What are you talking about?"

"I feel like I have made things worse instead of better."

"Without you I couldn't have lived through this week."

"I had half a mind to stay another day and give him a hand."

"He'll be all right."

"Sometimes it is just so hard to know what to do. I felt like I had overstayed my welcome."

"You've already said that, and you know it isn't true."

"Has he mentioned anything to you about the other night?"

"Not much."

"Do you think he took it wrong, some of the things I said?"

"We were all saying things. I thought he would have talked to you by now."

"He is so much like Montrose, you know. When you most want him to talk, he won't say a word."

Suddenly her eyes were wet with rising tears. In an instant remorse and grief added ten years to her face. "Sometimes I just wish he would tell me what he's thinking. I have already lost contact with Travis. I know I have."

"Listen to me, Lee. Don't talk like that. Grover is changing. He has changed a lot. We are all changing. And he is going to call you. I guarantee it."

I knew she saw his fate and well-being inextricably bound up with my own. The way her blue blue eyes searched mine as we said all this, I think it took some effort not to ask me if I knew what I intended to do next, not to give me more advice along those lines, remind me of what she would do or would have done at my age if she had known what she knows now. I was glad for that, though I could hardly bear to watch the face of the mother who felt estranged from both her sons. I had no clear vision of tomorrow or the next day. I did not want to lie to her about this, couldn't lie, to Lee. I did not want to have to admit it either. I told myself I was waiting for a sign.

She blinked back the impending tears and said, with a thin smile, "I can take the kids again, you know, almost any time."

"My God, you've already done so much! I wouldn't think of it."

"I'm not saying I want 'em tonight, you understand. But if you get in a squeeze you can always give me a call. The main thing is, I want you to stay in touch. Maybe in a week or two we can meet somewhere for lunch."

"I'd like that."

"Just a salad. Something light."

She took my hands, giving me, without any more words, her full support and allegiance and understanding. My arms went around her then, my ally, my mentor, my wisdom figure, in my spirit family the heart mother. In the cool sun outside the fire station we held each other in a long embrace.

As I watched her drive away, small and erect behind the high wheel of the Land Cruiser, swinging onto the state road, heading inland, it occurred to me that if Grover and I finally came to a parting of the ways, something in my relationship with Lee would

surely change, though neither of us would want it to. I wondered
then, as I still wonder, if these things, these loves, can ever be disentangled. When people come to you in clusters, where do you
find the line between love for one and for the other?

I couldn't answer, didn't try. Alone on the riverbank I felt the
need to talk. I should have held her there with talk a little longer. I
had not said nearly all I had to say. Craving more talk, I moved to
the telephone, thinking this would be as good a time as any to call
some of the numbers on a list Grover gave me, customers of his,
suppliers of this and that, business colleague/friends who needed
to be contacted and reassured. The dial tone must have shifted me
onto automatic pilot. When the first voice said hello, I did not
recognize it. A woman's voice. It frightened me. I could not speak.
The second time she said hello I realized I had called Maureen.

"Holly," she exclaimed, when she heard my name. "Is this
long-distance?"

"In a way," I said.

"Are you calling from New York?"

"I'm out here at the fire station on Revolution Road."

"Did you get to New York?"

"I did."

"Well, what happened? When did you get back?"

"You'll never believe it."

"After this week I will believe anything. Are they rationing
your water yet?"

"We're on a well."

"You're lucky. The worst flood in history and now there's a
water shortage."

"How could that be?"

"Something about the reservoir. When the power lines went
down, the pumps stopped pumping from someplace to someplace
else. A slide tore some piping loose. So now it is, Don't wash your
car, and Don't brush your teeth if they are merely off-white, wait
until they turn yellow. And only flush your toilet when it is absolutely necessary—whatever that means."

"How about you? Your apartment? You survived okay?"

"The apartment is great. Sunburst always survives. Me? Who knows? You remember that guy I told you about who had crabs and was hinting so politely that I ought to take better care of my bod? Well, he just called, literally five minutes ago, trying to get me all week, he says, but with the phones out, and so forth, and he wants to apologize because he has located the carrier, and he is sorry he ever suggested it might be me. By way of apology, he says, he thought of giving me a present. But then he says—now get this—he says, I was going to buy you something to express, well, the feeling between us. But then I remembered that you are a Cancer, and Cancers have such exquisite taste, I knew I could never pick out anything that would be equal to the things you already have. His name is Larry, by the way. And I immediately say, Larry, Larry, I am only on the cusp, I have Scorpio rising, and Scorpios have terrible taste. It didn't do one bit of good. He said he would drop by the bar some night and buy me a drink."

We laughed in our sisterly way, and yet it sounded like something I had heard a long time ago, a sound out of the past. I felt a gulf between us. I wanted to cross it. I wanted to get back to her, or bring her closer to me, but I could not do it over the phone. There was too much to tell. She wanted to meet that afternoon.

"The club has been closed all week. No power means no lights. No sound. No ice. But today we are having a grand reopening. We're staging a benefit too, for the flood victims. Twelve hours of country music. All the bands are volunteering. Everybody is going to be there. You ought to be there too, Holl."

"Can I get in free?"

"You're a flood victim, aren't you?"

"I hadn't thought of it that way," I said.

It didn't take me long to go down Grover's list. Most of the people weren't answering. The whole county was running at halfspeed, and some of the connections were still bad, depending on the district. Ten minutes later I was standing in front of the pickup studying the river, as I so often do. The main bridge had endured a fierce battering. Thanks to someone who had taken a chain saw into the log jam, neatly cut limb chunks were strewn along the banks with the flotsam from farther upstream. A stump too thick to cut still broke the flow. It made a rippling V that held me mesmerized. I can think of three things that cause people everywhere to stop and stare—fire, serious damage, and moving water, which I believe is here on earth as a gift. It quenches our endless thirst, and it also helps visualize some of the basic facts about life and death.

I thought of all the creeks in the world emptying into the multitude of rivers that flow like this one across the continents to join up with the all-surrounding sea, thought how it all goes on forever and yet every ripple only happens once. The thousand gallons just then veeing past the stump, would they ever pass this way again? Would this day? Would I? No. Of course not. Not in my present form. Not as Holly Belle.

As Lee was ready to depart I had almost broken into tears. Now they flowed out silently, another kind of river, flowing to another kind of sea. The thought of how quickly all things come and go overwhelmed me. Hearing what Maureen had just said, about flood victims, I was thinking, Yes, yes, all of us, carried forward in the daily flood.

I climbed back into the pickup and started driving. I had to take it slow until I passed the last fallen log and last stretch of one-way, directed traffic. When those tears passed, I was marvelously unburdened. My eyes felt bright. The salt had burned them clean. I was on the road again, following the river.

28

Traveling Music

Where the trees thinned out, I picked up speed and switched on the radio, playing with the dial, wanting to hear all the stations at once, after our week-long media silence. As the sky opened, and as the town came rushing toward me, my mind was rushing too. Though I had a hundred things to take care of, I felt on the loose again, and I found myself thinking about Ray, as I still do, from time to time, when I am driving—how we met, or failed to meet, by accident, and yet by some uncanny design.

Why did I meet him? Why do you meet anyone? Was he sent to me for that low moment? Or did I seek him out? I fantasize what it would have been like to remain in New York City. I was only in his van for about ten minutes, but when I think of it now, it is the memory of myself in free-float, on my way to the subway station with this man, this total stranger who is very good-looking and with whom I have shared one of the intense mornings of my life. In my fantasy those minutes stretch out over days and weeks, Ray and I at large among the boroughs, driving the streets, listening to the radio. Sometimes while he is up on the third floor servicing an apartment I walk the neighborhood gazing into shop windows, buy something, have a cup of coffee, read a magazine. The morning sun is slanting in, and I am anonymous. These are images that only come to me when I am driving alone, with certain songs on the radio to stir the imagination.

That is what does you in, the old imagination, always running ahead or around you, back and forth in time and space, dancing along this road and that road, saying, "Try it," saying, "Do you have any idea what lies down that alleyway there? Do you have the nerve to look?" If there are people whose minds do not work that way, I envy them. I think I envy them. I wonder if they are more content. Obviously you cannot follow every one of those imagined paths. You cannot even follow two or three. You have to pick, and whichever you pick, there is always another one you did not pick, the other station you aren't listening to. There is always a Ray. There is always a Howard. And yet you know that if you had chosen another path, the one you're on would be shining in the distance. Sooner or later you make some kind of choice. Or perhaps you choose at the moment you are chosen. And this is the riddle of your karma. That is what Lee would call it. I don't know. I am only guessing. It is always mysterious, and you can spend a lot of time explaining these choices to yourself. It can obsess you—the way things turn out—because it seems random and also predictable. Sometimes it all seems foreordained. This is how we get fanatics in the world. They make some kind of choice, then get so eager to prove to themselves they made the right one, they have to persuade all the rest of us to move along in that same direction. They sit down next to you in the airline terminal, like the Light Steward, and begin to talk.

I understand the impulse. I understand now, as I get close to the end, why I had to write all this. But I am not a fanatic. I would never go so far as to say my life should be a pattern for anyone else's. I am a firm believer in the fact that each relationship only happens once. This is why we have so much trouble getting the hang of getting along with another person. The world is full of books and songs on the subject, and this has not changed the hard truth that the only way you can learn how is by trying it. Suddenly it has started, here it goes, you are in right up to your heart, juggling what comes at you from one moment to the next.

Safeway was my first stop. As I swung out onto the crosstown freeway I could see it in the distance. A great gush of warm affection flowed through me. No. Affection is too mild a word. This was closer to patriotism. I almost wept again, and I learned something else about myself. When you live outside of town, it is easy to feel superior to those who cannot let go of sewer lines and shopping malls. Though you may only live a mile beyond the city limits, it is easy to feel more kinship with old-time mountaineers than with the softies still hooked on goods and services.

The red Safeway logo came into view, a stylized S that is really a thinly disguised version of the interlocking teardrops of yin and yang, Asian symbol for the law of opposites. For the first time it made sense to me. In that moment I surrendered to all contradiction. I surrendered to the great supermarket I had not seen for an entire week. This was my homecoming and my true reward.

Curving off the exit ramp, I pulled into the parking lot, among the rows of empty cars, astonished at how light my body felt. The glass door, swinging with its quiet hum, cleared a path into a world that was magical and wondrously familiar, magical because at home we still were using kerosene and here was a door that opened and closed by itself a thousand times a day, familiar in the haunting way an old landmark can touch the heart when you have not seen it for a long long time.

It was more than nostalgia. It was erotic. As I crossed the threshold all my appetites were stirred. Walking in made me feel sexy. I realized this had been going on for years. In the brilliant light my eyes were wet with an unspecific lust. My clothes felt loose against my skin. Unfettered. I found my wire cart and began to stroll from aisle to aisle, with the brightly labeled merchandise piled overhead, looking at the labels as if for the first time, selecting things I would not ordinarily select, not because I needed them but simply for the pleasure of buying. This too was an aphrodisiac. A pound of thin-sliced pastrami from the gourmet butcher, a papaya, a new brand of Spanish olives, big green ones, the size of robin's eggs, a jar of British marmalade.

I had given myself to the shopping, thinking of nothing else. In Aisle Five—COFFEE, COCOA, SPICES—I decided to go back for a second bag of nine-grain breakfast rolls. I was making the turn into Aisle Six—BREADS AND PASTRIES—when I almost had a heart attack. Sarah stood halfway down the aisle examining a package of cookies—the last person I wanted to see, and obviously the person I was not going to be able to avoid. She had been sent to me, I thought later, or perhaps we had both been sent into this market at the same time for the same reason, though at the moment I did not have the presence of mind to see it that way. I almost changed my course, almost moved off behind some shelving that would conceal me. But I couldn't. In the few seconds before she felt my gaze and turned, I stared as if she were a statue in a gallery.

I had seen her only twice, a week earlier, from the side, in the auditorium, and at that party the previous July. The way she looked that party night had stayed with me. Yet what I saw did not resemble my memory much at all. She was smaller, her breasts were larger, her waist slimmer. She was wearing jeans, a long-sleeved leotard, and a down-filled vest. She reminded me of someone. I could not think who.

She looked up, turning, and our eyes met. Hers filled with fear. I knew what she was feeling. Like a fugitive, she looked behind her. When she turned toward me again, her eyes had changed, hardened. She had swallowed her fear. She was smiling. I saw then who she reminded me of. It was Leona. They were almost the same size. The hair was darker, longer perhaps. And the eyes. The eyes I had remembered correctly, calculating, still made up in the feline lift. In all other ways she could have been Lee's daughter, or Lee herself as a younger woman.

Seeing her fear did not give me any confidence. I too wanted to flee. But I was magnetized. I already knew her, knew a great deal about her. This resemblance told me I knew even more, things I did not want to know. It was the same feeling I'd had at age eleven, the morning my father walked out the second time. I knew it before I knew it, and I wandered through the house afraid to speak.

She said, "You're Holly."

"I thought you were gone."

"I heard the same thing about you."

I did not like the way she said this. It sounded arrogant.

"Are you back for good," I said, "or just passing through?"

"I haven't made up my mind yet."

"Maybe I can help you make it up."

"You're carrying a lot of anger, Holly. Did you know that?"

"Don't tell me what I'm carrying."

"Are you by yourself?"

As she said this she looked around again, checking again for an ambush from behind, or perhaps checking for Grover.

"I'm shopping. I'm doing a very big shopping for four people."

"Listen. Holly. I am glad we ran into each other. I really am. I feel like you and I should talk to each other. But this isn't such a terrific place to talk, considering the kinds of things we need to talk about."

I weighed this. Spending any time at all with her seemed sordid. Being near her made my skin crawl.

"What are you thinking of?" I said.

"There's a coffee shop across the parking lot."

"I mean, what do you think we have to talk about?"

"I just feel like I know what you've been going through."

This came as an invitation, as if we were already intimate, as if there already existed between us some unvoiced and kinky alliance.

I was repulsed. There are certain people you despise on sight, they make you want to kick out and argue. Small women can affect me this way, reminding me of what I take to be my own inadequacies, reminding me that size in a female can be a hardship, that in male eyes the trim and compact woman is somehow more womanly, more feminine, reminding me that size and youth were both on Sarah's side.

I was disgusted. She was a punk. I was also attracted, though it is difficult, even now, to admit that. They say opposites attract. They say two people who have slept with the same person are somehow bonded, whether they like it or not. Though I could not bear the thought, I must have felt the link. Another sister. The shadow sister. The darkest one.

"How could you possibly know anything about what I have been going through?" I said.

"Grover has talked a lot about you. He has been wanting me to meet you. He says we have a lot in common."

"I can't imagine what that would be."

"He has been wanting the three of us to get together."

I had a sense of déjà vu. I heard echoes. As her eyes held me, I remembered Maureen's account of her last days with Charlie.

"Tell me something, Sarah."

"Sure." She smirked, defensively, it seemed to me, a mask to cover any show of weakness.

"Do you love him?"

This took her by surprise. For a moment nothing in her face moved. Her smirking grin froze. Inside the grin her lips moved. "Yes. I do. Very much."

"Do you want to marry him?"

"He is a very beautiful person, Holly."

"People who are in love usually get married."

"Things like this, you have to take them one step at a time."

"What do you think is the next step?"

Her face opened in a wide smile she believed was her most charming smile. Later it occurred to me that this might have been her only smile, one she used on both men and women. It had obviously worked with other women, or she would not have used it just then. It almost worked on me. I could have surrendered to her. She had that kind of power. I could have let her lead me, and him, into a darkness that seemed, from this threshold, delicious. While her voice said, "One step at a time," her eyes and lips were saying, "Join me. Join me in something wild and outrageous and decadent." It must have been the smile she gave Grover when she suggested they hop a plane to Cuernavaca. How had he resisted it? I could scarcely resist it myself. Sarah was more than dangerous. She had something I had never possessed. She knew her looks were desirable in the blinding way. She could make a man go blind and crazy and then encourage him to call his blindness love and lead him around until the blindness lost its entertainment value. But she had never loved anyone. I could see that. She was closed to love. I did not know why. On that day I did not want to know why. I simply wanted her out of my life.

I should say out of *our* life, because it was just at this moment that I decided to stay with Grover, at least give marriage one more chance. The decision took the form of a huge sob that rose within me and almost stopped my breath.

It has taken me some time to figure out what happened there, why that should have been the turning point. I have gone over it in my mind, searching for words to describe what I felt and thought I saw. For one thing, I finally understood why I had started seeing Buddy in Grover's eyes. It was not the long-lost female that Sarah had encouraged to come out, but the boy within, the boyish Grover looking for a secret place to hide. In her presence he could be twenty again, or younger. Much younger. Ten. And she could be both playmate and vicious mother, the one who offers punishment. Grover called that mother out of her. And if I turned away, to let these forces run, he could end up crawling on his hands and knees. There might be nothing left.

I sucked in a double breath, like a swimmer hyperventilating before the starting gun, and found my strength, and said, "The three of us are not going to get together."

"You can ignore things, Holly . . ."

"And I don't much care for your arrogance."

"But that doesn't mean they are going to go away."

"It means you are going to go away. It means you are going to get out of his life completely."

"What makes you so sure of that?"

"I am going to see to it."

I felt a cruel rage rising. My hands were locked around the push-bar of the shopping cart. If she had said the wrong thing then, or said anything at all, I would have jumped her. I was ready to attack. She must have known that. She didn't speak, though something similar had been ignited inside her. In her eyes I could see it blazing. Looking back, I don't think she wanted Grover anymore. But at that moment she was willing to do battle for him. We both were. If I had already decided beyond the shadow of a doubt to walk out on him forever, I would have fought with her to keep him, to own him, if only because she desired him or seemed to or seemed as if she might desire him again.

It had not yet occurred to me to be angry with Grover for allowing himself to fall into her clutches and be deluded into thinking he could ever have loved such a female. That anger would come out later. I was aiming all of it, everything I had, at Sarah, and this turned out to be a blessing. I overpowered her, right there in the supermarket, not with any word I uttered but with a raw surge of feeling, something in my face that I could see reflected in her face.

She dropped her eyes and glanced down at the load of groceries in the cart that filled the space between us.

"Have you ever done this kind of shopping, Sarah? Do you have any idea what is involved? It is very serious business. Lives depend on it. Have you ever done anything another life depended on? Have you ever given a thought to another life but your own? Don't bother to answer. Just think about it. And listen to what I am telling you."

She smiled a little smile that looked to me like a sneer of pity for the hapless housewife, while she was somehow of a different breed, emancipated and beyond the snare of rampant consumerism. I was not going to let her get away with such a look. I had been where she was, looking down my nose at daily life.

"Stay away from Grover," I said. "Don't call him. Don't write to him. Don't stop him on the sidewalk or come looking for him to talk about being his friend. Do you understand? This is a warning, and one warning is all you get. If I ever hear or see the tiniest clue that you are anywhere near his life, I will find you and strangle you. Do you follow that? I will strangle you until your face turns purple. With these two hands."

I showed her my hands, palms up and dirty. Little streaks of mud had somehow moved from the riverbank or roadbed onto the floormat and from there to the steering wheel and into the creases of my hands. She looked at them and looked up at me with that pitying smile, as if I were a crazy woman roaming around Safeway. At that moment I probably was. Mad Holly, at large and raving, somewhere in Aisle Six.

She stepped back a pace. Another woman was watching us, with two loaves of sourdough French clutched to her bosom, watching me as if she were ready to drop the loaves and call the manager. I took another deep breath and said, "Goodbye, Sarah. I'm glad I ran into you."

She nodded and dipped her head and stepped past me. The other woman had not moved. I forced a smile and said, "We are in the same acting workshop. One of the exercises is, any time you run into someone from the workshop you spontaneously rehearse a scene. You're welcome to join us. You might enjoy it. We meet every Wednesday from seven to nine at the community center."

I was on the road again, with the groceries loaded and the heater up and the radio blaring, when the aftershock hit me. I felt weak. My arms were trembling. I had never done anything like that, or spoken like that. Six months or six weeks or six days earlier i would have been impossible for me. I have always claimed to dislike rivalry, for what it calls out of people, but I would have fought with Sarah for almost anything. The bag of cookies. A shopping cart.

I learned something else about love that day, learned again how little I understand. I am talking now about winning and losing. If there is a line between possessiveness and love, I wish someone would point it out to me. In a world of transcendent beings, of course, we would all be capable of the unconditional love you hear so much about. I have not personally seen much evidence of it. Maybe by the time I am Lee's age, or a bit older, I will be better at it: love with no strings attached. I am working on it. As I sit here writing out these final pages my mind understands it perfectly. But not my body. How long must I wait until my mind and my body are one?

I wanted to tell Maureen what had just happened. I knew she would approve. I knew she would have a sly opinion on the subject. I could hear her voice. But I wanted to see her rascal face as she spoke. I had a lot to tell Maureen. That was when I decided to stop at The Last Roundup before heading home. The club was on the other side of town. So was the supply yard. I would pick up the cement and the cable and then catch part of a set at the flood victims' benefit. Maybe I would sing a song or two. I felt like singing. There was going to be a lot more singing from here on. Already I could see that. In my heart, in my throat I could feel notes rising. Old notes. New notes.

I needed some traveling music. I brought in my favorite station sharp and clear, to fill the cab and immerse myself in the songs that give me guidance. You will never hear unconditional love mentioned in country music, by the way. It is all about men and women with warm and tender bodies who do things behind closed doors.

It was another moment of startling synchronicity. The sequence of tunes the deejay picked spoke directly to this day and hour in my life. First a Nashville lady said, "If I didn't love you, I would have left you a long long time ago."

Then Merle Haggard came on behind a strong and lonesome pedal steel singing, "Today I started loving you again."

Hank Williams was and still is the one who brings tears to my eyes just about every time I hear him. I find myself driving faster whenever Hank starts to sing. I had joined the flow of crosstown traffic, going seventy in a fifty-five-mile-an-hour zone, just for the hell of it, for the rush of motion under the cloudless sky, and Hank's voice was on the radio saying, "I can't help it if I'm still in love with you."

I didn't make it through to the end of that song. My arms were trembling again. I had to pull across to the outermost lane, the one marked EMERGENCY PARKING ONLY, and sit by myself awhile, with the radio and engine off, and let those words sink in.

A Note About the Author

James D. Houston is the author of four previous novels, including *Continental Drift* (1978), completed with the aid of a writing grant from the National Endowment for the Arts. Among his non-fiction works are *Farewell to Manzanar* (1973), coauthored with his wife, Jeanne Wakatsuki Houston, and *Californians: Searching for the Golden State* (1982), which received an American Book Award from the Before Columbus Foundation. He lives in northern California.

Catalog

If you are interested in a list of fine Paperback
books, covering a wide range of subjects
and interests, send your name and address,
requesting your free catalog, to:

McGraw-Hill Paperbacks
1221 Avenue of Americas
New York, N.Y. 10020